LUCKY PENNY

MIRANDA VAUGHN MYSTERIES #3

ELLIE ASHE

PRAISE FOR ELLIE ASHE

"Smart, sexy, and so suspenseful! The Miranda Vaughn Mysteries take you on a wild ride through the world of big-money crime, and you won't believe whodunit!" *–Traci Andrighetti, USA Today bestselling author of the Franki Amato Mysteries.*

"High stakes, high energy, and a highly humorous good time! From Belize to Macau, this is one globe-trotting adventure you don't want to miss!" *—Gemma Halliday, New York Times bestselling author.*

Winner of the 2015 HOLT Medallion awards from the Virginia Romance Writers for best first novel and novel with romantic elements.

LUCKY PENNY
by
ELLIE ASHE

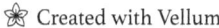

CHAPTER ONE

I gripped the handle on the courtroom door and took a deep breath before forcing myself to pull it open and walk into the silent and solemn room. The gallery was about half-filled, and several audience members turned to watch me come in. I glanced around quickly, trying to locate my boss, Rob Fogg, in the area reserved for spectators. From the middle of a row near the back of the room, he nodded and waved at a few empty seats near him. I squeezed past other spectators who had come to watch the trial.

"Glad to see you made it," he whispered as I sat down.

"Parking," I mumbled.

It was a common excuse in the busy downtown blocks around the federal courthouse, but it was also a lie. I'd found a prime parking space in the lot across the street. I'd also hit every green light on the way there. There was no excuse for my tardiness except my own nerves.

I wasn't even sure why he wanted me to join him. Rob's specialty was criminal defense, and as far as I knew, he had no connection to the civil trial that was underway in front of Judge Smith. And I had never wanted to set foot in this building again.

It had been more than a year since I'd been in the same courtroom, facing the same judge, on fifteen federal fraud charges. With Rob defending me, I'd been acquitted. I hadn't planned on ever returning to the scene of my utter humiliation and near destruction. If Rob weren't practically family now that he was engaged to my Aunt Marie, I probably would have come up with an excuse not to join him.

I swallowed hard and looked around the too-familiar room, trying to dampen the ghosts of old feelings that had rushed back —fear, nervousness, and even shame, though I had known that I hadn't done what I'd been accused of.

Get a grip, I told myself. *It's been more than a year. No one will even recognize you.*

Unlike during my two-week trial, the courtroom was crowded, especially for a civil lawsuit over a business deal. Rob's brief summary hadn't given me much background on the lawsuit, except that it was one business partner suing another over the dissolution of a start-up tech company.

A phalanx of lawyers and their paralegals sat at each of the counsel tables, surrounded by binders and boxes of exhibits that would be entered into the record. The jurors, who sat in two rows in the elevated box along the side of the room, looked bored out of their minds as the attorney at the podium wrapped up his questioning of the man on the witness stand.

The witness was excused and one of the other lawyers stood.

"The plaintiff calls Ms. Dorothy Russell."

An assistant hurried out of the courtroom, then returned a moment later with an older woman wearing a black Chanel-inspired suit and a leopard-print scarf. Her short spiky hair was dyed an odd shade of brassy orange that matched the scarf perfectly. The assistant, a lawyer so young he looked like he was wearing his father's suit, tried to direct her to the witness stand, but the petite woman raised a hand to stop him.

"I got this, sweetie," she said in a deep, gravelly voice that carried through the hushed room.

She looked to be in her seventies, but Ms. Russell walked to the front of the courtroom with a confident stride. She stood in front of the clerk, then raised her right hand without being asked.

"I solemnly swear to tell the truth, the whole truth, and nothing but the truth. So help me God." The pledge was over before the clerk could stand to read the swearing-in statement.

She sat in the witness stand and, unprompted, bent the microphone toward her. "My name is Dorothy Elaine Russell. That's spelled R-U-S-S-E-L-L."

The plaintiff's attorney at the podium looked up from his notes. "Good morning, ma'am. Would you please state your name for the record?"

"She already did that," Judge Smith said. "Try to keep up with your witness, counsel."

"Oh, uh, right," the attorney said, flustered.

"Why don't you ask me what I do for a living," Ms. Russell suggested.

This time, the jurors' giggles were full-fledged laughs. Even the judge bit his lip and looked down, trying to suppress a smile.

"Please let Mr. Walters ask the questions, Ms. Russell," he said.

"Sure, sure," she said with a wave of one wrinkled and bejeweled hand.

The attorney stammered a few more words, then sighed. "What do you do for a living, Ms. Russell?"

She beamed her approval as he finally got with the program. "I'm a forensic accountant."

"And what does a forensic accountant do?"

"I do the math that lawyers can't handle."

Despite my nerves and discomfort, I smiled at the truth in

the woman's words. That was pretty much what I did for Rob. After I'd been acquitted, he had started taking white-collar criminal cases. My job was to help him examine the financial evidence against his clients, such as bank records and company profit-and-loss statements. It seemed to be as close as I was going to get to my old job as an investment analyst, at least until the stigma of being handcuffed and arrested on the job faded. Which was likely to happen, oh, never.

The direct examination proceeded quickly, with Ms. Russell leading the jury through her examination of the business's finances. Though it was dry material, she ran through it quickly and concisely, and painted a clear picture—both partners had control over the bank accounts, but one of them was skimming off the top and stashing the proceeds overseas. The two men were now pointing fingers at each other, hence the lawsuit.

The courtroom doors opened, and two more people found seats in the audience. I shifted in my seat, uncomfortable in my suit. It wasn't the formal dress that was making me fidget, it was the growing crowd. I was starting to recognize some faces I'd seen during my trial as more court staff and attorneys drifted into the room.

The plaintiff's lawyer closed his folder and thanked his expert witness. As he sat down, the defense attorney stood up, adjusted his jacket, and made his way to the podium.

"Good morning, Ms. Russell. My name is Lyle Styler, and I represent the defendant in this lawsuit, Mr. Griffith," he said. He spoke slowly and loudly, as if the older woman might have problems understanding him, though there had been no hint that Ms. Russell was slowed by her age. "I suppose I should clarify your name. Do you prefer to be addressed as Mrs. Russell?"

"If you want to get formal, I suppose it's Dorothy Willis Stanford Chapman Scolari Lively Russell," she said with a wink.

"Been married five times. But you can call me Dottie. Everyone does."

The jury giggled again, and the man at the podium shifted, probably wondering whether the panel was laughing at him or the witness.

"Well, let's start with your testimony about the bank accounts you studied. How did you come to the conclusion that my client, Mr. Griffith, was the one who was siphoning off money?"

Dottie adjusted her reading glasses and glanced at the papers in front of her.

"On paper, it could have been either Mr. Griffith or Mr. Hart who was transferring money to the offshore account. But when I examined the personal checking account and credit card records, certain patterns appeared. That led me to Mr. Griffith's penchant for day trading," she said, leaning in toward the microphone and dropping her voice a little. "He's not very good at it."

"Uh, um, well that doesn't mean he was embezzling from his business partner," the lawyer said, thrown by the candid answer. "And didn't you find similar information about your client, Mr. Hart?"

"Sure did. Mr. Hart likes the ladies. Well, the ladies at the Tip Top Club, at least," she said with a shake of her head.

Mr. Hart's lawyer jumped to his feet. "Objection. That's not relevant."

"Overruled."

"So you discovered that the plaintiff in this matter, Mr. Hart —" Here, the lawyer motioned dramatically to the slumped plaintiff sitting at the counsel table. "—was frequenting strip clubs?"

The jury and audience leaned forward like we were enjoying story time at the library. Dottie lowered her chin and looked over the reading glasses at the attorney. "Glass houses, Mr. Styler."

The attorney took a step backward, and the rest of us in the courtroom held our collective breath.

"What did you say?"

Dottie shook her head and sighed. "Mr. Styler, all I'm saying is that it's not illegal to spend one's own money to watch some cute young thing shake her moneymaker," she said, then winked. "Good thing, huh?"

"Are you insinuating that I go to strip clubs?"

Judge Smith coughed gently, and I suspected it was to cover a laugh. "Mr. Styler, it's your choice, but are you sure you want to continue with this line of questioning?"

The courtroom was hushed as we waited to hear whether the attorney was going to get smacked down again by the tiny woman in the witness box.

"I'll move on," Mr. Styler said. "Ms. Russell, couldn't another employee have been the one to transfer the funds overseas?"

"No."

"Why not?"

She smiled, and the slumping plaintiff sat up a little straighter.

"Besides the two partners, the only other employee who had banking authority was the accountant."

"So it could have been the accountant?"

"No."

A frustrated sigh echoed through the room. "Why not?"

"When the transfers started, the accountant was Margie Griffith, who was married to Mr. Griffith. But shortly after the money began flowing overseas, Mr. Griffith left his wife, and she stopped working for the company. I suspect he thought it was a good way to hide assets from his wife in the divorce," Dottie said with a knowing nod to the jury. "You see this a lot in my line of work."

"Move to strike," Mr. Styler said. "Nonresponsive."

"Overruled. Ms. Russell's answer was responsive. You just need to phrase your questions better, counsel," Judge Smith said, leaning back in his chair and waiting for the next revelation.

Mr. Styler tried again. "The next accountant could have—"

Dottie waved an impatient hand. "No. There was no next accountant. The partners handled the bookkeeping until the company folded a few months later."

The defendant's lawyer didn't seem ready to give up digging a grave for his client's case. My discomfort faded away as Dottie's cross-examination continued. This was a subject that interested me, but I had degrees in finance and economics and had worked as an analyst at a financial services firm. Ms. Russell was doing the impossible—making this interesting to lay people.

"The money went to a numbered account, correct?"

"That is correct."

"So you can't say with any certainty that it was my client who opened that account, can you?"

Dottie tilted her head and paused before answering. "No, I guess I can't."

"And you can't say that it was Mr. Griffith who transferred the funds there and not Mr. Hart, can you?"

"I suppose that I can't say that with 100-percent certainty."

"And after all your poking around the personal finances of those involved in the company, you can't say that Mr. Griffith had control over that account," he said, his voice rising as his confidence returned.

"Uh oh," Rob whispered, nudging my elbow with his. "I think that was one question too far."

By now, I was hanging on every word, along with the rest of the audience. Dottie looked thoughtful, then shook her head.

"I wouldn't say that."

"What do you mean?"

"Well, I can't imagine who else would pay for Mr. Griffith's mail-order bride."

The collective gasp in the courtroom could have sucked all the oxygen out of the thirteenth floor. A delicious thrill ran through me as the smug lawyer was smacked around again by Dottie Russell. I was *really* starting to like her.

"I mean, unless you think Mr. Hart paid thirteen-thousand dollars last year to an internet business called Russian Brides For You, but I think that's unlikely, don't you? Mr. Hart has been married for seventeen years to Mrs. Hart, and as far as I know, he didn't purchase her online. And Mrs. Griffith, the new one I mean, is a recent immigrant from Russia. So that leads me to conclude that the person who had control over the account was your client."

The courtroom was silent as the attorney stood at the podium. He seemed unsure of whether to continue or give up. The only sound in the room was the shuffling of papers as Mr. Styler regrouped from the beating he was taking.

Oh yeah, this woman was my new hero.

"Any further questions?" Dottie asked.

"Uh, no." Mr. Styler turned and sat next to his client, who was resting his head in his hands.

"Ms. Russell, you're free to go," Judge Smith said. "We'll take our morning break now."

We stood as the jury filed into the room off the side of the courtroom. I had become so engrossed in Dottie's testimony that I hadn't noticed the room had filled to capacity, with a few people standing in the back. Word must have traveled through the building that there was something worth watching. After the door to the jury room closed, the judge disappeared into his chambers, and the audience began leaving, a low murmur of amusement rising as the attorneys and courthouse staff rehashed the testimony they'd just watched.

I followed Rob into the hallway, navigating around the crowds of courthouse staff.

"That was entertaining, but I still don't know why you wanted me here," I said.

"I want you to meet Dottie," Rob said. "She's an old friend of mine and one of the best forensic accountants in the state. It would be a good thing for you to get to know her."

He took my elbow and steered me toward the windows. Dottie Russell joined us in a cloud of Chanel No. 5. Though I was only five-foot five-inches tall, I towered over this tiny rock star of an accountant.

"You must be Miranda," she said, taking my hand and shaking it with great enthusiasm. "It's a pleasure to meet you."

"Thank you. I really enjoyed watching your testimony."

She laughed. "Those young pup lawyers have got to learn when to stop asking questions, right Rob?"

"I think they both learned a valuable lesson today," he said.

"Rob says you're working on his white-collar cases now," Dottie said.

"I help out when I can," I said.

In truth, though, Rob hadn't taken on a new fraud defendant in a couple months, so I wasn't working full-time any longer. My skills, which involved reading financial reports and studying bank records, just weren't needed in cases where our clients were charged with selling drugs or buying illegal firearms. I knew Rob was trying to keep me busy and earning some money, but there was only so much work he could throw my way.

This wasn't a huge problem for me as my overhead was fairly low. I was living in my childhood home now that Aunt Marie had moved in with Rob, and the house was paid for. So was my car, a semi-reliable decade-old Volkswagen GTI. I didn't have any debt except for property taxes on the house and my family's cabin at Lake Tahoe. I didn't need a huge salary.

But I also couldn't work part-time forever. I'd worked in finance and understood the need to build up a retirement nest egg.

Basically, I needed to rebuild my career, but I was still unsure as to what that career would be. Sure, I enjoyed the work enough, and it was nice that my best friend, Sarah, was Rob's paralegal. But it wasn't what I imagined my career would be. Unfortunately, financial services seemed to be out, since my arrest on fraud charges was so high profile. The fact that I'd been acquitted didn't matter to the human resources department at major investment banks. All the hiring committee members would recall was the image of me being led out of Patterson Tinker Investment Services with my hands cuffed behind me. I kept hoping that the stigma would fade, but a year after I was found not guilty, and I was still unemployable.

Dottie gave me a warm smile and handed me a business card. "I could use some help, if you've got some time. Rob said you'd be uniquely suited for this project."

I took the card. "Sure, I guess I could do that."

She looked me over with an appraising eye. "You like Lake Tahoe?"

My mind flashed back to happy childhood memories of hiking and camping and to my more recent acquisition of the Vaughn family cabin that sat far up a mountainside that over-looked the sparkling blue waters. "Of course, who doesn't?"

"I'm doing an internal audit of a family-owned resort. It's not a huge job, and I've worked with the family for years, so I'm quite familiar with the operation, but it would be nice to have another set of eyes on the books. If you're interested, come by my office after lunch, and I'll fill you in," Dottie said.

I nodded, but before I could voice my agreement, she was

speed walking toward the elevator, pausing occasionally to return greetings from some of the courthouse regulars.

"Have you worked with Ms. Russell?" I asked Rob. "And why did you recommend me?"

"You've had some time on your hands. That means you're spending idle time with Sarah, and nothing good can come of that."

He may have a point there. Sarah did seem to gravitate toward trouble.

"You'll like working with Dottie," Rob said, his expression hopeful that I'd grab the opportunity he had clearly engineered for me. "She's a bit unorthodox, but she's the best in the business. It would be good for your career to work with her."

"Are you firing me?" I asked, figuring it was better to get the bad news out there.

He laughed. "No way. You've been invaluable to the firm. But if I don't have enough work for you, I think it would be good for you to branch out a little. Dottie's got a good reputation. And plenty of work."

I mulled this over as we followed the crowd toward the elevators. It would be nice to earn a little more money. I wouldn't mind upgrading my car eventually. The little white hatchback had so many dents that Sarah had dubbed it the Golf Ball. And while I loved living in the house I'd grown up in, the two-bedroom bungalow needed some cosmetic renovations. With a little extra money, I could finally rip out the pink shag carpet in my childhood bedroom.

"I guess I could meet with her," I said.

"Good," Rob said with a nod. "Are you on your way to the bridal shop now to meet with Marie?"

"Oh, damn it," I said, grabbing Rob's wrist and looking at his watch. "I'm late. Gotta run."

"Tell my beautiful bride hello for me," he said, hitting the elevator button for me and then turning to greet another defense attorney.

"Miranda!"

I turned at the sound of my name, and my heart skipped at the sight of Jake Barnes striding through the crowd toward me. He was wearing a suit, which never failed to make my mouth water. Seeing the FBI agent standing tall above the rest of the crowd made my pulse quicken. It was a sight I should have been used to, since Jake had been living in the apartment over my garage for the last three months while his house was being reno-vated. Unfortunately, he had been out of town investigating cases or at training seminars for much of that time, so I'd spent more time with his dog, Hank. I hadn't actually laid eyes on the tall, dark-haired agent in more than two weeks while he was off learning new crime-fighting skills or something.

"What are you doing here?"

His greeting was sincere and warm. The glances from several prosecutors standing nearby echoed the same question but with suspicion. I could see it in the quick exchange of puzzled looks and the whispered asides. *Why was a federal agent chatting up a former criminal defendant? Why was she even here?*

"Rob asked me to meet him here," I said as the elevator doors slid open. I stepped in quickly to get away from the pack of attor-neys and courthouse staff who were studying us.

Jake followed me and hit the ground floor button for me, then another floor for a pair of federal prosecutors who joined us. We rode in an awkward silence about halfway down the building until the attorneys filed off to go to their offices.

"You coming, Barnes?" one asked as he stepped out of the elevator.

Jake shook his head. "I'll catch up with you later."

The young man glanced at me, smirked, and turned away. I moved to the middle of the elevator as the door slid shut.

"How have you been?" Jake asked.

"Fine. You?"

"Okay. It's nice to be home. Thanks for taking care of Hank."

"He's no problem."

I liked having the big mutt around. The house felt too empty with Aunt Marie gone. She'd left behind Kvetch, her ornery orange cat, but he didn't appreciate having me as a roommate. I didn't entirely trust him not to kill me in my sleep. Hank, at least, always seemed happy to see me. Even though Kvetch would be more of a threat to an intruder, the dog's massive size was enough to deter anyone who might want to break into the house.

The elevator continued its slow descent, and despite my extreme discomfort at the surroundings, my mind immediately flashed to some of the more...interesting times when Jake and I had been alone together over the past year. It was the first time I could remember wanting to be trapped in an elevator.

My hopes were dashed when the doors opened to let me out at the lobby. Jake followed me and then put a hand on my arm to stop me.

"Hey, I know we haven't really had much time to hang out this summer, but I'm done with traveling for a while. Would you like to get dinner tonight?"

My mouth went dry at the invitation. This was what I'd been craving for months—a chance to be alone with Jake, to move things along in our fledgling flirtation. And the timing couldn't have been more perfect. The construction on his house was running way over the deadline, so he was probably going to be living in my backyard until the end of summer. I had plenty of time on my hands, since Rob didn't have much work for me. We could put behind us all the drama and conflict that had kept us apart in the past.

I opened my mouth to answer as the door across the hall

opened, disgorging a half-dozen men who came in from the secured parking lot. They greeted Jake by name, and I recognized several as federal prosecutors and guessed by the thick necks, broad shoulders, and suspicious stares that the others were law enforcement. Again, the wave of uneasiness came over me as Jake returned their greetings.

Then a tall, slim woman in a dark pantsuit walked through the door, and our eyes locked. FBI Special Agent Bethany Boylan gave me a steady and unfriendly stare. Jake's stunning partner had no love for me. And it was mutual. It was hard to say what I was more jealous of—her supermodel good looks or that she spent her days working alongside Jake.

"The meeting's in ten minutes in the conference room," she said to Jake, pointedly ignoring me.

"I'll be right there," Jake said, making no move to follow the agents into a waiting elevator.

His eyes were still on me as his colleagues were whisked up a dozen floors. They were gone, but there would be more of them walking by any second. This was the federal courthouse where Jake's colleagues spent their days investigating suspected criminals—and where last year they had tried, and failed, to build a case that would have put me in prison for a decade. From the pounding of my heart, it was clear, I hadn't let that go yet.

"I should go," I said, backing away, my breathing shallow. "I have to meet Aunt Marie."

"Sure," Jake said, turning and stepping into an elevator to go back upstairs.

As the doors slid closed, I realized that I hadn't given him an answer.

CHAPTER TWO

I pulled the Golf Ball into the last parking space at Bella's House of Bridal Fashions, berating myself for staying at the courthouse so long and making Aunt Marie wait for me at the fitting for her wedding dress. She was so excited to get married to Rob, and damn it, I was going to make sure that everything went perfectly at the wedding.

I found Aunt Marie in the bridal showroom, still wearing her street clothes, so at least I hadn't missed the wedding dress fitting.

"I'm sorry," I said, giving her a hug. "I'm late. I'm sorry."

She hugged me back, enveloping me in the scent of fresh-baked cookies that told me she'd come straight from the Sugar Plum Bakery. Though she had planned to work fewer hours at her business now that she was living out on Rob's ranch, the thirty-year habit of waking early to bake pastries and bread was hard to break, and she came to oversee her bakery staff at least three days a week.

"Rob sent me a text. It's fine. I told them you would be here any minute, so they're getting the fitting rooms ready for us."

I breathed a sigh of relief. The ladies who ran the House of

Bridal Fashions operation scared me a little with their militant attitudes about deadlines, their encyclopedic knowledge of wedding etiquette, and their measuring tapes. I was sure that Rob and Marie would be married already if not for the four-month wait to have the wedding dress fitted.

"What do you think of these parasols?"

I tried not to grimace as Aunt Marie touched the lace-edged trim on a pale green organza umbrella.

"It's lovely," I said with as much enthusiasm as I could muster. If Aunt Marie wanted her maid of honor in a ten-gallon Stetson or a Spanish mantilla, I was going to wear it without complaint. Even if that meant I looked like Little Bo Peep during the ceremony.

"It might be warm. I don't want you to burn," she said, a worried frown on her face. "You always get sunburnt when we go to Lake Tahoe. It's the altitude, I think."

It was more likely my pale skin and Nordic genes. "I'll be fine. The ceremony's at sunset, and there's always a breeze off the lake. And I'll wear sunscreen. Don't worry about me. I've been spending so much time at the pool this summer, I'm practically beige."

I flashed her a shoulder, and she shrugged, apparently not impressed with my nearly flesh-colored flesh.

"About that," she said in a tone that I was far too familiar with. I braced myself for a parental chat. "Did you talk to Rob about Dottie Russell?"

Was everyone conspiring to get me another job? It was true that I was working fewer hours, but I hadn't been complaining about it. I figured things would pick up or that maybe eventually I could find a position in investment banking again. But with Rob and Marie both concerned about it, maybe I was fooling myself about ever getting back into finance.

"Yes, I met Dottie at the courthouse. She's interesting."

Aunt Marie laughed. "She's quite a character, but what a sweetheart. I made three of her wedding cakes, you know."

"Has she really been married five times?"

"That's the rumor. Divorced three times, widowed twice," Aunt Marie said with a shake of her head. "She's a character. But she's got a good heart. And a great mind. She's very smart and great with numbers. You're a lot like her."

"But without all the husbands."

"That's because I raised you to be independent. But don't be like me and wait until you're in your fifties to get married and then end up feeling foolish for wearing white."

"You look beautiful in white," I said, as the door to the fitting area opened, and I caught a glimpse of Marie's dress waiting for her fitting.

The sight of the floaty white fabric made my throat constrict with emotion. I was so filled with joy for Aunt Marie and Rob that I wasn't sure how I was going to make it through the ceremony without breaking down in sobs. At least she hadn't asked me to speak during the ceremony. I'd never be able to pull myself together for that.

"And you'll look beautiful in this," Aunt Marie said, admiring the pale blue halter dress that hung on the door of a dressing room.

It was a gorgeous dress—classy, sophisticated, and when I looked at it, I didn't care about the staggering price tag. The cool shade of blue brought out my eyes and complimented my fair complexion. All eyes would be on Marie and Rob, but I was going to look good at this wedding.

"Are you going to work with Dottie?" Marie asked, as the seamstresses waved us into dressing rooms.

"She wants me to work with her on an audit at a family-owned resort near Lake Tahoe."

"You should do it. She's very good at what she does, and at

her age, she probably wants to slow down a little. Maybe even retire eventually."

With the help of two stern women who ran the bridal shop, Aunt Marie and I put on our dresses and met in the main fitting area, where we stood on the raised platforms while the fabric was pulled and pinned. Marie beamed as she examined the dress in the mirror. Two layers of white gauzy chiffon floated over a shimmery off-white sheath and formed translucent elbow-length sleeves. One layer of the chiffon gathered in the front in a fabric flower that highlighted Aunt Marie's slim waist. It was a simple dress that would be perfect for a summer garden wedding on the shores of Lake Tahoe.

"You look so beautiful," I said, my voice choking up.

"Don't cry," said the woman jabbing me with pins. "You'll stain the fabric."

I blinked and tried not to weep on my bridesmaid dress.

"Thank you, sweetie," Aunt Marie said, her cheeks pink. "So do you."

"This bodice enhances your bust. See?" The seamstress yanked the pale blue halter straps on my dress upward to prove her point.

And as if by magic, cleavage appeared. "Wow. How'd you do that?"

With the speed and skill of a ninja, she skewered the dress with about a hundred more pins, then eased me out of it. After we returned to our far-less-glamorous street clothes, Aunt Marie met me in the front of the shop, and we walked out together to the parking lot, sizzling under the midday summer sun.

"I hate to bring up a sore subject," Aunt Marie said, standing at the door of her car, "but have you decided whether you're bringing a date for the wedding?"

It was the question I had been avoiding like crazy. Why did I need to bring a date? I was the maid of honor and Aunt Marie was like a mother to me, so there was lots for me to do at the wedding ceremony, and on top of all that, I had to find a man to drag along?

"I mean, it's just so I can tell the caterer. You could bring Jake," she suggested.

Of course I wanted to be there with Jake. Even the mention of his name made my stomach do a slow somersault. But my mind went immediately to the guest list and how many of Rob's work friends would be there. How many of them knew Jake professionally? Pretty much all of them. How fast would the gossip get back to the rest of the federal bar? Pretty much instantly.

And how would that affect Jake's job to be dating a former criminal defendant?

"When is the deadline to get back to you on that?"

Aunt Marie sighed and gave me a sympathetic head tilt.

"Early next week. But don't worry about it. If you don't want a plus-one, it's no problem," she said. "Good luck with your meeting. Say hello to Dottie for me."

Aunt Marie's assurance that it was okay for me to be a total loser at her wedding did not make me feel better. I waved as she drove off and then unlocked the Golf Ball. I left the door ajar for a few minutes to vent the hot air and pulled Dottie's card out of my purse.

The office of Dorothy Russell Accounting Services was a short drive from the bridal shop in a two-story complex with an interior courtyard that featured a koi pond and a couple of trees tall enough to provide shade to the succulents planted around the water feature. The tenants all seemed connected with the legal industry—attorneys, investigators, mediators, and a secretarial service. Dottie's door was in the corner of the upstairs balcony.

My tentative knock was greeted with a cacophony of yaps

from what sounded like a dozen small dogs on the other side of the door.

It was only two yappers, I learned when the door opened. One of the tiny canines had a pink bow gathering a tuft of brown hair on top of its head, and the other was in an argyle sweater vest. Dottie Russell followed behind the pair and picked up the dog with the bow.

"Come in, come in," she said, motioning to an open door to a conference room on the side of the small lobby. "This is the welcoming committee. This is Duchess, and that's Bub. They're all bark. Well, they're mostly bark, at least. Watch your fingers around that one."

She nodded toward the smartly dressed Chihuahua mix who was giving me a suspicious side-eye.

I stepped around Bub and followed Dottie into the conference room. The first thing I saw was a massive square glass ashtray on the table, a thick cigar perched on the side sending up a plume of smoke. I couldn't remember the last time I'd seen an ashtray that wasn't on a curb at least twenty feet from the entrance of a bar. This was California, proudly a nonsmoking state. Beyond the antiquated smoking accessory, a man stood. He was at least in his seventies, completely bald, and had a thick gold chain around what little bit of neck separated his square jaw from his broad shoulders.

"Miranda, this is Max Emmerson, owner of the Whispering Pines Resort and Spa," Dottie said, giving her introduction a flourish that caused the tarted-up pup in her arms to kick her legs for traction.

Max Emmerson walked around the table to shake my hand. He was barely my height but seemed at least as wide as he was tall. His handshake was firm and warm, as was his smile.

"It is lovely to meet you, Miss Vaughn," he said.

"I was just telling Max about how you're going to help me

with the audit," Dottie said, pulling a chair out for me at the conference table.

"Do you want me to send you a resume?" I said, unsure if our one-minute conversation in the courthouse hallway had already gotten me the job.

She shook her head, and her dangling earrings swung and bobbed. "Rob vouched for your attention to detail and your work ethic. That's all I need to know."

"You beat the feds. That's all I need to know," Max said, taking his seat.

My face heated up at the mention of my trial, but I forced a smile. At least they didn't seem to think I was a criminal. As far as I could tell.

"I'm not sure how that will help," I said.

Dottie took the seat at the end of the conference table, between Max and me. "Let me tell you what we're doing for Max."

She set the little dog on the floor, then opened a binder on the table and withdrew a glossy brochure, which she slid over to me. "Max's family has owned Whispering Pines since the 1940s. Have you heard of it?"

I nodded and smiled. "Oh, yes. It's beautiful. You can see the lodge from most of the lake, I think."

The resort loomed over Lake Tahoe, like a castle on the side of the mountain, nestled among the pine trees. It had one of the best restaurants on the lake, five-star accommodations, a world-renowned spa, a helicopter pad, and a view of the water and the mountains that would take your breath away. At least, that's what I gathered from the brochure. I'd only seen the resort from a distance, as I couldn't afford to eat there, let alone stay in the luxurious suites.

"It's a gem," Dottie said, and Max beamed with pride. "Max took it over in 1978, when his father died."

Dottie gave a deep sigh. "Unfortunately, Big Sal's death left some unresolved financial issues at the time, so the family lost its other property, the Lucky Penny Casino, in the '80s."

I tilted my head as the name jogged a memory. "It's down near the water, right? Is it still open?"

Max shook his head. "Nah, we lost it in bankruptcy, and then it got sold a few times. The last owners shut it down in 1996, and it's been empty ever since."

That was why I remembered the Lucky Penny Casino—the faded and defunct sign on the side of the neglected building, sitting behind a chain-link fence. The property must be worth a fortune though. It was on the water's edge, and I was surprised that someone hadn't bought it up, bulldozed the old building, and put up a sparkling new casino.

"The property's been tied up in legal battles between the partners who bought it last, and now both of them are dead, and their heirs are finally ready to sell it," Dottie said. "It's still hush-hush, but Max here is going to buy it and restore the Penny to its former glory."

Max grinned at the thought and patted Dottie's hand. "It's gonna be a show-stopper."

"That's wonderful," I said. "Congratulations."

Dottie pursed her lips. "Well, there are still a few wrinkles left to iron out. For starters, the family's going to have to leverage Whispering Pines to come up with the money," she said. "And then the Nevada Gaming Commission will have to approve Max's gaming license. We'll have to have plenty of investor interest to get the backing too."

Max nodded. "Dottie's going over the books with a fine-tooth comb to make sure everything is in order before I go to the bank and get a loan."

She slid a binder over to me, and I opened it to find a typical annual financial report. The sections were tabbed, and everything was neatly organized.

"I had to take a medical leave last year, and my nephew, Jordan, was in charge while I was gone," Max said. He shrugged. "Nice kid. Good looking, like my sister. But not too smart. Like my brother-in-law."

Dottie gave him a sympathetic nod. "Your sister was a real looker."

"God rest her soul," Max said.

They both looked down in silence, and I shifted uncomfortably in my chair.

"Anyway," Dottie said, breaking the moment of reflection on Max's good-looking dead sister. "The resort's numbers are a bit of a mess."

Max snorted. "That don't even cover it. They're a fuckin' mess. Pardon my French."

"So you're just reviewing the books?" I asked, flipping through the profit-and-loss statement. I didn't know much about resorts, but the P&L statement indicated that this one at least made a healthy profit.

"Sort of," Dottie said, and I looked up from the charts. She bit her lip, and her brow furrowed. "You know how today in court, I testified about the patterns of spending? It's a lot like that. When there are irregular patterns in the books, you want to know why. You want to know who is mucking things up. That's what we'll be doing, but instead of looking at two horny guys and their credit card statements, we're going to be studying the hotel's books. See what it tells us."

I nodded but wasn't sure what she expected me to do. I knew math, but psychology wasn't my expertise. At all.

"I've already looked over what Jordan prepared for the board. There are a few problems, a slight downturn in profits. It may just be that Jordan was inattentive. Or there could be some theft. It's hard to say yet if it's mismanagement or intentional."

I raised an eyebrow at this. Tracking funds was something I could do. Not only had I been in charge of transferring large sums between accounts while I worked in financial services, but after my acquittal, I'd put those skills to use to find the money that my former boss had skimmed from the investment bank. It wasn't quite what Dottie seemed to do, but it was close enough to give me some comfort that I could help her with this project.

"Dottie's been my go-to gal for finances for years. She knows my business better than I do. So if she says something ain't right, I believe her," Max said, then tapped the table with a finger for emphasis.

Dottie leaned forward and patted Max's hand. "Don't you worry, Max. Miranda and I will get you back on track and ready for the Gaming Commission."

He grinned and squeezed Dottie's hand. "Thanks, Dot. It will be great working with you again. Hell, it's great just to be working again."

Dottie gave Max a wide smile and then looked over at me. "Now, while I'm doing all the things I normally would do in an independent audit, this one is just for Max, not the banks. You know, to take the pulse of the business, let him know what he needs to do before inviting in the bank and the Gaming Commission. Those guys will bring in their own number-crunchers."

"You ladies will stay at the lodge," Max said. "We'd normally be booked solid, but my genius nephew rented out the place at the height of the busy season to some movie people. But on the plus side, we can get you each a room while you're working. And you don't pay for a thing at my resort."

Dottie laughed. "And that's the nice part of doing a personal audit. Max can take good care of us without it being a conflict of interest."

Now *this* was starting to sound like fun. I hadn't been to a spa in several years and never at someone else's expense. I hadn't had a vacation in far too long. Sure, I took an international tour of Macau and Belize last year, but chasing down a money laundering operation was not a holiday. I wished that I could get Sarah to join me but then reminded myself that this was a work trip and I really shouldn't be thinking about gambling and dancing and excellent shows and oh, the restaurants. I'd read about the world-class restaurant at the lodge and its amazing wine cellar.

Focus on work, Miranda. You need the job.

From Dottie's lap, Duchess perked up and alerted us to a sound from the lobby, and Bub let out a howl that belied his five-pound frame. Both dogs raced to the front door, and Dottie leaned forward to see who walked in.

"Come in, Frankie, we're back here," she called, over the furious tirade of high-pitched barks. "We're just wrapping up our meeting."

The man who joined the conference room was the opposite of Max in every possible way. He was tall, slim, and his thick, dark hair was slicked back from his hairline, which started low on his brow. He paid no attention to the little dogs jumping around his feet like they were on trampolines.

"Miranda, this is Frank Harvey, my assistant," Max said, standing.

I stood and shook hands with the tall man, who gave me a curt nod but said nothing as he studied me closely. He had the vibe of a bodyguard, rather than someone who retrieved coffee.

"The plane's fueled and ready to go," he said to Max.

"Yeah, we gotta get back," Max said. "Dottie, thanks for everything. I'll see you in a couple days, right? You too, Miranda?"

I nodded. Why not? It's not like I had work, or a social life, since I'd accidentally blown off Jake's invitation. I might be able to salvage that, but on the other hand, maybe a couple days away was a good idea. I'd spent too much time this summer waiting on him to return. A little turnaround sounded like a great plan.

"I can send the jet back if you want, Dot," Max offered.

A private jet? *Damn*. This job was getting better all the time. But Dottie shook her head, and my short-lived daydream of living like a rock star vanished.

"It's a two-hour drive, Max," she said.

"Wish you'd let me spoil you some," Max said, kissing her cheek. "Don't know what I'll do if you actually retire, sweetheart."

Dottie laughed. "I'll make sure you're in good hands."

Max and Frank left, and the dogs settled down again as soon as the door shut behind the two men.

"So, what do you think? Want to help out on this job?"

"Sure, but I'm still not sure what I can do," I said.

She tilted her head and shrugged. "It's not your typical internal audit. If there are problems, we need to clean them up. Everything has to be perfect for the application process. The Gaming Commission won't approve a license application if there's a hint of financial impropriety."

Dottie stacked the papers on the conference room table and then walked me to the front of the office.

"We'll drive up Thursday morning, check in at the lodge, and stay a couple days. Plan on coming home on Sunday. That's not going to interfere with any work Rob has you doing, is it?"

I shook my head. Unfortunately, my workload at Rob's office was very light. "I'll stop by the office and make sure my schedule is clear, but it should be fine."

Dottie picked up a few pages from the printer on her desk and handed them to me. "Look this over, and if that's an acceptable rate for your services, sign and return them to me by Thursday."

I glanced down and was pleasantly surprised at the hourly rate for the contract, with her business picking up all expenses. I'd earn more working for Dottie for four days than I'd earned last month at Rob's office.

Dottie walked me to the door, the little dogs mincing along with her, and I found myself in the courtyard wondering what I'd just gotten myself into. This morning, I was an underemployed assistant to a criminal defense attorney. By midday I was planning a trip to Lake Tahoe with a 70-year-old accountant and would be making real money to boot. What would the evening bring?

My head was still swimming with images from Whispering Pines's brochure as I drove the few blocks to Rob's office. It had been too long since I'd had a good massage. I hoped I'd have time for one there, where the masseuses were among the best in the world. When I arrived at the law firm, I found the small parking lot dominated by a large truck pulling a horse trailer. The truck was empty, but the trailer contained a passenger who snorted and stamped as I passed by. I immediately recognized the logo for the Bishop Ranch on the truck's door.

Damn. I'd done my best to avoid Quinn Bishop in the last few months. Not because I didn't like Quinn. In fact, it was quite the opposite. I liked him a lot. But things got a little complicated, and I wanted to put a little distance between Quinn and me until I figured out my feelings. Still, I couldn't help myself and smoothed my hair before opening the door to the law office.

The lobby was empty, but I heard laughter in Rob's office and steeled myself to face the man who I'd last seen in this same room, right after he'd kissed me. The memory of that kiss still curled my toes, but I gave myself a good shake and forced myself into Rob's office. Quinn sat across the desk from Rob, both men leaning back in their chairs, laughing. Rob's dog, Basil, lay at Quinn's feet while the casually dressed cowboy stroked the dog's ears.

"Hey, Miranda," Rob said. "Come on in."

"I don't want to interrupt," I said, hanging near the door. Maybe I could get out without confronting the fact that I'd been avoiding Quinn.

Quinn stood, and my mouth went dry. Holy hell, the man was just too good looking. Tall, lean, with a rogue's smile and tousled dark blond hair. Bright blue eyes that contrasted with his tan skin. He was dressed in jeans and a T-shirt that showed off nicely muscled and tanned arms. Some women might be put off by the felony drug conviction, but since I worked for his former criminal defense attorney, I knew the truth of how he'd ended up spending two years in federal prison. But regardless of those circumstances, that was several years ago, and he'd put it behind him. When he'd been convicted nearly a decade earlier, he had been a successful horse trainer who worked with Hollywood movie producers. Now he was running his family's ranch.

"Miranda, it's good to see you," Quinn said, his blue eyes locking on mine.

"You too, Quinn," I said. "What are you doing here? I mean, how have you been?"

Quinn's eyes crinkled at the edges. "Busy at the ranch, but it's all good. How about you?"

"Miranda may be branching out and doing some freelance consulting work with Dottie Russell," Rob said. "Quinn is on his way to the ranch to drop off my new horse."

Rob's small ranch sat on the outer edge of the county, where he raised a few head of cattle. It was peaceful and pretty and Aunt Marie was enjoying redecorating the old farmhouse where Rob had lived for the last few decades.

"How was your meeting with Dottie?" Rob asked. He seemed nearly as excited as I was about the job opportunity.

"It was good. I guess I'm going to Lake Tahoe with her on Thursday."

"No kidding? You need a ride?" Quinn asked with a grin. "I'm heading there this weekend too."

My heart did a small skip at that thought. I gave myself a mental shake. The charming and too-handsome cowboy liked to flirt, but I wasn't sure that I was ready to take it beyond that. Though he was a really good kisser.

No. That wasn't fair. To say I had unresolved feelings about Jake was a huge understatement. And maybe I could still salvage that invitation to dinner that I'd accidentally rejected.

"Why are you going to the lake?" I asked.

"I'm delivering a couple horses to a friend who has a ranch outside of Carson City. He's down a few men on the ranch, so I may take a couple extra days to help him out," Quinn said. "If you're going to be around for the weekend, we should get dinner."

"I'm not sure how much time I'll have to socialize, but yeah, that would be nice," I said.

"You've got my number. Give me a call when you get there. At least let me take you to dinner." Quinn apparently knew the way to my heart started with a good menu. He moved toward the door and gave me a wink. "I'm going finish up this delivery and get back to the ranch. Hope to hear from you, Miranda."

His eyes met mine, and I nodded mutely and then watched Rob walk Quinn to the door. Fanning my face, I went to tidy up my workspace before I left for my trip. I filed the few documents lingering on my desk and checked my email. I changed my outgoing voicemail message, even though I rarely got phone calls. It took fewer than ten minutes, and then I was out of things to do.

The rest of the office was empty. Sarah was at the courthouse pulling records, according to the note she left on the whiteboard next to her desk. Theresa, the receptionist, was out of town for a family reunion.

Yeah, I did need Dottie's job offer. It was barely mid-afternoon, and I shut down my computer and looked over the time sheet I kept for Theresa. My hours had steadily declined in the past few months, and some of the work that Rob had me do was stuff that Sarah could easily handle. It had been a nice place to land after the trial, but it wasn't permanent, and it was time to move on. I had no idea what I could do to help Dottie, but I was smart and had a gift for numbers.

Maybe a few days in the most peaceful place on the planet was just what I needed to figure out where to go next.

CHAPTER THREE

The mattress shook as the other body in my bed rolled over, stretched, and groaned. It was enough to barely wake me, and out of habit, I reached out to shake him to stop his snoring. I was greeted with an enthusiastic tongue bath.

"Ugh, yuck, Hank," I said, wiping my hand on the bedspread.

My companion flopped his head back onto the pillow, and moments later, the snoring resumed. The good news was that after a long dry spell, I finally had someone sharing my bed. The bad news was that it was Hank, the 120-pound mastiff mix, and not Hank's owner.

I sighed and swung my legs over the side, leaving the bed to the dog. I tripped over the half-packed suitcase on my way to the coffee pot. I wasn't meeting Dottie until 10 o'clock, but I still had no idea what to pack for the trip. Swimwear? Something fancy? Tourist-casual? I was only going to be gone until Sunday, so I was probably just going to throw everything into the bag.

It was barely light out, and I squinted out the kitchen window at the garage across the backyard. I couldn't see any lights on, but I had heard the low rumble of the garage door opening late last night, so I knew that Jake was home. We had been on the cusp of actually having a date Tuesday evening, when he got a call from Bethany Boylan and had to drop everything to go arrest someone. He dropped Hank off at my door, gave me a kiss that made my eyes cross, and bolted off with a promise that he'd be home the next day. But instead, I got a text message letting me know that he'd been delayed, and would I mind taking car of his dog for another night?

This was getting old.

I had so been looking forward to having a summer with Jake living in the backyard. He'd planned on renting the apartment over the garage until August, when the contractors would be finished repairing his house from an unfortunate incident with a pipe bomb that was totally not my fault. But the renovation was taking longer than planned. That was good for me, since whatever this thing was between us hadn't progressed much in the last few months.

I poured a cup of coffee as Hank staggered into the kitchen yawning. I opened the door to let him into the backyard, set out his large bowl of kibble, and then went to take a shower. Between the hot water and the hot coffee, I was nearly awake when I walked into the kitchen to get a refill.

Thankfully, I was also nearly fully dressed, because Jake was standing at the counter pouring a cup of coffee.

"Good morning." I set my cup next to his, and he topped it off and gave me a sheepish smile.

"Coffee maker's broken," he said, his voice as rough as the two-days of scruff on his jaw.

"Did you get your suspect?" I asked, watching him stir a heaping teaspoon of sugar into his coffee.

He looked up, his dark brown eyes still sleepy, and gave me a nod and a slow smile. "Yeah, we got him. Bethany took a fist to the face, but we got him."

I tried not to smile at the thought of Jake's snooty partner getting punched in the face, but the news brightened my day considerably.

Jake laughed softly and shook his head. "Don't look so happy about it. She's fine."

I'd have to work on my poker face.

Jake reached out and put a hand on my waist, pulling me close to him as he leaned back against the kitchen counter. "I believe I owe you a date," he said, a smile on the edge of his lips. "How about tonight?"

I groaned. "I'm going to Tahoe today. I'll be home on Sunday."

"Tahoe?" he asked, his smile fading. "Not with Sarah, I hope."

"I wish. No, I'm picking up some extra work with Dottie Russell."

Jake grinned, and I was still very aware of his strong hand at my waist. "I don't know if that's any better. I hear she's a wild one."

I laughed. "It's an audit. I'm sure I'll be fine. No casinos, no dancing. No fun."

He stared into my eyes, and my heart fluttered. "Okay, then, Sunday night."

I smiled. "Sunday night."

The flutters moved south at the thought. *Finally*. Months of dancing around our attraction, trying to navigate conflicts that kept us apart. We were both finally on the same page.

"Can you feed Kvetch for me while I'm gone?" After I'd spent so much time with Hank, I figured I was owed a little payback.

"Not fair. Kvetch hates me," Jake said.

"Kvetch hates everyone. Except Aunt Marie. But all you have to do is put his food out twice a day, and make sure he has fresh water. Just check to make sure he's okay. For some reason, Aunt Marie adores that ornery bastard, and I don't want anything to happen to him."

"Why didn't she take him out to the ranch with her?"

I shrugged. "I don't think he'd have mixed well with Rob's chickens. Or other livestock."

"Sure, yeah. I'll feed the cat for you. But I won't pet him."

I laughed. "He won't let you."

I caught sight of the clock on the stove and jumped back, away from Jake. "Oh, damn, I have to pack and get to Dottie's office. If I miss my ride, I'll have to hitch a ride with Quinn and his horses."

I moved away and heard Jake's unhappy exhale. "Quinn Bishop? He's going to Lake Tahoe with you?"

Immediately, I regretted letting Quinn's name slip out. The two men didn't know each other, except by reputation. Or by criminal history. Jake had warned me away from Quinn, but he didn't know the full story behind Quinn's past. I did, but I couldn't tell anyone.

"He's just going to be there at the same time, delivering horses to a ranch near the lake. I'm not going *with* him."

Jake set his cup on the counter and frowned again but didn't say anything. I stepped forward and set my mug in the sink. "It's not a big deal—"

Before I could finish my defense, Jake grabbed me and pulled me tight against him. My breath caught as I pressed against his hard body. One hand reached up and brushed my hair, still wet from my shower, away from my face. Then he leaned in, and I met him halfway. His lips were soft against mine, and my heart thudded at the contact. I might be biased, but I was pretty sure we were really good at this.

With a sigh of regret, I pushed away from Jake's chest. "I really have to—meet. Drive."

Great. One kiss and I'd lost the ability to speak.

"I'll get you to Dottie's in time," he said, pulling me back for another mind-melting kiss.

It was heaven. The tiny flutters in my belly grew into tremors as I ran my hand up his chest, to his neck, and then raked my fingers through his thick, soft hair.

Jake pulled away first, and the absence disoriented me.

"Go get dressed." His voice was hoarse and low.

"Dressed?" My body and a lot of frustrated hormones had other ideas.

"I don't want you to miss your ride," he said, picking up his coffee cup and heading to the door. "And I need to go get a shower. A cold one."

Oh God. This was going to be the longest four-day business trip ever.

Jake was true to his word, though, and two hours later, I was standing at the curb in front of Dottie's office while he hefted my suitcase out of the back of his truck.

"Jesus, what did you pack?"

"Everything. I didn't have time to pack light. *Someone* distracted me."

He grinned and gave me a wink. "Didn't want you to forget me before Sunday."

That was unlikely. If the kisses were that amazing, I was really looking forward to actually having a date with Jake.

"Miranda!"

I turned to see Dottie, walking toward me pulling a small, wheeled carry-on.

"Hi, Dottie," I said. "This is Jake Barnes, my, uh, neighbor."

"Uh-huh," she said, giving him a once over that reminded me of the look Bub had given me. "You're the FBI agent, right?"

"Yes, ma'am," Jake said. "It's nice to meet you. I saw you testify in the Ramirez trial. It was impressive."

"Not impressive enough. He got convicted."

"Not on all the counts," Jake said.

"Were you the case agent on that? I don't remember you

being there. I'm sure I'd remember that," she said, still eyeing him.

"No, that was Agent Boylan's case," Jake said. "I just happened to be there that day."

"Well, we need to hit the road. Miranda, did you pack for a month? Are you going to be able to lift that suitcase?"

Geez, everyone was a critic. "It has wheels."

Jake pulled up the handle on the bag and handed it to me, our hands brushing. "See you Sunday."

My mouth went dry at the promise in his voice. Suddenly, Sunday sounded so far away.

I followed Dottie to the private parking lot, where she opened the trunk of a powder blue, mint-condition classic.

"Nice wheels, Dottie," I said.

"Thank you. It's a 1955 Ford Thunderbird," she said, running a hand along the chrome trim of the hardtop. She eyed my suitcase and then frowned at the trunk, which was half-filled with the spare tire.

After a struggle, I managed to fit both my suitcase and Dottie's small carry-on bag in the limited space, and minutes later we were pulling out of the parking lot.

"So what's up with you and Agent Dollface back there?" Dottie asked as I fastened my seat belt.

"What? Oh, nothing. I mean, maybe there's something, but he lives in the garage. It's an apartment over the garage."

I was rambling but couldn't seem to control it.

"Good for you," Dottie said, turning onto the freeway onramp.

"Well, we'll see. It's complicated."

"Sweetie, when a man looks like that, it's not complicated. You jump on that and ride to the buzzer." As I choked on a response, Dottie gunned the engine, and the little car leapt forward.

"Have you spent much time in Tahoe?"

"Sure, I have a cabin on the west side of the lake. Well, not near the water, but I can see it from my deck."

"That's nice. How about South Shore? Stateline? The casinos?"

I nodded. "Yes, many times. Not in a few years though."

"You're in for a treat. Whispering Pines is an institution. One of the oldest lodges in the area. You know it was designed by a guy who studied with Julia Morgan. You know, the woman who designed Hearst Castle."

I raised an eyebrow. "Really? I've never been up there, but it's sure beautiful from a distance."

"It's gorgeous. And Max and his family have taken real good care of it too. I don't think you'd find a more exclusive resort anywhere on the West Coast."

"Why is he willing to risk that to buy a casino?"

I knew little about the casino business, but it sounded, well, like a gamble. Much more risky than a nice resort and spa with an excellent reputation.

"The Penny is not just a casino. It's a legend. And Big Sal owned it in its heyday. It was a classy place. Sinatra used to come stay at the lodge and play the Penny at night."

I could picture that—the celebrities hanging around the sun-drenched swimming pool, out on the classic wooden boats, the nightclubs filled with men in tuxedos and women in stylish dresses.

"So Max wants to bring all that back?"

"That's the plan. And he's got the swanky clientele from the lodge to make it happen." She paused and adjusted her over-sized sunglasses. "There are just two hurdles. He's got to show the banks that the hotel is in tip-top financial shape. And he's got to show the Gaming Commission that there's no hint of financial impropriety around his existing property."

"But he doesn't have a casino now," I said.

"Right. But when Max lost the Lucky Penny, there was talk. Nothing proven, mind you, but there were rumors about Sal having mob ties."

"What do you need me to help with?" I asked.

"In many respects, what I do for Max is very similar to the rest of my work. I go in and look at the books. Identify areas where there are inadequate controls, so the company may be losing money, and look for indications that there may be fraud or theft or just mismanagement," Dottie said. "It's not really much different than looking at someone's credit card bill to tell if they're cheating on a spouse. It's just a bigger credit card bill."

"I audited departments when I worked in finance," I said, feeling like I was on firmer ground now. It hadn't been my primary job when I worked at an investment bank, but the tasks required were familiar, and I could handle it.

"Good. We should be in and out in a few days," she said.

"Max must be really attached to this casino," I said. "He's going through a lot of trouble to get approved."

Dottie laughed. "It's not all sentimental. Do you do much gambling?"

"No, not really. As you said, I'm good with numbers, so I know the odds are in the house's favor."

"Smart girl. If you're going to play, blackjack, poker, and craps are the best options. At least there, you've got some strategy to employ," she said. "Even then, the house wins eventually. If you keep playing."

She passed a black muscle car as the wide interstate began a slight incline as we left the valley floor.

"Casinos make money on the tables, and it's good money. But the great money is keeping people in the house. Shows, restaurants, shops, spas, hotel rooms. It all turns a profit. And Max and his wife Angie have done amazing things with the resort. If he can get the Penny back, they'll make it huge."

"I can't wait to see it up close," I said, as the landscape zipping by the sports car changed from valley suburban strip malls to the rolling foothills of the Sierra Nevada mountains. "I spent a lot of summer vacations at Tahoe but mostly at campgrounds and my family's cabin on the west side of the lake. The resort always looked like a castle up on the hill, like a fairy tale."

Dottie nodded. "It's quite a landmark, and the Emmerson family has developed it into a treasure."

The little car purred as we climbed in altitude on the interstate. The evergreens grew thicker along the side of the highway, and the road curved gently around in a familiar route. We started our descent on the other side of the ridge, and Donner Lake came into view, then slipped past us as we headed toward Truckee. There, we turned, continuing toward the edge of Lake Tahoe.

The road would eventually lead to Stateline, Nevada, where the large casinos were wedged between ski lifts and daring downhill runs on the east, and private lakeside golf courses and public beaches to the west. It was a vacation paradise, no matter what time of the year, and one of my favorite places in the world.

We rounded a corner, and Dottie pulled over to a vista point, parking the little coupe in the shade of a copse of evergreens.

"Come on, I want to show you something," she said, getting out of the car.

I followed her, and we walked out to the edge of a scenic overlook, where a low stone wall enclosed the visitors' area. Below us was a 40-foot drop that ended in the icy lake water, and in front of us was a view as majestic as I'd ever seen. I took a deep breath, savoring the familiar scent of the pines. The tension in my shoulders evaporated, and I smiled as the sun warmed my shoulders.

"Isn't it something?" Dottie asked, the awe in her voice matching my own feelings.

"It's my favorite place on earth," I said.

"No, I meant the Penny."

I looked where she was pointing to the left and saw a faded building in the distance, sitting back from the water's edge behind a chain-link fence. The exterior was worn by the weather—frigid winds and snow in the winter and high-altitude sun in the summer. A wall of dark windows rose several stories high and curved out toward the shoreline, and behind it, the building rose several more stories and stretched back toward the highway. Weathered balconies faced the water, and I could imagine that the Lucky Penny's guests had paid a premium for those hotel rooms.

"That's the Lucky Penny?"

I squinted into the bright sun at the abandoned casino and hotel. In its prime, I could see why it had been popular. It sat in a great location—just close enough to the action at Stateline to draw casino traffic—yet apart and a little exclusive. Just a bit out of the reach of the everyday gambler. If you drove down the curved drive to the grand entrance, which we could barely see from this angle, it must have felt like a world away from everything.

"And there's the Whispering Pines Resort," Dottie said. She raised a hand to point but didn't have to.

I'd have to be blind not to see the cream-colored walls and peaked red roof that contrasted with the dark green trees and bright blue skies. My gaze went between the two properties— Whispering Pines, a sparkling gem rising like a silver cloud above the lake, and the Penny, crouched in the shadows of the trees and the rocks.

"Well, let's get a closer look," Dottie said, then turned and strode back to the car.

I gave the Penny a backward glance and wondered how much work it would take Max and his family to restore the neglected casino to its former glory. Or even make it habitable after it had been closed for nearly 20 years, and neglected for who knew how many years before that.

A few miles down the winding lakeside highway, Dottie pulled to the right into a driveway with a huge sign warning that this was private property, patrolled by security, and there was no camping allowed. She followed the driveway to a locked gate and pulled up to the side so I could see out the passenger side window. I rolled down the window and felt the breeze from the lake rustle my hair.

A marquee on the front of the entrance had lost about a third of its now-faded and crooked letters but appeared at one point to have said, "Thanks for the memories." The white background was now streaked grey and brown.

But there was something about the architecture that was appealing. It had been designed to sit among the trees, not compete with them for attention. It seemed to be in harmony with the landscape. Or maybe it was that the landscape was reclaiming the man-made building. But it didn't look like a box had been dropped onto the shore, like other casinos along the lake.

Dottie backed up the Thunderbird, and we slowly drove back up the shady narrow road to the highway.

"It really was special," she said, her voice so low I wasn't sure if she was talking to me or herself.

I didn't respond, just kept my eye on the empty casino until we turned the corner, and it disappeared from view. We continued in silence for another few minutes, until Dottie turned left onto a steep curving road that led away from the lake. This, too, was a familiar drive to me. Aunt Marie and I had explored the top of the ridge many times—either in our hiking boots or our snowshoes, depending on the season. But we weren't heading all the way to the top of the ridge. Instead, Dottie signaled a left turn through curved stone walls, upon which the resort's name was set in a cursive script.

I had never passed through these gates before, and I leaned forward in anticipation of what lay beyond. The shady road curved through the pine trees for another half mile or more, then burst out of the canopy and into a bright green manicured meadow that stretched out, the L-shaped lodge at the other end. The road crossed a small creek that flowed under a rustic bridge. The water then tumbled over an artificial waterfall made of boulders from the nearby mountains, then into a pond that shimmered in the rolling green meadow.

And then beyond that idyllic scene were the creamy walls and red roof of the Whispering Pines Resort. As amazing and fairy-tale like as it was at a distance, the lodge was even more impressive up close. It was huge, much larger than I realized, with a wide veranda along the front of the building. It was multiple stories high and L-shaped, with a long wing stretching back away from us.

"Welcome to the Whispering Pines Resort," Dottie said with a laugh at my open-mouthed stare.

"It's gorgeous!"

"Yes, it is. Wait until you see inside."

We pulled up to the front under a sweeping portico, and a young man in a uniform jacket hurried out to greet us. He loaded our bags onto a cart then gave Dottie a valet ticket, and another employee escorted us to the lobby through the largest set of wooden doors I'd ever seen.

Inside, a cavernous room was made almost cozy by the natural wood walls and a stone fireplace that was a center-piece of the room. Cozy couches and comfortable club chairs sat in groupings around the lobby with arrangements at the windows that looked out onto a lush green lawn that rolled away with the bright blue waters of Lake Tahoe in the distance.

The room was quiet, and I glanced around and realized we were the only people in the lobby.

Dottie led the way to the counter, where a smiling young woman checked us into our rooms.

"It doesn't seem very busy," I said, looking around at the empty room. It was impeccably furnished, warm, and inviting— but other than a few scattered employees and me and Dottie, it was empty of people. Maybe my recent middle-of-the-night viewing of *The Shining* was a bad idea.

The girl behind the counter smiled wider. "I know, it's really exciting. They're filming a movie here right now, so we don't have many guests who aren't involved with the production."

"That's really cool," I said. "What movie is it?"

"I don't know what it's called, but it's a drama set during World War II. Or is it World War I? I always get those confused," said the girl, whose name was Kayla, according to the tag on her vest. Her brow furrowed for a moment, but then she smiled and leaned forward with a conspiratorial whisper. "It's so neat! Reece Muir is here."

It was Dottie's turn to frown. "Who?"

"Reece Muir. He's an actor. He was in that action movie that bombed last month," I said.

"Didn't see it. Don't get out to the movies much. Too much crap," Dottie said. "They just don't make movie stars like they used to. Frank Sinatra, Elvis Presley. *Those* were entertainers."

"Reece Muir is hot right now," I insisted. "Despite that horrible movie. He's a good actor."

"You'll probably see him. In fact, they're filming in the library all day today, and if you look down the grand hall, you can see where they're set up," Kayla said. From the check-in counter, we couldn't even see the grand hall, but I looked around anyway trying to take everything in.

"Lots of Hollywood types come to Whispering Pines," Dottie said. "They don't get hassled here. It's a place to relax, get away from the cameras, and not have to put on a front. The staff here really take good care of you."

Kayla grinned and nodded. "You've been here before," she said with an approving nod. "I'll have someone take care of your bags, and if you'd like to follow me, I'll give you a quick tour and then show you upstairs to your rooms."

"No need," Dottie said. "I know my way around."

"You'll need to take the elevators or the front stairs from the lobby, because they're filming at the other end of the grand hall, and those stairs are closed," Kayla said, handing us the electronic keys to our room along with a map to the grounds.

Our shoes on the marble floor echoed through the lobby as we crossed to a pair of elevators that rose silently to the second floor. We stepped out into a hallway that was even more quiet than it had been downstairs. The thick carpet muffled our footsteps as we walked down the hall. Unlike the downstairs hall that ran straight through the bottom floor like a runway, the second floor hallway took a slight jog to the right, then after two sets of doors, to the left. This gave the upstairs a cozier feel, and probably provided more privacy, since you couldn't see every doorway at a glance. The walls upstairs were a warm creamy plaster with the same natural wood accents. Our rooms were across the hall from each other.

"Let's meet downstairs in an hour," Dottie said, unlocking her door. "Max wants to meet with us before we start our work."

I nodded and entered my own room, where my suitcase had been left near the closet door. Even though we were in regular rooms and not the suites where the movie stars were probably staying, the space was stunning and spacious and felt even larger because of the tall wood-framed windows that provided a sweeping vista of the sloping lawn, the trees, and the lake in the distance. A round table and two chairs sat near the window, and a four-poster bed dominated one wall, its crisp white linens inviting me to climb in and take a restful nap. I dropped my purse on the low rust-colored settee at the foot of the bed and took in the immaculate and peaceful setting. Who needed a spa? This room was enough to make me forget my troubles.

Then I saw the bathroom—and decided to forward my mail here. They'd have to drag me kicking and screaming from the Whispering Pines Resort and Spa. Pale green and blue glass tiles lined the shower, which featured several showerheads, and a bathtub big enough for two was lined with lavender-scented toiletries and a pyramid of fluffy white towels.

Max had done us right.

I quickly unpacked my clothes, kicked off my shoes, and lay down on the bed with a deep sigh. I love hotel rooms. There's just something about checking in and playing house for a few days. Not to mention having someone to clean up after you every day.

But this room was a cut above any other I'd ever stayed in and so romantic that it was a crime I was here alone. On the plus side, I wouldn't be sharing the bed with Hank. But I also wasn't sharing it with Jake, which was a crying shame. I quickly pushed that thought away. *Sunday*. Just a few days away, and then I'd be out on a date with Jake.

I stretched out across the king-sized bed and heard a soft knock at the door. I walked barefoot across the soft carpet and opened the door without checking the peephole, but it wasn't Dottie on the other side.

A uniformed bellhop carrying a large vase of lilies and roses smiled at me. "Miss Vaughn, these are for you."

"Oh, how nice. Are you sure?"

He smiled. "Your name is on the card."

He set the vase on a side table, and I found a few dollars in my pocket for a tip. As he left, Dottie's door opened, and she walked into my suite.

"Nice digs, huh?" she said, then spied my flowers. "Hey, you've already got an admirer?"

"I can't imagine that this is right," I said, opening the card. I saw the message, and all the air in my lungs left in a rush. "Oh."

Dinner tonight? Call me, Quinn.

CHAPTER FOUR

The restaurant where Dottie and I were going to meet Max was on the lower level of the resort, below the lobby. We were early, so Dottie pointed out the hall that led to the resort's gym. Then she led me past the unopened doors to the restaurant, Angelina's, and to a pair of tall, frosted glass doors that led to the resort's spa.

As soon as we entered the spa's quiet lobby, I sensed the change in atmosphere. The room was lightly scented with lavender, the walls were a soft blue-green, and the low couches were light khaki and faced the smooth, curved wooden reception desk. A woman behind the counter stood and welcomed us.

"Dottie, it's so nice to see you," she said, coming around the desk for a hug.

"Thanks, Angie. This is Miranda Vaughn, my new assistant."

I shook hands with the woman, who looked like she was in her 60s, but well preserved. Like she was too relaxed to ever incur wrinkles. Of course, if I worked here, I'd probably be so relaxed that I was boneless.

"Angie Emmerson is the genius behind the spa's success. She's also Max's wife," Dottie said to me, then turned back to the spa's hostess. "But I didn't expect to see you behind the counter here today."

She laughed, and finally I saw a few light lines around her pretty blue eyes. "I gave most of the staff time off until the filming is complete. There's not as much work for them right now. And I can always fill in in a pinch."

Dottie picked up a menu from the counter, and I glanced at the list of services the spa offered—everything from head to toe, literally. I could have my hair cut and colored, get a facial, a full body massage, get anything and everything waxed, and end with a manicure and pedicure. There were also various types of mud baths, saunas, steam rooms, meditation coaches, yoga classes, and aromatherapy.

"I recommend the hot stone massage," Dottie said.

"If you'd like to schedule an appointment, I can put you on Margarit's schedule," Angie said. "And how about you, Miranda. Would you like to schedule a massage?"

There was no price list on the menu, and I hesitated, wondering how much a massage at the most exclusive resort at Lake Tahoe would set me back. That sort of extravagance surely wouldn't be included in the all-expenses-paid offer by Max. I should pass on the spa treatment and find my relaxation by curling up in one of those plush chairs in the lobby with a good book and enjoying the view.

On the other hand, I was making a nice chunk of change for my work with Dottie. Maybe I could afford to splurge a little. Sensing my hesitation, Angie gave me another gentle nudge toward indulging myself.

"The Swedish massage is Margarit's specialty. It's very popular," she said.

I agreed to schedule the massage for the following afternoon, which I justified by telling myself that I'd need it after a day of poring over the Whispering Pines accounts. Angie closed the ledger that contained the spa's appointments and gave us a warm smile.

"Are you meeting my Max for lunch?"

Dottie nodded. "Yes, we were a bit early, and I wanted to show Miranda around a little."

"Don't let him order the steak," Angie said, walking us to the door. "He's not supposed to eat red meat, and I keep telling the waitstaff that, but he sneaks around and does it behind my back."

Dottie laughed. "A man's got to have some vices, Angie. And I don't think I could stop him if I tried."

"I suppose as vices go it's not as bad as some. He did give up cigars and bourbon," she said with a warm laugh. "Enjoy lunch, and I'll see you around. If you need anything, just pick up a phone and the front desk will help you with anything at all. It's a good time for you to be here, Dot. It's never this quiet in the summer."

"I've never seen it this quiet at any time," Dottie said.

"Have you run up to watch the filming yet?" Angie asked, and Dottie and I shook our heads. She fanned herself. "That Reece Muir. What a hottie."

She waved us through the doors with a girlish giggle back into the dark-wood enclosed entryway.

"There you are!" Max stood in front of the glass and mahogany doors of Angelina's. His booming voice echoed in the empty vestibule, bouncing off the dark wood-paneled walls and marble flooring. Then he gave his wife a little wave with wiggling fingers that contradicted his tough-guy suit and softened his scowl.

The plaque on the door said it wasn't open until 5 o'clock, but Max yanked the door open and waved us through. Inside, a sea of cozy tables covered in white linen tablecloths stretched out, a contrast to the dark wood-paneled walls. A waiter appeared and escorted us to a corner booth.

"There will be four of us," Max said, and another restaurant employee appeared nearly instantly with an additional place setting for the generous table.

Before I could ask who would be joining us, a tall, dark-haired man in a tailored suit walked in, paused, and then walked in our direction.

"Dottie, you remember my nephew, Jordan Swift," Max said. "And this is Dottie's new associate, Miranda Vaughn. Jordan was acting CEO while I was on leave, and now he's our vice president of operations."

Jordan shook hands with Dottie and me as I wondered what that title meant for this business. On the surface, there was little that would indicate he shared any genetics with Max, except for the sharp, nearly black eyes that didn't miss anything. He was a handsome man, as Max had said, with a set of cheekbones that would make a supermodel jealous and those piercing eyes. The dramatic good looks were softened by a hint of grey hair at his temples and a few fine lines around his eyes. When he smiled, two perfect dimples appeared on his tan cheeks, but the expression didn't quite warm his eyes, which appeared tired on closer inspection.

"It's nice to see you again, Dottie. It's been too long since you've come for a visit," he said, and his rich voice sounded sincere.

But did he think we were here on a social visit?

"Miranda is my newest employee," Dottie said with a smile, and I nodded quickly. *Sure, okay.* I wondered who else she employed, other than maybe Bub and Duchess. "I thought with Max coming back to work, it was a great time to bring her to meet my favorite client."

Dottie reached over the table and squeezed Max's hand with affection.

"Congratulations, Miranda," Jordan said with a nod.

"Thank you," I replied, reaching for the bread. Maybe if my mouth was full no one would ask me questions about my new and still unfamiliar job. Plus the bread looked and smelled like it was just out of the oven, and it had been a long time since breakfast.

"Is this a business trip or are you on vacation?" Jordan asked.

I glanced at Max and felt the frisson of tension between uncle and nephew. Jordan didn't seem to know Dottie and I were there to examine the books and study Jordan's management of the resort while Max was away. With Jordan still in management, this could get sticky.

"A little of each. I wanted to get Miranda acquainted with the operation so she can help out in the future."

Dottie gave him a wide smile, and Jordan gave her a weak one in return. The waiter approached the table, and talk of business faded away. The rest of the meal passed with small talk that didn't give me any more information about the family dynamics. The food was incredible, which distracted me from the thoughts of why Max and Jordan seemed to be glaring at each other across the table. The sea bass marinated in miso and grilled over applewood just about made my eyes roll back in my head. While we had yet to look at any of the finances, so far, it looked like the resort hadn't suffered under Jordan's temporary stewardship.

"Normally, we'd have a concert to entertain you two this evening, but our normal summer schedule was disrupted by the film schedule," Max said. "But there's plenty to do just down the hill. If you see anything at any of the casinos that interests you, just let the front desk know, and they'll make sure you get what you need—reservations, tickets, a limo. Whatever you want."

It was a generous offer, but it was the first part that caught my attention. The film production was clearly a bone of contention between the two men.

Jordan kept his face neutral, but his eyes were hard as he looked at his uncle. "It was a good opportunity to get the resort's name out there," he said, the defensive tone evident. "And they're paying to use the buildings. And the food, the spa, everything."

Max snorted. "What food? You see those women? You think they eat?"

Jordan glanced between me and Dottie, then back to Max. "Well, you know my opinion, Max."

An uncomfortable silence descended over the table, and then Jordan glanced at the gaudy watch on his wrist. "I'm afraid I have an appointment to make. It was nice to meet you, Miranda. I'm sure I'll be seeing you both around."

With a curt nod to his uncle, Jordan left the empty restaurant. Max watched him stalk through the doors and then shook his head.

"This whole Hollywood thing was his doing," he said. "We haven't done anything like this before, and frankly, I don't like it. This should be our busiest season, and instead, we're turning down our regular customers because those people booked up half the rooms, and we had to reschedule the concert series so they could shoot at night."

He exhaled a frustrated sigh. "He says it's good publicity, but I don't see why we need that. Whispering Pines has been here for nearly seventy years. We're the premiere resort on Lake Tahoe. Why do we need more publicity than that?"

Dottie patted Max's hand. "It's just for a short time, Max. Think about how nice it will be to see the lodge on the big screen."

He waved a dismissive hand. "I know, I know. That's what Angie says too. I should just relax and enjoy the fact that there's a little peace and quiet around here in July for a change. Everyone comes here to relax, but making that happen causes me and the rest of the staff a lot of stress," he said, giving me a wide smile. "Don't mind me, Miranda. I'm just a cranky old man."

He walked Dottie and me to the elevators and pressed the button for us.

"I'll get you ladies set up in the office. Then I've got a doctor's appointment in Reno. I'll be back tonight, though, and maybe the four of us can have dinner together."

"Oh, I'm sorry, I think I have plans," I said.

"Good for you," he said. "Where are you going? Need tickets to anything?"

It was disconcerting how often the people at Whispering Pines wanted to take care of everything for me and Dottie. I shook my head.

"No, I don't think so, but thank you," I said.

We stepped out on the main floor and walked past the empty front desk, where Kayla still stood at attention, waiting for guests that weren't coming—at least according to Max—until after the movie wrapped up its production. We entered a door marked "authorized personnel only" and then walked down a hallway, past plaques on the wall indicating the offices for human resources, accounting, marketing, and other business offices. At the end, we reached a conference room, and Max unlocked the door, then gave Dottie the keys, along with two employee badges.

"Everything should be here, but if you need anything—"

"I know. We'll call the front desk," she said.

He nodded and gave me a wink, then turned and headed back down the hall. A tidy row of binders and a closed laptop sat at one end of the conference table. The room's single window looked out over a view similar to the view from my room. If the lobby had been quiet, the business office was tomblike in its silence. The scrap of the chair that Dottie pulled away from the table echoed through the bare room.

Dottie handed me a key and one of the temporary employee badges, then smiled.

"You ready to get to work?"

CHAPTER FIVE

I closed the last binder on the conference room table with a long sigh, then squeezed my eyes shut and rubbed my forehead. My brain ached from trying to absorb four years of profit-and-loss statements and Dottie's explanations of what we were trying to discern from them.

"Yeah, there's a lot to learn," she said, snapping shut her laptop. "But you need to see the big picture before you dive into the details."

We had the large conference room to ourselves all afternoon, and other employees of the business office treated us with such great deference that I wasn't entirely sure if Dottie hadn't told them we were with the IRS. The couple times that Dottie had picked up the phone and asked for more information, it had been delivered promptly by friendly, yet somewhat nervous office workers.

Dottie stood and patted my shoulder.

"Don't worry. Tomorrow morning, we'll just be focusing on the receipts," she said, then slid something across the table at me. "Here ya go."

I picked up the plastic card with the Whispering Pines Resort's logo on it. "What is this?"

"Your room account card," she said. "Use it for food here, car services, the spa—it will all get billed to your room. I'll come by and get you at eight tomorrow, and we'll get breakfast before we start work."

"The spa? Really?"

Dottie laughed. "Just tip your masseuse. Otherwise, spa services are included. I negotiated that as part of my fee."

I was suddenly energized as I helped Dottie stack the paperwork on the table and pack up our computers. Maybe I would give that hot stone massage a try. I made a mental note to get a spa menu and see how much I could fit in before we finished the audit. When we left the room, Dottie locked the door behind us and pocketed the key. The business office was nearly empty as we walked back to the lobby.

"Everyone seems scared of us," I said, as we walked to the elevators.

She laughed. "Yeah, well, the big boss just brought in auditors. That's never good. They probably think we're scouring expense reports. Max was out of the resort for a year and a half while he recovered. Some of these people were brought in by Jordan, and they know of Max by reputation only. So they're probably not real secure about their jobs right now."

Kayla was no longer at the front desk, replaced by a young man with dark hair. He gave us a friendly nod and smile as we passed by. I waited until the elevator doors closed before asking the question that had been on my mind most of the day.

"What was wrong with Max, if you don't mind me asking?"

"He had cancer, but he's doing great now. Totally cancer-free and probably healthier than he ever was, even in his prime," Dottie said. "I don't think Jordan expected him to make such a comeback, so he made some big changes to the resort, brought in his own people to help him. It's causing a rift between them."

We rode the elevator in silence to our floor then stepped out into the wide, quiet hallway that led to the suites.

"By the way, I didn't mention it earlier, but just a reminder not to talk to anyone about what we're doing here," she said, pausing at the threshold to her suite.

"Of course," I said.

"I knew you'd understand, working for Rob and all," she said with a smile. "Now go have some fun! I'll see you in the morning."

I felt the knot in my shoulder and considered her advice about hitting the spa. But instead, I collapsed on the wide king-sized bed with a view of the lake and called Quinn to accept his dinner invitation. We needed to talk anyway. His flowers made me wonder if it was smart to accept the offer, when I had no intention of getting involved with him. Well, more involved. We had shared a flirtation and a very nice kiss once, but that was it. I really did enjoy his company. I just didn't want our relationship to continue in a romantic direction.

I showered and dressed in a pair of skinny black capris and a shimmery silver tank top with a draped neckline. It was dressy but in a casual way. I never thought of Lake Tahoe as a formal place, and this was comfortable but wouldn't get me kicked out of a nice restaurant. I found a pair of long silver earrings that paired well with the sleek top and brushed my hair.

Quinn arrived right on time, and I let him into the room, where we had a stellar view of the late evening sun just starting to approach the horizon.

"Nice place you got here," he said, admiring the view below, where the low, early evening sun was casting long shadows across the wide green lawn below. I tried not to ogle my own view of him—dressed in an open-collared dress shirt and a pair of tailored grey slacks. It was a far cry from the ranch attire I'd seen him in before. He turned back to me, and I hoped he hadn't caught me staring.

"What are you doing here again?" he asked.

"It's an audit." Since I wasn't allowed to talk about my job, I decided that the less said, the better.

Quinn had made reservations at The Golden Chalice, a popular fine-dining destination at the Royal Palace Casino, the most popular casino on the tiny Stateline strip. The hub of Lake Tahoe's nightlife was less than a half-hour drive from the resort but had a different energy entirely. Quinn took my hand in his, keeping me close as we wove through the crowded casino floor to the restaurant. We were seated at a table by the windows, perfect to watch the vibrant pink and orange sunset fade over the mountains in the distance. After we ordered cocktails, I bit my lip and leaned across the small table between us.

Quinn followed suit, leaning in with an amused smile.

"I need to talk to you about something," I said, unsure how to tell him.

"Are you breaking up with me?" he asked, his teasing grin causing his blue eyes to twinkle.

I gave an embarrassed laugh. "Sort of?"

"Does this mean that federal agent finally made his move?"

I shrugged and looked down at the table to avoid his eyes. "Yes. I mean, I think so."

"You're not sure?"

"It's complicated," I said, looking up and meeting his gaze. "I just feel like I need to see that through."

He nodded, his eyes turning more serious. "It shouldn't be complicated, Miranda."

I hated that he was right.

"Well, it's just that he's been busy with work, then there were conflicts with our jobs, but I think things might work out now."

"Then I'm very happy for you," he said. "As long as you're happy."

I nodded quickly and took a long sip from my mojito. "I feel a little weird talking to you about this. About Jake."

I might as well say his name, but that didn't make it feel any less awkward.

"Why? We're friends," Quinn said.

"Yes, but we're friends who kissed. So that's a little strange."

Quinn laughed and raised his cocktail. "To friends who kiss."

"Kissed," I corrected, raising my glass.

He laughed again.

The waiter returned to take our orders. When he walked away, Quinn leaned back in his chair. His handsome face was relaxed, and I didn't get the feeling that my confession about Jake broke his heart. Which was both a relief and a little off-putting. I mean, not that I wanted a dramatic scene where he declared his feelings for me. But that would have been a little flattering.

"So you and Barnes, you're taking things slow?" he asked.

"Yes, a little." That was one way to explain it.

"Look, feel free to tell me to go to hell, but it doesn't seem like you're all in with this relationship," Quinn said.

"No, I am."

I wasn't sure how to explain my warring feelings about Jake. When we were alone together, it was perfect. But as soon as we were in public together, at least, anywhere around his colleagues, I was supremely uncomfortable.

"What else is keeping you and Special Agent Barnes from moving forward in your relationship?" Quinn asked. He raised his drink and took a sip, eyeing me over the rim of the glass with a kind expression. I looked down at the table again, suddenly emotional as I realized he understood exactly what was going on.

I took a deep breath before answering. "His job. And my reputation."

Quinn nodded. There was no one else I could confide in about these feelings. Sarah didn't fully understand my concerns and just urged me onward, damn the haters.

"You were found not guilty. You don't have a criminal record," Quinn said, echoing what Sarah had told me a thousand times.

It was true, but to many of Jake's coworkers the acquittal simply meant that I'd slipped out of their net, not that I hadn't done anything wrong. The stigma didn't dissolve when the jury found me not guilty. And if anyone could understand living with that stigma, it would be Quinn—once a successful horse trainer who worked with Hollywood studios, until he was arrested on drug charges. Though he seemed to be moving forward just fine now, I wondered how long it had taken him to put it behind him —or how long it took to perfect his act of nonchalance.

"So you're just not going public with this," he asked, his voice gentle.

"It's not like that. We're not sneaking around," I said, hating that I sounded so defensive. "I just would hate for his career to suffer because of my history with the criminal justice system."

Quinn smiled and reached across the table to take my hand. "Like I said, as long as you're happy."

He gave my hand a squeeze and then let go as the waiter returned with our first course. During the rest of the meal, we avoided any discussion of my might-be relationship with Jake. Quinn was good company, entertaining me with stories of working on movie sets and on his family's ranch, which he now ran. He wasn't hard to look at either. And with the help of a couple tasty mojitos and a good meal, I was recovering from my embarrassing admission earlier in the evening.

When we walked out of the restaurant and returned to the casino floor, the crowds had grown. We passed by a Sinatra impersonator crooning to a nearly filled cocktail lounge. The roulette table was three deep in cheering revelers, and the black-jack tables were filling up too. It was nearing 9:30, and as we passed the doors to the poker parlor, I could see the tables were filled. I wondered if the Penny's casino had been as popular.

"So what would you like to do now," Quinn asked.

"Want to play cards?"

"Strip poker?" Quinn asked with that rogue's grin.

I laughed and shook my head. "I was thinking blackjack."

He slipped an arm around my shoulders. "Whatever you'd like. Lead the way."

———

The exciting party vibe was a great distraction from my thoughts about Jake and why I was conflicted about him. Even though it was a Thursday, the Lake Tahoe casinos were busy with summer tourists eager to spend their extra money, or any money. The Royal Palace was even busier than when we walked through earlier, but Quinn found us two seats at a blackjack table and pulled a chair out for me. The dealer, a young man with slicked-back, dark hair smiled and welcomed us. His nametag said he was Monty, which seemed like an odd-choice name for a young man in his twenties. Two older men sat to one side of us, and on the other side were two guys who looked like they had flashed fake IDs to get in the door.

Quinn and I put our money on the table, and Monty dealt. I didn't have a lot of experience gambling in casinos, but when I was in the mood to play and could afford to lose the money, I preferred blackjack. Not that I was a bad blackjack player, but I just never liked the idea of gambling. It seemed too much like a get-rich-quick scheme, and I had enough financial experience to know that there was no such thing.

I glanced at the two cards in front of me, dealt face up. King, ten. I waved my hand over the cards to indicate that I would stand. Quinn studied his cards—nine and three. His brow was slightly furrowed, and he motioned for another card. The jack of spades flopped onto the green felt and he let out a frustrated sigh at his bust.

"Sure you don't want to reconsider my strip poker offer?" he asked with a rueful grin.

"You'd be naked already," I said, then immediately regretted my quick retort as my cheeks warmed at the thought.

Quinn laughed and placed another chip on the table. An hour later, I had a stack of chips double the size that I started with. Quinn wasn't doing quite as well. The two kids lost their stakes and sauntered off, leaving paltry tips for the dealer.

A couple took their seats—a man in his 40s and a young blonde woman who couldn't have been over 25. She flashed me a smile framed by deep dimples, and I couldn't help but smile back.

"Hi, I'm Carly," she said in a cheerful chirp. Her blonde curls bounced around her pretty face and bright blue eyes.

"I'm Miranda," I said. "This is Quinn."

At the name, Carly's date looked over and did a double take. "Quinn Bishop."

Quinn startled at the sound of his name, then laughed. "I don't believe this. Mark, how are you?"

The two men shook hands.

"Miranda, this is Mark Tripp. We used to work together on movie sets," he said. "Mark was a gaffer, the head electrician on set."

Mark's handshake revealed the rough hands of someone who didn't work in the office. His short brown hair was cut so short it looked almost military. His face was tan, giving him the look of someone who worked outdoors.

"Man, it's been a long time, Q. Those were some fun times."

Quinn grinned. "Yeah, it was. So you're still crewing?"

Mark nodded and raised a hand to flag a cocktail waitress.

"I'm still in the game," he said, then put an arm around the petite blonde. "This is Carly Malone."

She eyed Quinn with a look I knew well. Her wide blue eyes widened, and her lips pursed slightly. It was almost a reflex, an involuntary reaction. He was a devastatingly handsome man, and women couldn't seem to help but admire him.

"Nice to meet you," she said. "Did you work in production too? What did you do?"

"Quinn was the best wrangler I ever worked with," Mark said. "Remember that film *Grace of the Mountain*? He trained all those horses, managed all the livestock, even managed to train the talent to sit in a saddle without having panic attacks."

I remembered that movie—a beautiful historical biopic of a strong pioneer woman who single-handedly built a ranch. The movie had been critically acclaimed, though it had little success at the box office. But it had put its star, Lorelei Arens, on the map. She went from indie princess to actual movie star after the film won some obscure award.

It was also the movie that Quinn had just finished working on when he'd gotten arrested, returning from Mexico with his girlfriend—Lorelei Arens.

It had been her drugs hidden in the suitcase, and Lorelei, a Canadian citizen, begged Quinn to say that they were his so she wouldn't be deported. Only Quinn hadn't known about the drugs, and when he told the Customs officer that they were his, he had no idea that Lorelei Arens was more than just an up-and-coming starlet—she was also an illicit pharmaceutical rep to the stars. He ended up in federal prison for two years. She got an eight-figure offer for her next film.

"Uh, duh, of course I know *Grace of the Mountain*!" Carly laughed and hit Mark in the arm.

"Hey! Siskel, Ebert. You come here to play cards or review cinema?" one of the old men at the table snapped, flipping a chip onto the table and giving Quinn a dour stare.

Carly eyed my stack of chips. "Wow. Looks like you're having a good night," she said, then looked over at Quinn.

He gave her a wide smile. "Don't look over here. I'm not doing nearly as well."

"So you haven't improved your game any, huh, Quinn?" Mark said, clapping his old friend on the back.

He threw some chips in for himself and Carly and Monty dealt everyone in. A half-dozen hands later, I was up about two hundred dollars.

"I'm out," Quinn said, with a laugh that was half groan, pushing his last chip toward the dealer for a tip.

"Well, hey, let's grab a beer before you two take off for the night," Mark said, collecting his winnings.

Quinn gave me a questioning look, and I smiled. "Sounds fun."

We made our way toward the fireside lounge. Carly and I settled in chairs in the corner while the guys headed to the bar to get drinks.

"Do you work in the movie industry too?" I asked her, hoping she wasn't a celebrity who I just failed to recognized.

"Yes, but I'm totally behind the scenes," she said, applying a layer of an expensive brand of gloss to her cherry red lips. "I'm a PA."

I smiled and nodded and tried to look like I knew what that meant. She flashed that wide, dimpled smile again. She must have been a cheerleader in high school. She just had that energy about her. I could totally imagine her being tossed from the top of a pyramid. She was petite—probably just over five feet tall without her three-inch heels—but curvy and cute. She didn't have that hungry actress look to her.

"A personal assistant," she said, seeing through my act. "I work for actors and help them navigate the world now that they're famous and can't do simple things for themselves without getting mobbed by paparazzi."

"Oh, that's interesting," I said. I wasn't that up to speed on celebrity culture, but I saw the headlines and watched a little bit of reality TV. Okay, maybe more reality TV than I'd care to admit. And I might check in with some entertainment news websites on occasion. "Who do you work for? Or can you say?"

She looked around as if the three other tables of elderly gamblers might be spies. "I really can't say, but I used to work for a pretty well-known actor. Like, always in the tabloids. I just changed jobs a few months ago, though, and now I'm working for an actress who is really great. It's so much nicer working for a woman."

Mark and Quinn returned with our drinks and sat down.

"This is a fun place, isn't it?" Carly said, taking the spear of fruit from her daiquiri and laying it on the napkin by her drink.

"The Royal Palace or Lake Tahoe in general?" I asked.

"Both, but I just love Lake Tahoe. It's awesome. So charming and beautiful," she said. "It's so nice to get out of LA."

"Yeah, I've heard that," I said. I'd spent time in Los Angeles but had never lived there. After a week or so there, I was always ready to leave. "Are you here long?"

Carly sipped her drink and nodded.

"We're here for a shoot."

I nearly smacked myself in the head. "Oh, the one up at Whispering Pines?"

Her eyes widened. "You know about that? We've been trying to keep it quiet so there's not like a crush of paparazzi there."

"I'm staying there for work," I said. "It's a beautiful place for a movie."

She nodded. "It's the best place to get away. A lot of actors and musicians go there to relax and, you know, rejuvenate after a tour or a movie. But this is the first time they've ever allowed a film to be shot there, and it's going to be perfect. See, it's about a married couple who are separated by World War I, and it's so romantic. It's totally low budget, but oh my God, the script is amazing. Did you know that Lionel Merriweather is playing the butler? Can you believe that? He's been retired for like five years, but when he read this script, he decided to come back to California all the way from London."

I had a feeling I'd come to the right source for information on celebrity gossip. I only had a vague notion of who Lionel Merriweather was, though I knew he was a British actor. Rather than ask, I nodded, took a drink of my margarita, and glanced over at Quinn, who was deep in discussion with his old friend. Carly continued her lesson.

"I really think it was Whispering Pines that drew him to the movie. I mean, the script is amazing. But the part's pretty small, you know? And it's not like he needs the money, right?"

I nodded again. "And it has Reece Muir in it."

She leaned in with a smirk. "I used to work for him," she said, her voice low. "It's fine and everything. We're still like mega close. But I just got a better offer. It had nothing to do with *Attack at Dawn*."

I didn't know the first thing about how personal assistants in Hollywood worked, but I was having a hard time imagining cute little Carly Malone breaking up with Reece Muir, who, despite his recent box-office flop, was considered one of the top actors of his generation. But maybe a really good personal assistant was hard to find.

"So, Miranda, what do you do?" Carly asked. Mark glanced in my direction at the question.

"Oh, I work for a law firm, doing accounting and stuff like that," I said, taking a drink of the tart margarita. I never knew how to explain my job. It wasn't exactly finance, and it didn't feel like legal work. And since I was now working only part time, I really seemed to lack a job title.

I didn't have to worry that Mark and Carly would ask follow-up questions because, from their expressions, my job must have sounded as boring as watching dust being formed from rocks. And in comparison to the world they lived in, it probably was.

"Quinn, you still working with horses?" Mark asked.

Quinn shook his head. "In a manner of speaking, yes. I'm running my family's ranch in Northern California. I'm still training horses but not working on films any longer."

"It was a shame what happened, man," Mark said, his voice sounding sincere. "I can't tell you how great it is to run into you here. We're close to wrapping this indie up. Maybe a week or so, weather permitting, of course. And as long as none of the talent goes off on a bender or otherwise decides to throw a fit about a non-vegan choice on the catering table."

Quinn laughed and shook his head. "I sure don't miss that business."

"Hey, since you're staying at the resort, you should come by and watch tomorrow. They're shooting a key scene, and you can totally get a behind-the-scenes view of the movie," Carly said. "Give me your number."

She whipped a high-end phone out of her Kate Spade clutch and then punched my name and number into her contacts. "I'll text you tomorrow and get you on set."

"Sure, that would be great," I said.

She giggled and gave me that cute dimpled smile again,

leaned closer and dropped her voice. "Bring your boyfriend. He's totally hot."

I opened my mouth to respond to Carly's mistaken impression, but Quinn put an arm around my shoulder before I could answer.

"Sorry to break up the party," he said. "But I've got to get up early tomorrow. Maybe we'll see you Saturday though."

Mark and Quinn exchanged phone numbers and shook hands. We said our good-byes and Carly and Mark strolled away, looking for the nightclub.

Quinn and I walked out to get his truck from valet parking.

"Are you busy tomorrow night?" Quinn asked, helping me into the cab.

"I don't know," I said. "I'm meeting Dottie for breakfast, and then we're reviewing reports. I'm not sure when I'll be done."

"Well, if you find yourself without plans, give me a call," he said, giving me a smile.

I paused and looked up at him and he laughed. "Just as friends. I promise. You're better company than a half-dozen grizzled ranch hands."

I laughed and nodded. "Sure. I'll call you."

It was nice hanging around Quinn, even just as friends. Even if he wasn't the man I wanted to be spending my evenings with.

CHAPTER SIX

The buzzing of my phone on the nightstand jolted me out of a deep sleep, and I fought my way out of the smooth sheets to turn off the alarm.

"Miranda?"

It wasn't the alarm, I realized, as I heard the faint voice.

"Jake?" I croaked.

A night spent in the smoky casino and lounge made me sound like a young Kathleen Turner or an old bar fly. I hoped it was the first.

"Are you okay?" Jake sounded concerned.

I cleared my throat and tried to speak normally. "Yeah, fine. Just sleeping."

His gentle laugh pulled me further out of my drowsiness. "Sorry to wake you, but I wanted to check in with you before I head off to court."

"What time is it?" I sat up and blinked at the alarm clock and saw that it was ten minutes before my alarm was set to wake me up.

"Time for you to get to work, I'm sure," Jake said.

I snuggled back down in the pillows and closed my eyes with

a sigh. It was a very comfortable bed, and I wasn't ready to get out of it yet. Had Jake been with me, instead of just on the phone, I wouldn't have tried.

"How is the new job going?"

"It's good. I've only done a few hours of work so far, but it's interesting."

"What are you doing?"

"Just a routine audit," I said, not wanting to accidentally betray any confidential information. "What are you doing in court?"

"The usual, putting bad guys in prison, saving the world, that sort of thing," he said with a low chuckle.

I smiled and closed my eyes, sinking deeper into the soft pillow. "My hero."

"Did you and Dottie stay out of trouble last night?"

"Dottie went to dinner with the client and his wife," I said, then paused. I wasn't sure if I should continue talking about my dinner with Quinn, even though nothing happened. I scrunched up my face and hoped that Jake didn't ask any follow up questions.

"And you?"

Well, hell. He was a trained interrogator.

"I had dinner with Quinn."

There was a long pause. "Oh."

"It wasn't a date or anything. I told him that he and I can only be friends," I said. Why did I feel guilty for meeting Quinn for dinner when Jake and I were still...whatever we were.

"You did?" Jake's voice sounded a little more relaxed.

"Yes."

"How'd he take that?"

"Fine. It's not like we dated." I paused, hearing the rustle of paper in the background of Jake's end of the call. "What are you doing?"

"I'm opening a bag of cat food to feed that hateful beast of yours," he said. "And I was just asking about Quinn because —*Jesus*!"

A yowling screech interrupted Jake's words. It was followed closely by the sound of something tearing, then very loud cursing and then crashing as the phone hit the ground.

"What's going on there?"

"Damn it!" Jake's muttered curses grew louder and so did Kvetch's growled protest. I could hear a hiss and then more cursing.

"Are you okay?" I sat up in the bed, helpless to assist in Jake's battle against the angriest feline in the city. For a cat that Aunt Marie raised since before his eyes were opened, he sure wasn't grateful to the human race. "Jake, are you there?"

I heard some faint sounds of scuffle, then Jake's voice again.

"Bethany, hand me that towel."

My eyes narrowed. Bethany Boylan was at my house? And he was worried about me hanging out with Quinn?

I pictured the willowy brunette agent and my rage grew. I was sure, or at least not completely unsure, that Bethany Boylan was an upstanding citizen who paid her taxes and never ran red lights. And maybe she volunteered at soup kitchens and saved abandoned puppies in her spare time. But she also snubbed me whenever she got the chance and made it clear that she believed that I was guilty of the fraud charges her office had brought against me. Having to see her around the courthouse and working with her for Rob's clients was hard enough, but knowing that she was spending her days with Jake and could be whispering her thoughts about my criminal tendencies to him was just about too much to take.

"Oh my God, are you bleeding?" Bethany asked, her voice distant in the background of the call.

Ugh. Even that faint sound set my nerves on edge.

"Miranda, let me call you later," Jake said.

"Oh, sure. Whatever," I snapped.

I pressed the disconnect button on my phone and wished there were a more satisfying way to hang up on someone. So I threw the phone onto the bed, where it bounced once and then landed on the thick plush carpet without making a sound.

That, too, was highly unsatisfying.

God, what was wrong with me? I had never been the jealous type. Why was Bethany Boylan bringing it out in me? It wasn't really a rhetorical question—I knew the answer. Jake seemed to respect her, even like her. And that meant he might listen to her opinion about me.

The alarm next to the bed went off, and I slammed the off button, which made me feel a little better. I staggered into the bathroom and turned on the shower in the marble and glass enclosure. But not even a long hot shower with high-end, lavender-scented soaps could lessen the scowl on my face.

I tried my best to be pleasant while having breakfast with Dottie. Between the strong, dark and freshly brewed coffee and Dottie's energetic recounting of her dinner with the Emmersons, I had pushed Jake to the edge of my mind.

Dottie used her silver resort card to pay for our breakfast. Then we returned to the business office to begin the most tedious part of the audit. My job was to examine the outgoing payments and the receipts that justified them. Jordan wasn't the most detail-oriented person, and I had more questions than answers by the time lunch rolled around.

I ordered lunch in from the Pines Cafe and kept working, while Dottie slipped out to make her massage appointment. In the quiet of the conference room, it was easy for my mind to wander back to my call with Jake that morning, but each time I found my thoughts going there, I gave myself a mental slap and focused on the numbers in front of me. Numbers were constant.

they were something that I could work on without getting emotionally involved. I didn't have to worry about emotions, attachments, or jealous feelings. I poured all my energy into the figures, and by the time Dottie returned, I had questions for her.

I laid out in a chart the information that I had compiled that day, and then I walked her through it.

"This is table revenue from three years ago—see? Everything is pretty stable. Then here is where Max goes out on medical leave, and still everything continues as normal for about six months," I said, running my finger along the laptop screen. "You start to see a slight dip in revenue about six months after Jordan takes over, but it bounces back almost to the baseline."

Dottie nodded, and I flipped to the next screen. "But it gets more vague when you break it down further."

"How so?"

"Well, Jordan's not exactly a micromanager, and there are a lot of unanswered questions here with some of these payments," I said. "He brought in this accounting firm, on contract, to take over the books after the CFO retired, but I don't think they did a very good job."

Dottie frowned and tapped the report between us. "This is their report?"

"Yes," I said, turning to the pages that I had marked with a sticky note and opened the bound report, spreading the spine as wide as I could. Where the pages were bound there was a page missing toward the end of the document—cut out with a razor so close to the binding that I almost hadn't caught it.

"Oh, hell."

Dottie sighed and ran her finger down the seam to feel the edge of the missing page.

"Yeah. Someone didn't want that information in here."

She pursed her lips together. "Jordan. He was taking these

reports to Max to keep him updated on the resort while he was undergoing treatment."

"But why hide it? I mean, it's going to come out eventually."

Dottie shrugged and frowned. "Maybe because he knew there was mismanagement."

"They're not losing money, just not making as much as it used to," I pointed out. "Maybe they would have done a more thorough report for the end of the financial year, but Max fired them before they completed that work."

She shook her head. "This doesn't look good. The Gambling Commission doesn't want to approve companies that can't manage their books. The banks don't want to lend them tens of millions of dollars."

Dottie tapped her pencil against the table and stared out the window, her mouth in a thin line. She motioned toward the report, and I passed it to her.

"What do you think of this company's work?"

I shrugged. "I'm not familiar with how resorts work, but there's a lot of information in here that would be useful to Max. I'd like to see the missing section."

"Give them a call and have them send over the whole document," Dottie said. "In fact, maybe you should go pick it up in Reno, rather than having them mail it here."

I nodded. If Jordan was the person who cut out the pages, then he could swipe the report again before it got to me and Dottie.

"It would help if Max would modernize the company's financial systems. I don't understand how a company that has such a robust electronic reservations system is still using this old computer system for accounting." I waved at the laptop with frustration. I'd quickly realized that it was next to useless in reviewing the company's finances.

"Max is old school. He has been doing this for his whole life and he can tell you all that, just from his experience," Dottie said.

"I'm not criticizing Max," I said, though I clearly was. "I'm sure he understands Whispering Pines better than anyone. But that's exactly the problem. He went out on leave and the company's profits continued based on momentum for a time but then started to drop because no one else here knew what Max knew. There might not even be a problem to solve here, now that he's back at the helm."

Dottie leaned back and pursed her lips.

"I see what you're saying," she said after a long pause. "Maybe we should talk with Jordan."

I raised an eyebrow. From our uncomfortable lunch the day before, I didn't get the idea he was going to be happy about working with us. "Think he'll talk with us?"

"Yeah, you may be right. He sees me as Max's ally." Dottie tilted her head and her topaz earrings sparkled. She studied me with a serious expression. "But maybe you could talk to him."

"Me? I'm the new person."

Dottie shrugged and stood up. "Perfect. Ask him to explain the drop off. He knows you don't know Whispering Pines as well as I do—"

"Or at all."

"—and maybe he'll explain what he sees happening."

"I'm sure he's going to be busy, so should I make an appointment with his assistant? Also, does he know we're auditing his work?"

"Yeah, I made Max tell him this morning. No sense in hiding what we're doing here."

I wasn't afraid of confrontation. Hell, I'd worked in finance, a nearly all-male office with more testosterone than was advisable and could hold my own with the most belligerent of traders. But I didn't know Jordan at all and wasn't sure how he'd react to a stranger confronting him with the missing pages or even some criticism of his management. Maybe I should go get that massage first. Before I could pitch that excuse to Dottie, she reached over and picked up the phone on the conference table.

"Hi, it's Dottie. Can you connect me to Jordan? Thanks." A short pause, then she smiled. "Hi, Jordan. You busy?"

Five minutes later, I was in the elevator going down to the lowest level of the resort to meet the vice president of operations in the security center. The elevator doors opened to a long bare hallway dotted with unmarked doors. As soon as I stepped into the hall, one of the doors opened, and Jordan walked out.

He greeted me with a polite smile and handshake.

"Thank you for meeting with me so quickly," I said, walking with him down the hall. He had told Dottie that he had a few minutes between meetings with security personnel, and he could spare some time if I'd come to him.

"No problem," he said, though his voice indicated otherwise. "What can I do for you?"

I glanced around the empty hall, and he shrugged. "It's okay to talk here. Not too many people work on this level."

The security office was a small windowless room behind an unmarked door, not far from the heavy handcrafted door to the resort's wine cellar. We were directly below Angelina's, the restaurant where we had dined the day before. Inside, there was a small bank of screens that showed the lobby and the exterior of the resort from various angles. In all, there were probably a dozen screens, and the videos they showed were slightly grainy and either too dark or too light to see what was going on.

Jordan motioned to a pair of chairs by the screens, and I sat. He took the chair next to me and logged into the computer system.

"Do you normally work in the security office?" I asked, taking in the view of the resort from the low-res cameras.

He shook his head. "Trying to find some footage of an attempted car break-in last night."

A long exasperated sigh escaped from his lips, and he picked up the phone and hit a button. "Yeah, it's Jordan. Camera nine is pointing at the sky again," he said. While he waited for the other person to respond, I looked at the monitors and quickly located the camera in question that was showing only the tops of trees and some blue sky and puffy white clouds. "I don't care why. Just fix it, okay? Thanks."

Jordan hung up the phone and went back to his computer, as if I weren't there.

"Does that happen often?"

"What?" he asked, still ignoring my presence as best he could.

"Car break-ins, criminal activity, the sort of things that this surveillance system would help you prevent," I said. I was about done with his attitude.

"No, our security team doesn't have much to do but roust out tabloid photographers once in a while, maybe shut down a private party that gets out of hand," he said. Then he leaned back in his chair and fixed his green eyes on me. "So what do you need from me?"

His tone wasn't friendly but was assertively neutral, as if it was hard for him to remain polite.

"I had a couple of questions about the last report from the accounting firm," I said, uncomfortable in the room that was barely more than a closet. "There are some pages missing at the end."

He looked away from the computer with a brief scowl, then shook his head. "It was a letter from one of the accountants. It didn't have anything to do with the year-end financials, and it shouldn't have been included with the report."

I paused, waiting for a further explanation. It was possible that a memo could have been accidentally included in the report, but he could also have meant that the letter was about something he didn't want included.

"What was it about?"

He turned back to me, and his annoyance snuck through the carefully maintained polite exterior. "Nothing that concerns the audit."

"Everything concerns this audit. Max wants everything in order before the banks come in and do their own investigation of his finances."

Jordan rolled his eyes, looking more like an insolent teenager than a businessman. "Max isn't going to get the loan for the Lucky Penny. And even if by some miracle a bank will lend him the tens of millions that he needs to buy it, the Gaming Commission isn't going to sign off on his application. No way. This is all just a pipe dream."

I sat up straight in the uncomfortable office chair, startled by his frank answer. "Why do you say that?"

Jordan shook his head, looking more tired than angry now. "When my family lost the casino, there was talk, rumors, that things were being mismanaged. Max was at the helm when all that happened. There was even talk of an investigation, but then we lost the casino, so it didn't go any further."

"But that was years ago," I said. "Even if Max was in charge when the casino was sold—"

"Lost in a bankruptcy proceeding," Jordan corrected me. "There's a difference."

"Right, but it was still decades ago. And the resort has been highly successful since then, which shows he's a good business-man." If Max had immediately applied for another license, any misconduct at the Penny probably would have influenced the commission's decision.

Jordan shrugged. "If given a choice between a consortium of

investors with squeaky clean backgrounds and returning the Penny to the Emmerson family and rumors of our mob connections, the commission's probably going to go with the corporate investors."

Something about Jordan's dismissive attitude rubbed me the wrong way. Max wouldn't have hired his own forensic accounting firm to prepare for the purchase of the casino unless he thought he had a chance to buy it. He seemed way too smart to do that. But was nostalgia for the old Lucky Penny getting in the way? I made a mental note to learn more about the Gaming Commission's rules for potential owners.

"Who are the other bidders going to be?"

"It's private, no one knows," Jordan said. "But there's talk about a group of A-list Hollywood types who are considering it. And there's a gaming operation from Laughlin that is thinking of expanding. But until the current owners make their decision, it's all speculation. Except for Max, of course, who tells anyone who will listen how badly he wants the casino back. Which is a *great* strategy."

Jordan stood and opened the door for me—my cue to leave.

"I'll let you get back to work. I'm sure you and Dottie have a lot to do on your audit," he said, not bothering to hide the smirk this time.

I stood and walked to the door. "We need to see that letter."

The polite facade slipped away completely. His lips tightened, and his eyes narrowed slightly. "I'll make sure you have it by the end of the day."

CHAPTER SEVEN

I wrapped myself in the fluffy white towel that Whispering Pines was kind enough to provide and padded to the middle of the room. My body felt extra loose from the one-hour Swedish massage that afternoon. All the stress from dealing with Jordan and spending hours hunched over spreadsheets had melted away under Margarit's expert hands. A person could get used to living like this.

Two dresses lay on the bed, and I studied them, trying to decide which one to wear to dinner with Quinn at Angelina's. One was a jersey dress with a wide belt. The coral color gave the illusion that I had a tan. The other was a blue halter dress with a plunging neckline. Since I was waiting on Quinn for dinner, and not Jake, I knew I should choose the coral dress. Its simple style said, "hello, friend." The blue dress, on the other hand, had more of a "hello-o-o-o sailor" vibe.

I glanced at my silent phone. Still nothing from Jake since that morning when we spoke. My probably unstable mind filled with images of Jake spending time with Bethany, and I looked back to the blue dress.

I was overreacting to hearing Bethany's voice on the call. She was his partner, for heaven's sake. I should get over it already.

And yet, I couldn't seem to stop myself from feeling this way.

I turned to the closet to put away the sexier dress option as the phone on the bed buzzed.

Unfortunately, it wasn't the person I wanted to hear from. Rather than Jake, it was Carly Malone, the PA to the stars I'd met the night before.

If you want to meet Reece Muir, come down the back stairs in about 20 minutes, and I'll get you on set.

Hot damn!

Sarah was going to be crazy jealous when I told her I met Reece Muir, the handsome, brooding movie star. He'd gotten his start on a television series, playing the mischievous middle son of a typical sitcom family. But his black hair and green eyes and deep dimples had taken him well beyond teen heartthrob status. He played a drug-addicted bank robber in an indie film in his early 20s, which helped him leave his sitcom past behind. He'd made a career as a serious dramatic actor since then, with a long list of emotionally wrought performances. Along the way, he'd dated models and actresses and heiresses and graced the cover of many a tabloid. Still, his name sold movies. He might have made a poor choice with that action-adventure bomb this summer, but he'd bounce back.

I checked the time. I could easily run downstairs and meet up with Carly and hang out on set until I met Quinn in the lobby. *Perfect.* I dropped the robe and slipped the blue dress on, adjusting it so what little cleavage I had was shown to its best advantage. Within minutes, I had done my hair and makeup and slipped on a pair of wedge sandals. I transferred the essentials— lipstick, powder, room key, ID, cell phone—to a simple clutch and left to meet Carly with a few minutes to spare.

The stairs that Carly directed me to were at the other end of the building from the lobby, and a velvet rope hung across the opening with a note asking patrons to use the stairs by the entrance due to filming. I unhooked the rope and let myself through and walked quietly down the carpeted stairs. As I approached the bottom of the flight, I could hear the low murmur of voices and panicked. Would I be walking onto the set, like into the frame? While they were filming?

I turned my phone on mute and then sent a text to Carly to confirm that I wasn't going to disrupt the shoot.

No, it's fine. Come on down. I'll be right there.

I took a deep breath and then a few more steps to the bottom of the staircase, then peeked around the corner. The film crew was set up in the ballroom just off the wide hall that ran the length of this wing of the resort's main building. There was a flurry of activity going on inside the room, but the wide double doors were opened enough that I could watch the action without being in the way. Thick black electrical cords snaked out of the ballroom's three sets of double doors, all of which were opened, and down the hall, and I stepped carefully over them and made my way closer to the entrance.

"Quiet on set!"

I looked around to make sure I wasn't in anyone's way, but all the action seemed to be in the ballroom. I couldn't see what was being filmed but could hear the voices.

"When are you leaving?"

"I'll depart this evening."

A gasp and an anguished sob. "Why so soon?"

"You know why, Frances."

It sounded like a heartbreaking scene, and I wished I could get closer to see it unfold, but from my angle all I could see was the back of the crew members.

"But Henry, you don't understand..."

"I know what you did."

"You have no idea what I have done."

That last line was delivered with a tremor in the voice that made the hair on the back of my neck stand up. Only a true talent could deliver that line and make the listener believe it, even without seeing the performance.

My attention was diverted from the drama that I couldn't quite see by Carly Malone waving at me from another set of doors. She motioned for me to join her about fifty feet down the hall, so I walked quietly down to where she stood. She took my arm and steered me about two feet to one side, where I had a perfect view of Reece Muir.

He was standing in the corner of the ballroom, which was made to look like a library. His back was to a wall of bookcases, and he was looking out the windows, which were shaded by trees outside and what looked like black shade cloth that was keeping the glare from bouncing into the star's eyes. At his side was a young woman with long, dark hair wearing an old-fashioned nightgown of thin cotton or linen. She was barefoot and barely came up to his shoulder.

The woman had her back to me, so I didn't have as good a view of her, and frankly, my attention was on the stunningly handsome man in a World War I military uniform. His dark hair was slicked back, and the lighting emphasized his famous cheekbones. The dimples that made him a teen idol when he was 14 years old were absent as he stared out the glass with a moody expression. I had to suppress a sigh. He should trademark that expression. It really worked for him.

"Cut. Take five minutes. Then let's do it again," the director yelled, and there was instant movement and noise from every direction.

"Oh my God, Carly, thank you so much for inviting me. Is it okay that I'm here?" I turned to her, and she grinned and nodded.

"Give me a minute. Just stay here, and you should be fine. If anyone asks, tell them you're with me," she said, then slipped past a guy wielding a microphone on a boom and walked up to the actress, handing her a bottle of imported water.

I tried to take in everything that was going on in the room, but what was probably a choreographed operation looked like utter chaos to me. Make-up people brushed powder across Reece's forehead, then a wardrobe person tugged at his collar and a woman fixed a single strand of hair into its place. Meanwhile, cameras were moved to change the angle so the next take could feature the actress more, rather than focusing on Reece.

"Are we ready? Let's get this moving. We're close to wrapping this up on time, let's not ruin it now," the director said, pushing through the crowd to one side where he could watch the scene on a small computer screen. He was younger than I'd expect for a movie that was set in World War I, with dark-rimmed eyeglasses and short, but unruly black hair.

Carly put a hand on the actress's shoulder, leaned close and whispered something, then walked away with the water bottle and headed back to where I had dutifully stayed during the break.

The woman turned back to get direction from the man in the glasses, and as she did, I felt the ground shift beneath my feet.

I knew her.

Well, I didn't *know* her. I mean, she was an A-list Hollywood actress, twice-nominated for Academy Awards. Her face was on more magazine covers than most supermodels. Her wide, bright blue eyes were iconic, and her long black hair had inspired a generation of young women to cut their hair into thick retro-style bangs after she grabbed a Golden Globe nomination for her leading role in *Grace of the Mountains*.

I may not know Lorelei Arens personally, but it felt like I did.

Not just because of her celebrity, but because I knew things about her that the general public didn't, and would never, know.

Including how she set up Quinn Bishop to take the fall for her drugs. How she had begged him to say that the drugs in their shared suitcase were his, so that she wouldn't get deported to Canada. How he spent two years in prison for her.

Carly joined me at the doorway before I could react, and a hush fell over the room again. My breath caught in my chest as I watched Lorelei transform herself in an instant into a woman who was losing the love of her life to war.

And as much as I hated her, and I really did hate her, I couldn't turn away. From my vantage point, I could see the screen in front of the director, and it kept me riveted, even as I wanted to leave.

When the scene ended, I stole a quick glance at my phone and saw that Quinn should be arriving any moment.

"Isn't she amazing?" Carly asked, grabbing my arm with excitement. "Have you ever seen anything like that?"

I shook my head.

"She's something," I managed to get out.

"Okay, let's break this down," the director said. He moved toward the actors to talk with them, and Carly watched them carefully.

"I'll be right back, okay? Don't go anywhere. I'll introduce you to Reece," she said, bouncing off into the fray like a veteran.

I glanced down the hall toward the lobby but didn't see Quinn, so I lingered as instructed by my hostess. Mark Tripp was directing a crew of about four men. He smiled and waved when he saw me, gave one last instruction to his crew, then jogged over to me.

"Did you get to see that last scene?"

I nodded. "That was really cool."

"I think Lorelei Arens is probably the best actresses I've ever seen, and I've been doing this job for twenty years, worked on a lot of films," he said. "She has a gift."

I didn't say anything but nodded again. It was hard to deny that. But I felt disloyal even thinking it.

"Quinn around?" Mark asked, craning his neck.

"No, not yet. He's going to meet me in the lobby in a few minutes." I checked my phone again and bit my lip. The last thing I wanted was for Quinn to be surprised by Lorelei Arens' presence, as I was. But it would be worse for him. A decade ago, he had been in love with her. And that had cost him dearly. "Hey, can you do me a favor? Tell Carly that I appreciate the offer to meet Reece Muir, but I need to go meet Quinn."

Mark raised an eyebrow. "You're turning down a chance to meet Reece Muir? For Quinn? That must be serious," he said with a laugh. "But I'll tell her, if you tell Quinn that we have to catch up before we wrap this job."

"When do you think that will be?"

"We're a little ahead of schedule, just a few scenes to shoot outdoors, and the weather forecast is great, so probably a week at most."

Great. I'd be gone by Sunday, and I just had to keep Quinn away from the film set until then. No problem. I thanked Mark and promised to tell Quinn to call him and hurried toward the hall.

"Miranda, wait!"

I turned to see Carly pulling a WWI soldier toward me and felt my eyes grow wide.

"Reece, this is my friend, Miranda," Carly said, her blonde curls bouncing around her face. "Miranda, this is Reece Muir."

He extended his hand, and on autopilot, I shook it.

"It's nice to meet you, Miranda," Reece said. His green eyes were fringed by thick black lashes, and because of all the times

I'd ogled him on magazine covers and in movie theaters, they were oddly familiar.

I opened my mouth to respond, but all that came out was a giggle.

Get it together. He's just a man.

A phenomenally beautiful man.

"Hi."

Okay, at least it was a word.

From behind Reece and Carly, I heard a wail, and all heads in the room turned toward where Lorelei and the director were standing by the window. Carly bolted to them, and Reece rolled his eyes. The crew members still in the ballroom averted their eyes and made for the exits, and within seconds, I found myself nearly alone with the personal assistant and two movie stars, one of whom was sobbing uncontrollably. With the room cleared, Lorelei's wailing echoed off the walls.

"Uh, is this method acting?" I whispered to Reece.

"No. This is a temper tantrum." Then he looked down at me with a tight smile. "Sorry you had to see this."

Carly stepped in, embracing the waif-like actress and soothing her while she sobbed. Reece nodded toward the door, and we crept out into the hall, where the crew mingled, coiling the electrical cords and doing what work they could without access to the ballroom. From their nonchalant conversations, it didn't seem as if the outburst was unusual. Reece walked off with a polite nod. The warm tingly feelings from meeting my big screen crush were dampened by the squalling actress. Another reason not to like her.

I started toward the lobby but was making slow progress through the crowd when I saw a familiar figure walking toward me in the grand hall.

Quinn.

Damn it. I couldn't let him see Lorelei.

My eyes were locked on his as I hurried past the middle set of doors to the ballroom. I dodged a burly man carrying what was probably a very expensive piece of lighting and stumbled over a cord. Quinn gave me a puzzled look, but I just waved to let him know I'd come to him.

Stay there, I prayed.

I found an opening in the crowd as I approached the last set of doors to the ballroom and slowed my pace to something resembling normal. Well, a brisk normal. I still wanted to get him out of the hall as quickly as possible, but it would be better not to break my neck while doing that. I was just passing the last set of doors when a blur of white linen and long flowing dark hair burst out of the ballroom.

A crewman carrying a ten-foot ladder walked between me and Lorelei, keeping me from getting to either her or Quinn. If I could get to him, I might be able to distract him before he saw the tiny actress. Or if I could get to her, I could shove her back into the ballroom and let Carly take care of the fallout. Instead, I watched helplessly, trapped by the ladder, as Lorelei came to a stop in the middle of the hallway. She faced Quinn, who was only thirty feet away. Quinn stopped too, the warm smile on his face evaporating as he recognized Lorelei.

Sensing that something was happening, the crew hushed, many of them staring at the couple facing off in the hall.

"Quinn." The quavering whisper carried through the hallway, above the sound of the crew and even over the sound of my pounding heart.

He stood still, his face unreadable.

Lorelei hiccupped and raised a hand to her mouth. Despite her crying jag, her eyes were wide and teary, not swollen and red. She was a little pale, and her face was streaked with tears. But damn it, she was still stunningly beautiful.

I looked between the two former lovers. Quinn still hadn't moved.

"Oh God. Quinn," she gasped again.

Then she launched herself the remaining few yards and threw herself at him.

CHAPTER EIGHT

Carly rushed past me to the couple embracing at the end of the hall, and I followed as quickly as my wedge-heeled sandals would let me. *Crap.* How had I let this happen to Quinn? All I had to do was get him out of the building before he saw his ex-girlfriend.

"Lorelei, honey, are you okay? Maybe we should get downstairs for your spa appointment," Carly said, trying to unfasten the actress' arms from around Quinn's waist.

Lorelei held fast. Quinn patted her back gently, the shock fading from his expression replaced by confusion.

"I can't believe you're here," Lorelei murmured, her eyes on his face. "You're really here?"

Quinn gave her a half-smile. "I'm here."

She rested her head on his chest with a deep sigh.

"Okay, sweetie, let's get you back to the room," Carly said, trying again. She shot Quinn an apologetic glance and was able to pull her employer away from him.

Lorelei allowed herself to be pulled away by Carly, but her eyes were still on Quinn's face.

"When can I see you?" she asked, her voice soft and pleading.

Quinn looked up at me. "I don't know..."

"I need to see you," Lorelei implored him. "I need to talk to you. With you."

My eyes met Quinn's, and he gave me an apologetic shrug. "We'll see," he said.

"Please."

He looked back to the frail woman in front of him and then nodded. Her shoulders slumped in relief, and Carly pulled her to the elevator. I could see exactly how Quinn's fate had been sealed a decade ago—Lorelei's pleading, Quinn's acquiescence. I felt the frown on my face grow.

"Quinn, I'm so sorry," I said.

He shook his head and gave me a smile. "Not your fault. And it's no big deal. You ready to go to dinner?"

He offered his arm, which I took, and we walked toward the front lobby of the lodge. Though the resort was closed to the public for overnight stays, the restaurants and the spa were available if any tourists wanted to make the 15 minute drive up the side of the mountain. Under normal circumstances, I'd never be able to get a reservation at Angelina's on a few hours notice, but without having to compete with a lodge full of guests, we got a table by the windows overlooking the sunset.

We ordered a bottle of wine and listened as the waiter recited the specials. A slight breeze snuck in through the screened windows behind me and carried with it the scent of pine and fresh-cut grass and something else that I could only describe as unique to Lake Tahoe. It was something that tickled my memories and made me smile and think of long summer days at the lake, lounging on warm sand and cooling off in the cold, crystal-clear water. I relaxed by a few degrees.

I had a good view no matter where I looked—out the window at the pink clouds on the western edge of the mountain range, or across the table at Quinn, handsome and smiling.

"It is a big deal," I said.

His smile grew. "What are you talking about?"

"Running into Lorelei Arens. Being surprised by that. It is a big deal." How could he think otherwise?

Quinn sipped his glass of red wine and didn't say anything.

"Had you seen her since, you know?" I asked, suddenly unsure about talking to Quinn about his past. He'd always been so upfront and honest with me about his arrest and conviction, even his time in prison.

He sighed and looked over at me, his expression relaxed. "It's okay, Miranda. I'm fine."

"Well I'm not," I said. "I had no idea that she was at the resort, or in that movie, until just before you arrived. I wouldn't have put you in that situation."

He leaned forward and placed his hand on mine. "I know you wouldn't. But it doesn't matter. I'm okay."

"How can you say that?"

He laughed. "Because it's true."

"But you're acting like nothing happened."

"It was a long time ago, and I've made my peace with it."

"She set you up! You went to prison." I leaned forward and lowered my voice so the few other diners wouldn't hear our conversation.

He nodded. "I know."

"You don't hate her?"

He shook his head. "No. That takes a lot of energy that I'm not going to waste on Lorelei Arens."

I blew out a frustrated sigh. "Well then, I'll hate her for you."

Quinn laughed, and the sound reassured me. "Thanks for looking out for me."

He didn't sound traumatized by the encounter. He certainly looked relaxed.

"I know it's none of my business, but are you going to see her again?" I asked.

Quinn shrugged. "I don't know. I imagine that if there's something she needs to say to me, it's for her benefit, not mine."

"You mean to apologize to you?"

He nodded. "There was something about her though... I don't know. She didn't look well."

I agreed. She had been a mess, and that was before she laid eyes on Quinn. "She had a meltdown on the set, after they stopped filming. It was disturbing."

He frowned. "Well, she was always high-strung."

"I'm surprised Mark didn't tell you she was here," I said.

Quinn shook his head. "He didn't know Lorelei and I were seeing each other. No one did. We kept it secret during the filming. When the movie wrapped up, we went to Mexico together for a short vacation, and I got arrested as we returned."

"So she never acknowledged that she was with you?"

He shook his head again. "No, it never came out that she was there."

It remained a secret because Quinn had pleaded guilty for a reduced sentence, rather than go to trial. With his statements to the airport security officer claiming responsibility for the drugs in his bag, it would have been hard to convince a jury to acquit him. And Lorelei had never stepped up to take responsibility for the pills. Rob had negotiated a good deal, one that Quinn could live with, and he had taken it and moved on with his life.

Our conversation trailed off as the waiter brought our salads and refilled our wine glasses. When we were alone again, Quinn raised his glass.

"Let's change the subject," he said. "To your new career."

I smiled. "Thank you."

"How do you like being, what is it called? A forensic accountant?"

"Yes, that's it. And I like it. I think I'm good at it, or I could be once I get more experience," I said. "Dottie says it's equal parts psychology and math. But so far, it seems more like solving a puzzle using math, and I'm good at math."

Quinn smiled. "I'm glad there are people like you out there who like math. It was never my strong suit. Do you think you'll keep working for Dottie?"

So far she hadn't mentioned that, but it had only been a couple days. "If I prove myself on this job, I think so. Between working for her and for Rob, I should be able to piece together full-time work."

"How much longer will you be up here?"

I frowned. "It's not going as fast as I thought it would. I'm trying to get a copy of an accountant's report, but they won't have it until Monday. I was supposed to be home by Sunday."

And I was supposed to be going out on a real date with Jake on Sunday. The thought sent a stab of anxiety mixed with guilt through me. I was out having a romantic candlelit dinner, watching a beautiful sunset with another man. As friends but I still felt that bit of guilt over it. Also, I'd have to call Jake and let him know that I wouldn't be home on Sunday.

"Why are you frowning?"

I looked up from my glass of wine into Quinn's sparkling blue eyes. "Oh, I just remembered that I had plans for Sunday night that I have to cancel."

He smiled and leaned back. "Plans with Barnes?"

I nodded.

"I'm sure he'll wait for you."

I gave an embarrassed laugh. I hadn't meant to bring up Jake every time Quinn and I were together. I raised my glass. "Let's change the subject."

He laughed and touched his glass to mine. We kept the rest of our conversation over dinner in safer territory, talking about his horses and his friend's ranch that was just over the mountain in Gardnerville, and Rob and Marie's wedding.

"Are you coming to the wedding?" I asked.

"I wouldn't miss it. Rob's a great friend, and I've never seen him so happy," Quinn said.

"I know. I'm so happy for them," I said. "I told Aunt Marie I'd go visit the wedding venue before I came home. Since she refuses to have a wedding shower or a bachelorette party, there's not a lot for me to do as maid of honor. I can at least go check in with the wedding planner and see if she has something for me to do."

"Let me know if you need a ride," Quinn said. "I'm just a short drive away, and I'm happy to help."

"When are you going back home?"

"It's open-ended right now. My friend has a few openings at the ranch, so I'm helping him out a little. He's got a few men coming in over the next couple days, and if they work out, then I'll take off and get back to my ranch," he said.

"You don't need to be at your ranch now?"

"Nah, my parents are back for the summer, and my dad can run things while I'm away. I've got a great crew there who can handle anything that comes up."

I'd been out to the Bishop Ranch several times, and Quinn had taken me on a long horseback ride around the valley where his family had run a cattle ranch for over a hundred years. It was a beautiful setting in the foothills of the Sierra Nevada mountains. As we enjoyed the scallops tossed with fresh pasta in a light white wine sauce, Quinn entertained me with stories from his ranch. The sun had dipped beyond the mountains, leaving in its path a sky streaked with red and gray.

By the time the waiter brought us dessert—tiramisu and a *pot de crème*—the sky outside was dark, and the windows reflected the restaurant, only about one-third full. After buying

Quinn's dinner with my Whispering Pines Resort card, we strolled through the quiet resort and outside to the wide veranda where we could see the moon rising over the trees.

"I should get back to the ranch. I told Charlie I'd help him mend a fence tomorrow, so I'll need to get up early."

I turned to Quinn in the dark and smiled. "Thanks for coming up here again. I'm sorry the evening got off to a bad start."

He gave a gentle laugh. "Again, not your fault. And it was a nice dinner. Thank you."

I walked him to the stairs, and he gave me a very warm but platonic hug and kissed my cheek. "Good night, Miranda. Stay out of trouble."

He disappeared down the path toward the parking area, and I headed the opposite direction, to the end of the covered porch that ran the width of the main lodge's entrance. The moon was full and high enough that it was casting shadows on the lawn and illuminated the path on the south side of the resort that skirted the grassy area and led to the trees. Below the resort, I could see the lake—inky black but for the reflection of the moon on its surface. The cool night air was soothing and silent.

"Oh, hey! Miranda! There you are!"

I turned to find Carly coming up the steps to the main lodge, waving at me.

"Hi, Carly. What are you doing out here?"

"I was looking for you," she said. "We're having a little party in one of the cabins. Want to come?"

She joined me at the railing. With my heels, I towered over Carly and felt tall for the first time in my life.

"How's your boss doing?" I asked.

"Wow, I know. What was that about? Did you know they knew each other? I mean, how awkward is that? Some random movie star just hurls herself at your boyfriend," Carly said, looking up at me with wide eyes.

"Oh, no—" I started to correct her again, but she kept talking as if she didn't hear me.

"I'm so sorry about that. Lorelei can be impulsive, and this shoot is really stressful for her because she's working with Reece, and it's only been about six months since they broke up," she said.

"They dated?"

"Oh yeah, for a few months. It was pretty intense. I met Lorelei when she dated Reece. Anyway, when they broke up, I decided to go to work for Lorelei," she said. "I'd worked for Reece for more than a year, and before that, I worked for another actor. It was time to work for a woman for a change. And Lorelei and I are, like, really close. Like sisters."

"Uh-huh," I said. I couldn't picture the morose and weepy Lorelei sharing genetics with the perpetually upbeat Carly. But whatever.

"So did you know that she used to date Quinn?"

I nodded. "He mentioned it."

"Well, if you guys are free now, you should come to the party," she said. "Lorelei's not going to be there. She was so stressed out, I think she just went straight to bed after her massage."

"Quinn's, uh, he went to bed," I said. Which was true, just not *my* bed. But I wasn't in the mood to correct Carly's impression, in case she passed that on to her boss. I didn't trust Lorelei Arens as far as I could throw her, though when I thought about it, I could probably toss her a fair distance. That thought made me happy.

I shook myself out of my daydream of throwing the tiny actress like a javelin and gave Carly a smile. "Anyway, I'd love to come to the party."

Carly clapped her hands together and flashed me that huge smile that showed off her deep dimples. "Yay! Let's go!"

She took me by the arm and pulled me down the stairs, chattering about how much fun we were going to have. We took the same path that Quinn had just walked down, but before it reached the parking lot, we veered left onto a footpath lit with low amber lights shaped like mushrooms. I hadn't yet seen the cabins, but the Whispering Pines brochure had described them as simple and rustic.

The brochure lied.

The "cabin" that Carly led me to was a multi-leveled chalet off the main resort road. It was private, set back from the road and shielded from view with a stand of tall pine trees in the center of a circular drive. From the outside, it looked like a typical million-dollar vacation home that you might find along the shore of Lake Tahoe. Once we were inside, I doubled that estimate.

A sweeping staircase curved along the edge of the round entryway, and a long, handblown glass chandelier dangling from the top of the second floor landing drew my eye up to the stained glass windows that stretched to the top of the turret. What had been a low murmur of voices outside the house grew to excited shouts in the living room, and Carly grabbed my elbow and steered me in that direction.

I'd been expecting a small pizza-and-beer get together among the cast and crew, but the scene in the living room was anything but that. Much of the furniture had been moved out to make room for a makeshift casino. A crowd of about a dozen people gathered around a craps table near the arched entry to the room, and behind them, three dealers in white shirts and black vests handled the dice and the chips. Beyond that were two blackjack tables, and in the far corner, six people played poker—and all those tables had uniformed dealers as well. A cocktail waitress delivered a tray of champagne to gamblers, and another server balanced a display of appetizers.

I recognized a few faces in the crowd from the set earlier, including Mark Tripp, who was sitting at the poker table in the corner. Reece Muir was at the second blackjack table, just a couple chairs away from Denny Shawn Weber, the director.

"Carly, who are all these people?" I asked, as we made our way to a bar, also staffed with a smiling server, in the dining room.

"Oh, you know, friends who are up in Tahoe for vacations, friends of friends, wealthy strangers," she said, with a vague wave. She smiled and waved at a vaguely familiar woman leaving with a glass of white wine.

"Was that—?" I asked, turning to follow the tall and thin woman with long red hair.

"Rosie Lindholm, the model? Yes, that's her," Carly said. "She and Denny are an item. There are a few of her friends here too."

She scanned the room and then turned back to me. "Do you like cards? Dice?"

I shrugged. "A little, but I hadn't planned on playing."

She pulled a small stack of chips from her purse and pressed them into my hand, then took two glasses of wine from the bartender with a grin. "I think there's a seat by Reece."

By a small miracle, I found myself sitting between the movie star and the director, placing a bet on a hand of blackjack.

"Hello again, Miranda," Reece said.

"Oh, hi," I said, that damn giggle threatening to return.

"Have you met Denny?" he asked, then introduced me to the director on my other side.

"Miranda is friends with Carly," Reece said.

"Carly is the best ever," Denny Shawn Weber said, his eyes serious behind his thick lenses. "I mean, she's just amazing. You know that, right?"

"Yeah, I know," I said. She was responsible for the current seating arrangements, so she was practically a saint in my book.

"I think this movie would be three months behind schedule and a couple million over budget, if it weren't for her," Denny said, splitting a pair of tens and dropping another chip on the table. He slurped down the last of his scotch and motioned for the waitress with the empty glass. "I mean, hell, she suggested Whispering Pines for the set even. I gotta figure out how to steal her away from Lorelei."

On my left, Reece snorted, but I was distracted by the terrible play Denny was making. I glanced up at the dealer, waiting to see if he was going to caution the director against it, but he merely dealt two more cards—a four and a seven.

I stood on my own pair of face cards, beating the dealer's hard nineteen.

"Do you play blackjack often?" I asked Denny.

He nodded. "It's my game."

The dealer shot me a look that cautioned me against helping Denny improve his game as the director whipped out his wallet and slipped a small stack of hundred dollars bills across the table. The dealer returned a stack of about ten chips, and I looked down at the clay discs Carly had given me.

Son of a bitch. They were $100 chips.

I collected my winnings and set aside the original five chips to return to her. I didn't know what a personal assistant made, but apparently it was more than a forensic accountant.

I played a hand with the chip that I won in my last hand and drew a four and a seven.

"You going to double down?" Reece asked me. It was the logical move, especially since the dealer was showing a seven, but I paused. A glance at the other cards on the table told me that the odds were good that I'd draw a ten or a face card. But it wasn't my money to gamble with.

"I don't know," I said.

Reece slipped a chip onto my stack, and the dealer peeled off the card—the king of hearts.

"That's how you do it!" Denny said, putting a heavy hand on my shoulder and giving me a squeeze.

I tried to split my winnings with Reece, but he shook his head and smiled. My inner teenage girl squealed with glee as he took my hand in his, then pressed the small stack of chips into my palm and closed my fingers around them.

"I'm cashing in for the night," he said. "Early call tomorrow."

He flashed me that smile again and a wink, sending my insides fluttering. "Good night and good luck."

It was time for me to get out of this party too, I decided. It wasn't my crowd, and I wasn't that comfortable playing among the high-rollers. I pushed a chip toward the dealer and cashed in the rest of my winnings, looking around the room for Carly. For once, the blonde whirlwind wasn't anywhere to be found, so I slipped out the front door and started back to the lodge.

The resort's grounds were a silent and empty contrast to the party. I followed the narrow lane back toward the lodge. It was a slightly longer route than the footpath, but it was nice to be outside in the cool and quiet night. The road wound past several cabins, all of which were set slightly above the lodge, deeper in the trees that shielded them from view. Most were dark, and I imagined that the occupants were still at the party I'd just left. Ahead, I saw a yellow glow and realized that one cabin was occupied. I glanced down the short driveway and saw a white truck parked along the side of the house.

I stopped in the middle of the road and stared.

I knew that truck.

And I suspected I knew who was staying in this remote cabin.

But why was Quinn visiting Lorelei Arens?

CHAPTER NINE

I stood staring at the white truck in front of Lorelei Arens' cabin for several minutes, biting my lip as I tried to figure out why Quinn had gone to her. Was he still in love with her? After ten years and a massive betrayal? He certainly hadn't seemed upset over dinner, but maybe I was missing something.

The goose bumps on my bare arms finally roused my feet to keep moving toward the lodge, and I walked the rest of the way back to the main building lost in thought. Quinn was a grown man, and if he wanted to hang out with a lying and deceitful actress who had already ruined his life once, why should I stop him?

I walked up the wide steps to the front doors and let out a frustrated sigh. Because he was a good friend and a good man, and I didn't want to see him get taken down that road again. But I didn't know what I could do to stop it. He hadn't even told me that he planned to see her again.

"Looks like someone needs another appointment with Margarit."

I turned at the sound of Dottie's voice and found her and Max in a pair of club chairs by the fireplace.

"Or at least a nightcap," Max said. "Come on over and join us, Miranda. Wipe that frown off your face."

I tried a weak smile and declined the drink but perched on the arm of the sofa near them.

"You look nice. Were you down at the casinos?" Max asked.

I shook my head. "No, I met a friend for dinner at Angelina's, then I was invited to a party with some of the film crew."

"Must have been some party," Dottie said. "I saw a limo pull in earlier."

Max frowned. "We generally don't permit guests to host large events in the cabins, because people come up here to relax and enjoy the quiet. But since they're all here for the same reason, and there aren't any other guests to disturb, I guess it's okay."

I nodded. "It was a pretty nice deal. I got to sit between Reece Muir and Denny Shawn Weber at the blackjack table, and I won a few hundred dollars."

When I thought about it, that was actually a pretty good night, so I should just get over my bad mood about Quinn and his questionable romantic choices.

"Blackjack?" Dottie asked, setting her glass down.

"Yes, and poker and there was a craps table," I said with a nod. "Nice event. There was even a catering staff."

Dottie and Max exchanged a glance, and from their expressions, I could tell something was wrong.

"Is everything okay? Did I say something wrong?"

Max shook his head. "Are they playing for cash?"

I nodded, opened my purse, and withdrew the hundred dollar bills I'd collected when I cashed in my chips—five hundred of which I owed to Carly. "It looked real to me."

Dottie looked around the empty lobby. The front desk was closed for the evening, and there wasn't a single staff member around. We were alone by the fireplace, which popped and hissed. Despite the nice warm glow, I felt the chill.

"Is something wrong?" I asked.

Dottie pursed her lips. "It's illegal to gamble without a license. This sounds like a professional operation but not a legal one. If the Gaming Commission gets wind of this going on at Whispering Pines, that could be bad for Max's gaming license application. How many people were there?"

I made a quick calculation from my memory. "About 65 guests, about 10 dealers and cashiers. A few more waitstaff and bartenders."

"Who was running the games? Could you tell?" Max asked, his eyes intense on my face.

I shook my head. "There was a man in a suit who wandered around the games, seemed to be in charge, but I don't know who he is."

"Which cabin?"

I described the location and Max nodded. "Cabin No. 7. They're all rented to the film crew, but I can see who is assigned to this one," he said and stood up. "I'll get Frankie to take care of this. I knew nothing good was going to come of this stupid movie idea."

Dottie shook her head. "Max, now wait a minute."

He sat back down but leaned forward with his elbows on his knees, his lips pressed together in a tight line.

"Let's think this through. You get Frankie and his boys up there to roust out the party, you risk someone getting pissed and calling the Gaming Commission."

"Yeah, so?"

Dottie tilted her head. "There might be an opportunity for you here. Why don't *you* call the Gaming Control Board and report the illegal operation?"

He gave a harsh laugh. "Rat myself out? Are you kidding me, Dot? Why would I draw a target on my own back?"

She held up a hand. "Think of it as assisting law enforcement."

Max squinted at her. "Why the hell would I do that?"

She gave an exasperated sigh. "Because you're an upstanding citizen who wouldn't permit illegal activity on your property, of course."

Max still looked suspicious, but he leaned back a few inches in the chair, waiting for her to convince him not to go bust heads.

"The Control Board is always on the lookout for illegal gaming operations. You're going to be applying to the Gaming Commission for a license shortly. What better reference than a Control Board agent who can testify that you've been an asset in fighting illicit gambling?"

"I can't even believe I'm considering this," he said. "They could turn this around, investigate me, and then I'm not a do-gooder, I'm the target of their probe."

Dottie leaned back, looked at me and then back at Max.

"What about if we called in the FBI instead?"

"I do not see how that is better," Max said. "Have you lost your freakin' mind, Dot?"

She laughed. "It falls under their jurisdiction too. Plus, we've got an in there."

Dottie looked at me again and smiled.

"Miranda knows an FBI agent. We can trust him, right?"

Oh, damn.

"Uh, yeah, but I don't how much of an 'in' I have there," I said.

"You trust him?" Max asked.

Jake Barnes had saved my life, on at least one occasion. He was honest and trustworthy. And I really didn't want to involve him in this. But I nodded.

"Yes, I trust him."

The room was silent for several long seconds, then Max nodded.

"Yeah. Call him."

Twelve hours later, I was standing on the veranda of the Whispering Pines Resort, watching Jake walk up the steps. Tall, handsome, and serious—he had his FBI game-face on. Even with that grim expression, my insides melted at the sight of him.

He had said little when I called him the night before. He asked a few questions to clarify my rushed explanation of illegal gaming, movie stars, a fancy resort, and my desire to keep my new job and keep my first and only client so far out of trouble. Then he said he'd make some calls and let me know what would happen next. I'd never reported a crime before, but I expected more urgency.

Then the phone rang an hour later, and Jake said to expect him the next morning.

He hadn't warned me that he'd be bringing Bethany, who trailed behind him as he approached me.

"You've been busy," Jake said with a grin.

I blew out a long exhale. "Yeah, I have."

I hadn't even gotten into the story about Quinn and Lorelei, which wasn't relevant to the FBI's investigation, but I really wanted to talk to someone about it. But I couldn't mention what I knew about Quinn's prior conviction because I knew confidential details that I couldn't share.

"Max and Dottie are expecting us inside," I said, nodding toward the door.

"We've got a couple colleagues who are right behind us," Jake said.

I frowned. "You brought reinforcements?"

"The local FBI office is interested in this, and he's bringing in a state agency," Jake said. "That a problem?"

I shook my head. "Not for me."

As we watched, a black sedan cruised up the curving driveway and then into the guest parking area.

"That's them," Bethany said.

I stood next to Jake, watching a man and a woman walk up from the parking lot. The morning air was still cool but would warm up soon, and there was only a slight breeze, but it was enough to ruffle my skirt. Glancing down, I saw a bandage across the back of Jake's hand.

Jake caught me staring and tilted his hand to show off his wound.

"Kvetch?" I asked.

"Of course."

"Sorry. He's sort of a bastard."

"I gathered that."

I looked up, and he smiled, sending a rush of feelings through me. I was hesitant to call Jake in when Dottie suggested it, but now that he was here, I was filled with a sense that everything would be okay.

Bethany jogged down the steps to greet the man and woman walking toward the lodge.

"So, how much did you lose at the tables last night?" Jake asked, his voice low.

"I won $400. On two hands." Then I frowned. "Do I have to give that back? I didn't realize it was illegal."

Jake's low laugh thrilled me through and through. "We'll work something out."

Bethany led the two other agents up the steps to where Jake and I were waiting.

"Agent Barnes, it's nice to meet you. I'm Alex Marquez, from the Reno office," the man said, shaking hands with Jake. He turned to me and tilted his head. He was in his mid-thirties, slightly shorter and broader in the shoulders than Jake, with short-cropped dark hair and deep brown eyes. His white teeth flashed when he gave me a smile.

"This is Miranda Vaughn. She called in the tip," Jake said, putting a hand on my back and leaving it there.

"Nice to meet you, Ms. Vaughn," Alex said. "This is Agent Gail Bonner with the Nevada Gaming Control Board."

We shook hands all around. Then I escorted the agents through the vast and empty lobby, past the fireplace, and into the business wing, where Max and Dottie were waiting in the conference room. We were the only people in the business area since it was a Saturday, so the agents probably wouldn't draw too much attention among the resort's staff.

"Thank you for contacting us so promptly, Mr. Emmerson," Alex said, after introductions were made. "This sounds a lot like an operation that Agent Bonner and I have been tracking in this region. I'd like to get as much information as possible about who was at the event last night."

Everyone in the room turned to me, and I had the uncomfortable feeling of being caught in a floodlight.

"Uh, right. Well, first, I didn't realize it was illegal gambling."

Alex smiled, but Agent Bonner frowned. "Gaming is only legal when authorized and regulated by the state of Nevada."

"I'm not a lawyer or a federal law enforcement officer, Agent Bonner," I said, trying to keep my voice steady when inside I was trembling, remembering how it felt when I'd been interviewed by the FBI after my arrest. I hadn't done anything wrong but still ended up on trial for fraud. No matter how hard I focused on the fact that it had been more than a year since I'd been acquitted of those charges, having three FBI agents and a Nevada state agent staring at me still made my heart skip erratically.

Jake cleared his throat, and I looked to where he sat at the end of the conference table. His eyes were concerned but warm, and I focused on him as I began to recount what I'd seen the night before.

"There were about sixty guests and about a dozen or so staff. Two blackjack tables, one poker table in the corner, and a craps table near the front of the house," I said, my voice sounding calmer than I felt. If I could keep up this pretense, maybe eventually I'd even believe it. "There was a bar and two bartenders in the dining room area. A cashier and a man who seemed to be in charge of the tables."

Alex Marquez took notes, and Gail Bonner asked the questions, focusing on the staff and then on the guest list.

"Did you see any guests who spoke to the pit boss?" she asked.

I thought about it, then shook my head. "No, not that I noticed. I wasn't there very long. Maybe a half hour."

"And you won how much money?" Bethany asked with a sniff.

"About four hundred dollars," I said.

"Pretty good hourly rate," she said, her eyebrow arched.

"Did you make that much on the pole?" I asked, giving her my best wide-eyed innocent smile.

Jake coughed, and Alex looked up from his notes, his eyes wide, and his mouth half open.

"Back to the investigation," Gail said, with an impatient scowl at Bethany and me. "Did any of the guests seem to be hosting the event?"

I shook my head. "No, not really."

"Who invited you?" Jake asked.

"Carly Malone. She's a personal assistant to an actress on the film. She didn't seem to be in charge of it, just invited me to tag along with her."

"She's the one who gave you money to gamble with?" Gail asked.

"Yes."

"Five hundred dollars?"

I nodded. "Yes, it was five chips. I figured out later they were hundred-dollar chips. And I'm returning the money to her."

But not the winnings, if I could help it. I mean, I won that fair and square. Well, illegally. Damn it, I was probably going to have to give that up or at least give it to charity.

"And she said the gaming operation would be back next weekend?"

"Yes. The film should finish up later this week, so it will be the last night everyone is together," I said.

Alex and Gail exchanged a glance.

"Next week..." Alex said.

They each smiled then turned back to me. "You've got an invitation to the party?"

I glanced between them uneasily. "Not an engraved invitation, but Carly said I should come if I was still here. But Dottie and I should be done with our work here by then. And my aunt is getting married next Saturday, so I need to be done before then."

Dottie shrugged. "Well, we don't know that for sure we'll be finished with the audit by the end of the week. And if there's a chance that Miranda could help with your investigation, I'm sure Max wouldn't mind if she stayed here a few more nights. Right, Max?"

Max nodded. "Anything to help the Gaming Control Board."

His smile couldn't have been more forced if he used his hands to shove his cheeks upward.

"And we'll make sure that you can get to your aunt's wedding, of course," Alex said.

Jake put his hands on the table and leaned forward. "How

about we talk about whether these people are dangerous? Who are they? What are their records? Have they been violent before? And when were you going to advise Miranda of the risks involved in going in undercover?"

Alex scratched his head and glanced at Gail, who pursed her lips.

"Thing is, we don't know who they are. We know their MO and we know they hire locals to serve at the parties, but we haven't been able to pin down any identities yet," Gail said.

Jake shook his head. "No. This isn't happening. You're not sending her in like that."

"Not your operation, Agent Barnes," Gail said, lifting her chin. "It's mine. Alex has been assisting me because they're operating in two states, but this is a Gaming Control Board investigation."

They continued to stare at each other, both determined and neither acknowledging me. Dottie and Max both shook their heads in Gail Bonner's direction, urging me to volunteer.

"I'll do it," I said.

Gail smiled. "Great."

I smiled back. "If Jake goes with me."

Bethany rolled her eyes. "How are you going to swing that?"

"She'll just say Jake's her boyfriend," Gail said. "No problem."

Slight problem, I thought.

"Uh, actually, Carly thinks I have a boyfriend. A different boyfriend," I said.

Jake glared at me across the table. "Why does she think that?"

"She saw me with Quinn and jumped to a conclusion, and I didn't correct her."

"No problem. We'll have Agent Boylan go in with you as a friend," Gail said.

"Ugh. No," Bethany and I said in unison. At least we could agree on something.

"Oh, get over yourselves, ladies," Gail snapped. "Fine. Mr. Emmerson, I need a room for Agents Barnes and Boylan. Maybe a honeymoon suite. If anyone asks, just say their reservations were made prior to the resort being leased out."

She stood with the ramrod posture of a drill sergeant, and the rest of us followed suit.

"You—" She pointed at me. "You're going to report back to me and Agent Marquez anything you hear from your friend with the purse full of chips. Try to find out who invited this crew up for the party."

Then she pointed at Jake. "You just cool your jets, turbo. Do some surveillance of the cabin, find good camera angles, and set up remotes for the night of the party. We're not going to let Ms. Vaughn walk into a dangerous situation without protection in place."

"And you," she said, her gaze resting on Bethany, who looked uncomfortable. "Try not to piss me off."

Then she turned to Max, who took a half step backward, despite the fact that he was a good five inches taller than Gail. "Let's talk about those accommodations. Do you have a government rate?"

CHAPTER TEN

The afternoon sun blazed into the conference room, and my eyes were growing heavy, tired after reading scrawled receipts and bank records. The box of receipts that Jordan had turned over to us were not organized in any fashion whatsoever. But with only a few minor exceptions, everything matched up with the bank records and vendor contracts.

It was taking everything I had to keep my focus on the books and not let my thoughts wander to what Jake was doing while I helped Dottie wrap up the audit. Maybe he was moving his bags into the honeymoon suite with Bethany Boylan. A sharp pain pulsed in my temple at that thought.

"You find something?" Dottie asked.

I looked up and realized I was frowning at the spreadsheets. "Oh, no. Everything looks good here."

Dottie peered over her reading glasses at me.

"Are you okay cooperating with the investigation? I don't want to put you in an awkward position here," she said. "I mean, Max really does need to cooperate, but if you're not comfortable, we can tell Agent Bonner to get someone else to do this."

It was a little late for that offer, since I'd already agreed, and somehow this all led to Jake staying in the honeymoon suite with my nemesis.

"No, it's fine," I said. "I mean, Ms. Bonner said I might not even have to go to the party. They just want to make sure that if it moves locations, they have someone who finds out about that."

Dottie smiled. "Well, keep a lid on the plans. Other than Max, only Frankie knows what's going on. He's not telling Jordan. I don't even think he's told Angie."

Max was even more reluctant to go along with this plan than I was. It wasn't in his nature to cooperate with the feds, he told me and Dottie after the agents all left—Gail Bonner and Alex Marquez to secure rooms in Stateline nearby, and Jake and Bethany to get their bags and check into their room. That thought made my stomach turn over again.

That was the source of my reservations about this operation, but Max's were more deep-seated. His father had been under investigation at the time of his death. The federal government was looking at his taxes, his bank accounts, interviewing vendors and employees. The Gaming Board was sniffing around too, trying to see if there was any substance to longstanding rumors that the Emmersons had ties to organized crime.

"It was all bullshit," Max had told us. "But it ruined my father's life. They were the reason we lost the Penny. Once news of that investigation leaked out, it was all over. We just couldn't recover from that."

Dottie and I had promised to keep any word of the investigation under wraps to avoid bringing that sort of attention to the Emmerson family again.

"You know, there's nothing pressing on the audit right now. We can't get that full report from the accountants until Monday, and we have all next week to look at the rest of the finances. If you want to go home tonight or tomorrow, you're welcome to take my car," Dottie said.

Normally, that would be a tempting offer. As nice as the resort was, it wasn't home. It would be nice to sleep in my own bed. I even missed Kvetch a little.

But since Aunt Marie would make sure Kvetch wasn't terrorizing the neighborhood or at least that he wasn't doing it on an empty stomach, there was no immediate reason to return to Sacramento. Plus, Jake was here, and he was the main reason that I had wanted to return home by Sunday.

"No, I'll stay around here. I spoke to Aunt Marie this afternoon. She'll take care of the house and the cat for me. And Rob said there wasn't anything going on at work next week, so I can stay up here a few extra days."

"Well, the offer stands if you change your mind," Dottie said.

That wasn't likely to happen as long as Jake was pretending to be a happy newlywed with Bethany. Not that I knew what to do about that.

"At least take tomorrow off, and go down to the lake or something," Dottie said, gathering up our paperwork and computers and locking them in an oak file cabinet. I kept a stack of binders with the bank statements, so I'd have something to work on later. "Do you have plans for tonight?"

"No, but I may try to get in to see Margarit at the spa." The knots in my shoulders had Bethany Boylan's name on one side and Lorelei Arens' on the other. "How about you? What are your plans?"

Dottie grabbed her purse from the table and herded me toward the door. "I'm catching a show with Angie down at the Royal Palace Casino, then grabbing a late dinner. Don't wait up."

That figures. I'd probably be in bed by nine, curled up with a year's worth of financial transactions.

We walked out of the business wing and into the lobby. I was starting to get used to how large the space felt with its empty chairs and our echoing footsteps on the stone floors. This Saturday afternoon was no different—the bored reception desk clerk was reading a paperback and twirling a long lock of brown hair around her finger. She looked up and gave us a smile and set the book down.

"Good afternoon, ladies. Can I get you anything? Reservations for dinner or the spa, maybe?"

Poor thing looked so happy to have something to do that I paused at the desk to let her make the call downstairs to the spa for me. Dottie waved and headed to the stairs.

"Can you see if Margarit can get me in for a massage this afternoon or this evening?"

"Of course!"

While she made the reservation, I leaned an elbow on the counter and took in the rustic, yet elegant decor. The tall wood-framed windows looked out to the wide veranda that spanned the front of the main building. It was warm and welcoming, but eerie when it was so empty of guests. The phone still rang, though, with people trying to get last minute reservations and inquiring about the spa services and the restaurants' hours. The resort staff had been juggling those parts of the business that remained open with the demands of the film crew.

The clerk hung up and apologized for having to take another call, then handed me the reservation card for the spa. "She can get you in about an hour from now."

I smiled, thanked her, and started to walk to the elevator, but then turned back. "Do you know where the filming is today? I might want to walk around, and I don't want to get in the way."

She nodded and smiled. "Outside the ballroom, on the north side of the main building, until seven or so. Just stay on the foot-paths, and you should be fine. They've put up signs to direct foot traffic away from where they're shooting. Not that that's a huge problem," she said, looking around the empty lobby.

She sighed and picked up her book. I was sympathetic. Nothing worse than a boring job.

The opening of the massive wooden front doors drew our attention, and I heard the sharp intake of breath from the young girl behind the counter at the sight of the tall man crossing the threshold. His blond hair was tousled, and he wore his T-shirt and jeans with a confidence that said he knew that his casual clothes wouldn't get him kicked out of a formal black-tie event.

"Hi, Quinn. What are you doing here?" I asked, walking toward him.

"I'm on my way back home but wanted to talk with you. Is this a good time?"

"Yeah, sure." I held up my armful of binders. "I wouldn't mind dropping these off at my room. Walk with me?"

Quinn took the binders from me and carried them to my room, setting them on the desk by the windows. He smiled at me, but his eyes were troubled.

"Is everything all right?" I asked, offering him something from the mini fridge. He accepted a beer, so I grabbed two, and we sat in the chairs by the window.

"When I was leaving last night, I ran into Lorelei," he said, leaning forward and looking at the bottle in his hands, not at me. "Well, that's not true. She was waiting for me, at my truck."

A small alarm bell rang in my head. Was that why Carly had tracked me down and invited me to the party? To distract me so Lorelei could lure Quinn away?

"What happened?" I asked.

He shifted in the chair and took a drink of the beer before answering, and my stomach dropped, anticipating his reply. Then he shook his head.

"Nothing happened. I drove her back to her cabin, and we talked a little while, but she was really out of it," he said. "She said she is just tired from working all the time, but I think there's something else going on there."

I nodded, remembering her catastrophic meltdown in the ballroom—what Reece had called a temper tantrum seemed less like an angry toddler and more like someone who was not in control of herself or her emotions.

"What do you think it is? A nervous breakdown? Drugs?"

Quinn frowned. "I don't know. I really don't know. And I know I shouldn't care, but she just seems so...lost."

We sat in awkward silence for another minute.

"Why did she want to talk with you?" I asked. Maybe Lorelei had finally apologized for setting him up. Maybe she'd come forward and clear his name. Not that it would do any good erasing his guilty plea, but it would be nice for Quinn to have that public acknowledgement that he wasn't a drug dealer.

"She wanted—" He stumbled over the words. "Uh, well."

He blushed, and I laughed, embarrassed. "Oh, right. Of course she did."

He smiled. "Sorry I went there, but it was sort of a shock to me."

"But did you—?"

"No! God, no! I mean, no, I wouldn't have, but in her condition, I'm not even sure it would have been legal. I doubt she could consent to anything in her state of mind," he said.

"Good," I said. "I mean, that sounds like a good decision."

He wasn't really thinking of getting involved with her again, was he? I stared at him, trying to figure out his emotions from the expression on his face, but I got nowhere.

"Also, I told her that you and I were involved. As a way to explain why I wasn't going to stay with her. I'm sorry. I shouldn't have brought you into this," he said.

"No, that's fine. It's not a problem," I said, relieved. If I had to pretend to be Quinn's girlfriend for a few more days, that was a small price to pay to keep him out of Lorelei's clutches. "Her assistant Carly already thinks that we're a couple."

He tilted his head. "She does?"

"She saw us together and jumped to that conclusion, and I didn't correct her," I said. "I thought if I told her you were single, she'd pass that on to her boss."

He smiled—a genuine and warm smile that made me relax. "Thanks for looking out for me."

I returned the grin. "Any time."

He took another drink. "So I need a favor from you."

"Sure," I said.

"You might want to hear it first, before you agree to it."

I laughed. "How hard can it be?"

He glanced down again, then back to me. "I want you to keep an eye on Lorelei, make sure she's okay."

Oh God. Not that.

"You said you're going to be here until Monday or Tuesday, so if you can, I don't know, just make sure she doesn't hurt herself," he said.

"I may even be here a little longer," I said. "But Quinn, I don't know how to help Lorelei. And I honestly don't really want to. I don't even understand why you do."

He set his beer down on the table and wiped his palms on his jean-clad thighs. "I have no right to ask you to do this, I know. But she's in trouble."

"She *is* trouble," I said.

He nodded. "Yes, and she probably doesn't deserve the help. But I'm asking that you treat her like you would any stranger who you thought was in danger."

Well, it was clear that Quinn was a better person than I was.

I tipped my head back and looked at the ceiling with a huge sigh. "Fine."

Quinn laughed. "Now who's the drama queen?"

"If I see her around, I'll watch her and make sure she's not overdosing or breaking down," I said.

"It's not just that I want you to be there to call 9-1-1," he said. "She's in a cutthroat business, and I don't trust the people around her. She's in a vulnerable state, and this is an industry that attracts sharks."

"I'll do what I can. If I see any red flags, I'll call you," I said but wasn't sure that Lorelei needed my protection when she had Carly Malone on her side. That girl would do anything for her boss and probably had completed Secret Service training on how to take a bullet for her.

"Lorelei is one huge red flag. But call me if you think she's getting worse," he said. "Why did your stay get prolonged? Is the audit not going well? What about the wedding?"

I shrugged and tried to come up with an excuse that didn't expose the investigation into illegal casino operations. "Uh, yeah, it's just going to take a little longer than planned. But I'll be done in time to get home and pack for the wedding. I just have to drive to Reno on Monday to meet with the resort's former accountant, and then there's...stuff."

Quinn laughed. "Accounting stuff, which I'm sure is riveting."

"Yes, accounting stuff that you'd find boring as hell."

A knock at the door sounded, and I stood up to answer it. "You want to stay for dinner before you drive home? My treat," I said, walking across the floor.

"Well, that does sound like a better offer than a drive-through burger," Quinn said.

I opened the door, expecting to find Dottie, the only person who knew where I was staying.

Instead, Jake filled the doorway.

"Can we talk?" he asked, his brown eyes intent on mine. My heart skipped a beat at the eye contact and the fact that he was so close.

"Uh..."

He looked up, beyond me, and his body stiffened.

"Is this a bad time?" he asked, his voice chilled.

"Quinn was just stopping by before he drove home," I said. "We're having dinner later."

"That's okay, Miranda," Quinn said, joining me at the door. "I appreciate the offer, but another time."

"Barnes."

Bethany Boylan appeared at Jake's side, carrying a small overnight bag, because the situation just wasn't awkward enough. She handed him a key card and nodded toward the set of doors across the hall and down a few yards. "We're in room 212."

I pushed the door open all the way, so we wouldn't be crowded around the doorway.

"Jake, I'd like you to meet my good friend, Quinn Bishop."

Jake stepped into the room and shook Quinn's hand, and the two men sized each other up. I'd seen something like it once in National Geographic. If my recollection was correct, any moment now, one would lower his head and charge the other.

Bethany watched the exchange with a cautious expression. I introduced her to Quinn too, and she stepped in to shake his hand.

"Bethany is Jake's partner," I explained to Quinn, letting the door shut behind me.

Quinn shot me a curious look but smiled politely. "You're with the FBI too?"

She nodded and smiled, the expression softening her pointy features. They were standing close to each other in the crowded entryway to my room, and Bethany was tall enough that they were practically eye-to-eye. I watched in amazement as she brushed her long brown hair back from her face and over her shoulder in a casual manner. It was an unconscious sign of attraction, and I would have bet that she had no idea she was doing it. Or that she was flirting with a felon.

"Yes, I am. And how do you and Miranda know each other?" she asked.

"Mutual friends," I said.

There was another knock at the door, and I eased past Bethany and Jake to answer it, wondering how I was going to explain the FBI's presence to Quinn. At least he was on his way out of town.

"Hey, Miranda! Oh, hi, Quinn!" Carly bounced into the room like a tiny blonde tornado, and the two FBI agents moved back, eyes widening at the appearance of the sudden intruder.

"Carly," I stammered. "Hi. How did you know where I was staying?"

She laughed. "I asked at the front desk. This place is pretty casual. I told them we were friends, and I couldn't reach you because you left your cell phone in my cabin."

She held up a high-end smartphone, her blue eyes sparkling.

"That's your phone," I said.

She laughed. "I know. But it worked!"

She spun around and looked at Jake and Bethany, who were still standing in stunned silence. "Hi, I'm Carly."

"Oh, I'm sorry," I said. "Carly, this is Jake and Bethany. Carly works for one of the actors on the film shoot that's going on at the resort."

They shook hands.

"I didn't know there were any other guests up here," Carly said. "How do you guys know each other?"

"Miranda and I went to college together. We're old friends," Bethany said with a warm smile in my direction.

I forced a smile in return and hoped it didn't look too fake. Quinn caught my eye and raised an eyebrow but didn't say anything. I moved close to him and put an arm around his waist, leaning in to him. I couldn't even look in Jake's direction, it felt like such a betrayal. But I couldn't blow up the FBI's investigation that had only just started. Quinn put an arm around my shoulder and gave me a slight squeeze.

"How fun," Carly said, then turned and grabbed my arm. "Well, this is just great. I talked Jordan into letting us barbecue at the pool tonight, and I wanted to invite you and Quinn to join us. It will be so much fun! You should all come!"

"Oh, I uh, guess, sure," I said, unable to come up with a reasonable excuse in the face of such unrelenting hospitality. "What time?"

"Jordan is going to get the pool set up so we can start grilling around eight," Carly said. She looked at each of us in turn. "You'll all be there, right?"

We all nodded. She squealed and clapped her hands together, bouncing on her toes. Yes, she was definitely a former cheerleader. "That's so awesome! I can't wait to hear all about your college days!"

She turned and bounced back out of the hotel room, her blonde curls bobbing. The door shut, and the room remained silent.

"That was Carly Malone?" Jake asked.

I nodded. "Yes."

"She's the one who invited you to the party?" Bethany asked.

"Yes."

"She's rather high-strung," Jake said. He moved toward the door and picked up Bethany's bag. "We should go unpack. It looks like we have a double-date set up."

He turned and looked back at me, still standing with Quinn's arm around me, before opening the door.

"I'll let you fill your boyfriend in on what's going on."

CHAPTER ELEVEN

"What the hell?" Gail Bonner's voice on Jake's speakerphone sounded staticky and angry. Mostly angry. "I have to expense another room? For another informant? Who I've never met?"

Jake and I stared at each other over the phone, which sat in the middle of the small round table. Quinn had volunteered to help Bethany bring up the rest of her bags, and she had accepted his offer in a fraction of a second, so Jake had offered to call Gail Bonner and let her know that Quinn was now part of the operation.

"Mr. Bishop was here when Ms. Malone came into the room. It would have raised suspicions to let him leave. He's willing to stay tonight to help us out. But he needs his own room," Jake said, his eyes narrowing.

"Do you know what the government rate is at this place, Barnes? Miranda, you and Mr. Bishop can't bunk together for a night?"

"No." Jake's answer was quick and firm.

Gail let out a frustrated sigh. "Fine. I'll call Max Emmerson and tell him to give Mr. Bishop a room. What do we know about this guy?"

I bit my lip but decided it was best to give her a full explanation. "He has a criminal record. He was arrested ten years ago for bringing some illegal drugs back from Mexico. He pleaded guilty and spent two years at Lompoc. He's been in no trouble since then. Or before his arrest."

There was a sharp intake of breath on the other end of the phone.

"Before he was arrested, he worked as a horse trainer on film sets. He knows several members of the crew here, and that's what got me invited to the party in the first place," I said. "They trust him. And they won't think twice about him being at the party."

Another long sigh.

"Do you trust him, Barnes?"

"I just met him." Jake looked at me, his eyes serious. "But Miranda trusts him."

"Fine. Give me any information you have on his prior, so I can get the file."

I rattled off the case number and the year.

"How do you know this?" Gail asked.

"My employer, Rob Fogg, was his defense attorney."

"Tell me what you know of his case," she said.

"I can't."

And I wouldn't. I'd love to tell her that he was innocent of the charges, that he was set up by a conniving bitch, but I couldn't. Everything I knew was covered by attorney-client confidentiality.

"Right. Barnes, what do you know?"

"Nothing firsthand, just gossip."

"I'll look it up," she said. "But he's going to have to answer some questions."

"I'll let him know," I said.

"Bishop may be a better source of information than Miranda," Barnes said. "He knows people on the crew, and they trust him. And most of them know about his prior arrest, so they won't think he's working for the government."

"Yeah, okay. Let me know how it goes tonight," she said, then disconnected the call, and Jake and I were truly alone for the first time since he had dropped me off at Dottie's office on Thursday.

He rubbed his forehead. "I don't suppose you have another beer in that fridge?"

I nodded and retrieved two beers. I had canceled my appointment with Margarit, so I was counting on the cold IPA to get rid of the tension in my neck.

"This wasn't what I had in mind for a date," Jake said, using the bottom of his T-shirt to open a bottle and hand it to me.

"I know. Me too," I said.

He shook his head and closed his eyes. "Well, at least we can get Quinn his own room."

"But not you and Bethany?" My eyes narrowed at the thought.

"We're in adjoining rooms," he said. "Since there's no one but you and Ms. Russell staying on this end of the second floor, adjoining rooms will be fine to convince everyone we're in the same room."

"I hardly ever see anyone in the main building. Are there other rooms being used?"

Jake nodded. "Some of the crew have rooms, but they're clustered at the other end of the building. I asked Max to get Quinn the room next to you, which is right across from our rooms."

"Sounds cozy," I said, taking a long drink of the beer. The IPA was refreshing, but it wasn't going to cut it. "Wait, you already arranged for Quinn's room? I thought you had to get permission from Gail Bonner first."

Jake looked away and looked uncomfortable, then turned

back to me. "If Quinn was staying overnight, he wasn't staying here. With you."

The breath left my lungs in a quick rush. "Oh. You..."

He nodded and reached across the table to take my hand. Then he stood and pulled me up too, still holding my hand in his. It was the only point of contact between us, but we were mere inches apart. My lips parted, and I struggled to breathe at the naked intention in his eyes.

"I know we haven't been able to make this work out yet—"

My eyes opened wide as he leaned forward. His hand moved up my arm, to my shoulder, then to my neck, pulling me closer.

"I was so looking forward to Sunday," he whispered.

My eyes fluttered closed at the promise in his voice. "Me too."

The sharp crack of a knock at the door broke the spell, and I jumped about a foot away from Jake as I heard the beep of the key card and then the sound of the lock sliding open. When Quinn and Bethany walked in with Quinn's large duffel bag, Jake was standing at the window looking out over the lawn below.

"I thought we were going to need a cart for Bethany's bags," Quinn said with a smile. Bethany laughed, and I stared in disbelief. I had never imagined her capable of laughter, but she seemed relaxed and happy. It was a side of her I hadn't seen before.

"Thanks for your help," she said with another toss of her long hair.

I wondered if her attitude would change when she realized he had a criminal record. If she did suddenly start treating him as she did me, I'd have to punch her in the face. No two ways about it.

"Did you talk with Bonner?" Bethany asked.

Jake turned and nodded. "Yes, Max is going to get the room next door set up for Quinn. It will be ready shortly."

Quinn nodded. "Did you tell the lead agent about me?"

The question was directed at me, and I jumped in before Jake could. "Yes, I told her."

Jake moved toward the door. "We'll see you at the pool around eight then," he said, barely glancing in our direction.

The door closed behind the agents, and Quinn turned to me.

"What's wrong with Special Agent Prince Charming?"

I shrugged. "He's fine. He just didn't expect to find you here, in my room."

Quinn smiled. "Yeah, I could tell."

He didn't seem the least bit upset about causing Jake that distress.

"You doing okay?" he asked, his expression more genuine.

I sat on the edge of the bed, then fell backward. "Sure, I'm fine. I just have to pretend to be best buddies with Bethany Boylan, who hates me. While Jake is sleeping across the hall in an adjoining room with her and pretending to be married to her."

The bed moved as Quinn sat down and then lay back next to me. "It's just for a couple of days. You'll be fine."

I frowned and turned to look at him. He was smiling at me.

"What's the story with Agent Bethany Boylan?" he asked, giving me that familiar grin, the one that I'd been charmed by on more than one occasion.

"Ugh. No."

"What? She's nice," he said, raising an eyebrow. "And she's cute."

"She is not nice."

And I feared that he was going to be smacked in the face with her attitude once she learned that he'd pleaded guilty to drug trafficking. She was horrible to me, suspicious and cold, and I'd been acquitted.

"I think that's a bad idea. She's a federal agent."

"Yeah, I know. Not my usual type."

"Quinn, no. You can do better. So much better."

He laughed. "Why don't you like her?"

"Let's just say it's mutual."

A knock sounded at the door again.

"Oh, damn it. What now?"

I rolled off the bed and stood up. I found Kayla, the reception clerk, at the door. She handed me an envelope for Quinn with his room keys and then wished us a good night.

"Well, that wasn't horrible," I said. "Your room is next door. Here are your keys."

I tossed the envelope next to him. Quinn sat up and grinned at me. "I forgot to thank you for getting me a free night at a really nice hotel."

"It's not free. The government is paying for it. And you're working for it, pretending to be my boyfriend."

Quinn stood and laughed.

"The last time the government paid for my accommodations, it wasn't this comfortable." He grabbed his duffel bag and patted my head on his way out the door. "I'll pick you up around eight."

I closed the door behind him and then collapsed on the bed again. I didn't have time for a massage now, so I opted for a nice long shower. I was still in my robe, lounging on the bed, when I heard a soft knock on the door.

There was just no chance I was going to get to relax this afternoon, I thought, padding across the room to answer the door. This time, I used the peephole.

Jake was standing in the hall, looking nervously in both directions.

"Hey, what's up?" I asked, opening the door for him.

He stepped in quickly, closed the door behind himself and pulled me toward him, tight against his chest, my thighs against his.

"Oh," I breathed, my heart pounding.

"What I was trying to say earlier," he said, his voice low, and his breath brushing by my ear, "is that I am sorry that this summer has been so busy that we haven't been able to find time for each other."

Yes. I shivered in his embrace and wrapped my arms around his waist. "Me too," I whispered.

He tipped my chin up, and his lips met mine. *Oh, yes.*

My world tilted on its axis, and I clung to him, solid and hot and oh so delicious.

"I just want to make sure we're both on the same page here," he said, pulling away a few inches.

"Of course," I said, sounding winded.

"Good." He kissed me again, and my mind started to disentangle itself from the embrace. Was I on the same page? I mean, I was pretty sure we were both thinking the same thing at that moment, while our lips were locked together. But what about when we got home and went out in public?

"Hey, can I ask you something?" I asked. It was my turn to pull back.

He smiled. "Anything."

"This is okay, right? I mean, it's not going to like, get you in trouble at work or hurt your career, right?"

His warm brown eyes narrowed a little. "If anyone asks about whether I was kissing our undercover informant, I'll just tell them that it wasn't the first time."

He pulled back, but I put a hand on his chest. The steady thump of his heartbeat beneath the thin T-shirt fabric distracted me for a moment. "That's not what I meant."

But damn, that was another issue.

"What are you talking about?"

Jake brushed a lock of hair away from my cheek and kept his other arm around my waist, so I was pinned against him.

"I mean, my reputation. The fact that I was on trial for fraud."

"You were found not guilty," he said, his eyes no longer teasing and laughing. "Miranda, that chapter is over. You need to let it go."

I swallowed. Easy for him to say. He wasn't facing down scornful looks at the courthouse or seeing the flash of recognition as the hiring committee suddenly remembered why my name was familiar.

"My acquittal doesn't mean much to some people," I said softly.

"Those people don't matter," he said.

Those people included his partner. I forced a smile, but I didn't believe him. I just didn't want to talk about it any more.

"Don't you have to get back to your *wife*?" I asked.

"I've got time," he said and kissed me again. This time, with more passion, more abandon, as if trying to convince both of us that we could make those doubts go away. It didn't work, but it was fun trying.

"So, maybe later I can ditch the ball and chain, come back here and see you," he suggested with a playful grin.

"You'll see me tonight at dinner," I said. "While you're pretending to be married to Bethany."

He grinned and played with the collar on the bathrobe and then froze at the sound of footsteps in the hall, just on the other side of the door we were still leaning against.

"Shit," he whispered.

He turned and looked out the peephole.

"Your wife trying to track you down?"

He shook his head and frowned but didn't answer. The footsteps faded after a few moments, and he turned back to me.

"Who was that?"

"Your little friend, Carly," he said. "She was scoping out the hallway."

I couldn't imagine why, since she knew where I was staying. Was she trying to figure out where my friends were staying too? She hadn't knocked on any doors, so it couldn't have been too urgent.

"Is she gone?" I asked.

"I think so, but maybe you should check, so she doesn't see me stepping out of your room."

I opened the door a crack, then stepped out into the hall and looked in both directions. I started to return to my room, when Bethany stepped out of her room.

"Hey, have you seen Jake?" she asked.

I looked back toward the half-opened door to my room and saw Jake shake his head. "No, I haven't seen him."

"Huh, all right. If you do, tell him I went out for a walk."

I nodded and ducked back into the room.

"You're dodging the little missus already?" I asked, leaning back against the door, my arms crossed in front of me.

"Yeah, I am. Bethany's a by-the-book sort of agent. I'd rather not put her in an awkward position, knowing about us," he said.

I struggled to keep my face neutral but must have failed miserably because he held up both hands to stop me from jumping to conclusions.

"Hey, no. It's not because I don't want her to know about us. I just —"

"You don't want her to know about us."

"Just until this case is over. We're in with this crowd, and we can probably get what we need and get out in a few days," he said, pulling me over to the bed and sitting down, keeping me standing between his thighs. "This has nothing to do with you. It's her. She'd insist on following the rules."

"What rules?"

"The rules that say I shouldn't have a personal relationship with a witness," he said, putting his hands at my waist.

"You're not supposed to be kissing me, are you?"

He shook his head. "Technically, there could be an issue there."

"You said..."

"I lied."

"Damn it."

"Come here," he said, his voice low again.

"Jake—"

But I leaned forward a few inches, and he reached up to meet me, and we rolled back onto the mattress. This was a terrible idea. He could get in trouble for being involved with me. If it came out, it could jeopardize his colleagues' case against the gambling ring,

"It's just a couple days," he said, his voice gruff. "We'll just lay low, and then once we get home..."

He let his words trail off as he kissed my neck.

"Oh, that's good." The words escaped my mouth on a sigh. "I mean, that's not good. I don't want to get you in trouble— Oh, God."

I pushed him away before my robe magically disappeared. I could hardly catch my breath when he touched me, and I needed to think. That required oxygen.

"I can't do this. I need to think about this," I gasped. "I mean, you're taking a risk—"

"It's fine, Miranda," he said, loosening his hold on me but not moving away. "It happens, and the Bureau knows that. I know of several agents who got involved with witnesses, and it worked out. A couple are still married."

I swallowed hard. "How about a date first?"

Jake laughed at my stammered answer but then stood up and pulled me to my feet.

"Why did you come by anyway?" I asked, straightening my robe.

He smiled and walked to the door and looked out the peep-hole. Turning back, he met my gaze. "Didn't want you to forget our date tomorrow while you're at the party, pretending to be with Quinn Bishop."

I squinted. Jealousy? That's what this was?

"What the hell? And what date tomorrow?"

"You promised. See you tonight," he said, then slipped out the door and into the hall.

"Damn it."

CHAPTER TWELVE

By the time Quinn came by my room, I was even more conflicted. Was Jake sneaking around his partner because she didn't like me? Or because he didn't want to have to fill out paperwork about a relationship that neither of us was sure had even started yet? Or because he knew I was right—that dating me would be the kiss of death to his career?

"Oh, come on," Quinn said, as we walked out into the hall. "I realize it's not a date with your federal agent, but try to look a little excited. We're a happy couple, remember?"

I smiled and took his arm. "Sorry. I was just thinking."

He kissed the top of my head as we walked toward the elevator. From behind us, a door opened, and I turned to see Bethany and Jake step into the hall. Bethany wore a blue and white striped maxi dress and looked like she'd just stepped out of a glossy magazine spread on what to wear in the Hamptons. Jake wore a simple short-sleeve linen shirt that emphasized his broad shoulders and bulging arms.

"Good evening," he said, giving me a wolfish smile as they joined us on the short walk to the elevators.

"Stop flirting with her," Bethany snapped. "You're supposed to be my husband."

I frowned at her. "And you're supposed to be my oldest and dearest friend from college. Why did you say that anyway?"

She shrugged. "It was Gail Bonner's idea. Seemed like the easiest cover to adopt at the moment."

Quinn put an arm around my shoulder as the elevator doors opened.

"I'm sure everyone can get along for one night," he said, giving Bethany a warm smile. Her pinched expression softened in response.

Huh. Who knew that Quinn was some sort of bitch whisperer?

The four of us stepped into the small elevator and rode down to the lower level in silence. The pool was located outside the gym in a meticulously landscaped greenbelt. Lounge chairs with deep green cushions surrounded the clear blue water, with pergolas spaced around the perimeter of the hard deck to provide shade for those of us, like me, who would burn to a crisp, no matter what strength SPF we applied.

Two large barbecues were set up at one end of the pool area, smoke pouring out from under the hoods. Several resort staff were setting up a buffet table near where a couple dozen people gathered by the bar. Mark Tripp raised a beer to Quinn and waved us over, and we walked around the scattered patio furniture to join him.

"Mark, this is my friend, Bethany," I said, hoping I sounded more convincing than I felt.

Mark smiled widely. "So nice to meet you, Bethany. What a lovely name," he said, holding her hand a few seconds too long.

"Thank you, it's nice to meet you, Mark," she said. "This is my husband, Jake."

Mark's smile faded, and he dropped Bethany's hand like it was on fire.

"Hi, glad you could both join us," he said. "What's everyone drinking? Get you a beer, Quinn?"

"You know it," Quinn said, putting an arm around my shoulders. "What would you like, sweetheart?"

I froze for a moment at the contact, my eyes meeting Jake's for a split second. It was brief, but I saw the flash of anger there, quickly replaced by a neutral expression that betrayed nothing.

"You should totally try the sangria," Carly said, popping up beside me, a tall glass of the red concoction in her hand.

"Yeah, that sounds great," I said. *The bigger, the better.*

"Bethany, what would you like to drink?" Quinn asked.

"I'll have the same," she said.

Drinks in hand, Carly led us to a table where Reece was sitting with Jordan Swift and a couple of female crew members. She introduced us and then bounced away again to make sure a new group of arriving guests were welcomed to the party.

"Miranda, how are you? Nice to see you again," Reece said, pulling a chair for me between him and Jordan, who gave me a curt nod in greeting.

I smiled back at Reece and tried to remain composed, but on the inside, I was squealing like a 13-year-old girl with a massive crush. Jordan squinted at me across the table. "You two know each other?"

"We met the other night at a little get together. One of the crew members had a party," he said, fixing his green eyes on mine. "You should have brought your friends. The more the merrier."

He threw his arms wide, and one of the women moved closer to him, leaning in so his arm was now behind her shoulders. Nice move, I thought. Reece took a long drink of the amber liquid in his glass, and I realized that my teen idol was pretty well into his cups.

"Next time, you all have to come by," he said.

"Sounds like fun," I said, taking a sip of the sangria. "When's the next time?"

"I dunno, maybe Wednesday or Thursday," Reece said. "Ask Carly. She knows everything."

Good advice. Carly did know everything. And everyone. I watched her move through the party with the skills of a socialite —a quick hug, kiss on the cheek, friendly wave, and then on to the next group. She was like a hummingbird, flitting from one social group to the next.

"Having a nice evening, Miranda?" Jordan asked, his tone neutral. I was sure he didn't have any idea that two FBI agents sat across the table from him but wasn't sure exactly what he knew about what was going on.

I nodded and smiled and took a sip of the sweet sangria. "Yes, thank you. How are you?"

He gave me a pained smile. "Oh, just great."

Quinn and Mark started chatting about mutual friends from the movie industry, and Jake and Bethany were scoping out the crowd. Reece's glazed eyes seemed most focused on the chest of the woman to his left.

Jordan lowered his voice and leaned toward me. "How's your work going?"

I nodded. "Good."

He nodded. "I probably shot my mouth off earlier, when we talked about the Penny. I shouldn't have, but it's hard to see Uncle Max get excited about something when there's such a slim chance it'll happen for him."

"I think he's in a good position to buy it back. He has assets to use as collateral." I was careful not to mention that the license approval was looking better since Max was working with the Gaming Control Board now.

Jordan shook his head. "It's not just that. There are other groups who are gunning for the bid. People with cash on hand who want to invest it."

He nodded toward a crowd at the edge of the patio, where Denny Shawn Weber stood with an elbow resting against the bar.

"He's investing?" I asked. "How do you know this?"

Jordan shrugged, and his glum expression marred his handsome face. "Just heard a rumor. A lot of Hollywood types are getting in on the action, apparently."

"How serious are they about this? And have you heard of anyone else trying to buy the casino?"

"Oh, they're serious. I heard they've raised several million in cash and have enough pledges that they're the ones Max is going to have to beat. It's down to Max and the movie people," he said. "Anyway, I just wanted to say sorry for being a jerk. It's not your fault that Max has his head in the clouds."

He pushed away from the table and headed to the bar, grabbed a bottle of beer, and then kept walking out of the pool area and into the lodge.

I was on my second sangria and starting to get restless when I saw Lorelei enter the patio from the gate that led to the gardens. She must have walked down through the gardens from her cabin, rather than through the lodge like most of the guests had. She was wearing a pale blue shift dress and a wide blue ribbon as a hair band, holding her thick, shiny, dark hair away from her porcelain face. Instantly, Quinn's arm around my shoulder tightened, and I couldn't tell if it was a warning to me not to cause her any harm or if he was trying to send a message to the actress that he was off the market.

Either way, his move was felt on the other side of the table as

I saw Jake mimic his action, placing an arm around Bethany's shoulders. She had matched my sangrias and seemed startled by Jake's sudden show of affection. Within a second, she had relaxed into his half-embrace with a smile.

Carly dropped into a chair next to Bethany and grabbed Jake's left hand, which was draped over Bethany's shoulder. "Hey, where's your wedding ring?"

Bethany nearly choked on her drink, but Jake just grinned. "We had to get them sized. We'll pick them up when we get home."

Carly's mouth opened in surprise. "You're newlyweds? Congratulations! We should get some champagne!"

I looked around to see if there was anywhere else I could possibly be when Carly toasted the happy couple, but before I could go anywhere, Reece excused himself, and his two female companions joined him, and Carly pulled Bethany with her to sit by me.

Despite the fading sun, there was enough light to see Bethany's expression fill with suspicion.

Carly leaned in, one arm around each of us. "Okay, now spill it. I want to hear all about your college days."

"Oh, there's not that much to tell," Bethany said with a modest laugh.

The sound annoyed me, beyond what it normally would. Not only was I annoyed with her for how she treated me, but I was pre-hating her for how I knew she'd react when she found out that Quinn had a criminal record. It wasn't logical, but strong emotions rarely are logical. And I felt very strongly about this.

"Well, there was the time you won that wet T-shirt contest," I said with a sangria-fueled smile. I could picture Bethany in college—the student who ran straight to the resident advisor to rat out everyone who was having fun.

Bethany choked on her drink, but to her credit, she recovered quickly and managed a half-mortified laugh.

"Well, you weren't going to take home the trophy," she said, glancing at my meager cleavage. "But you did clean up at that keg-stand contest. Three years in a row, if I remember correctly."

Oh, so she could give as well as she got. *Fine.* Game on.

"Four years," I said. "You probably don't remember that last one, because by that time of the night, you were usually, uh, indisposed."

I leaned toward Carly, who was eating this up with a spoon. "It took Bethie a few years to learn that she really couldn't mix pot and alcohol without projectile vomiting."

Quinn put a heavy hand on my shoulder, and the squeeze this time wasn't as gentle.

"Hey, I think the grill-master is ready for us," he said, standing and pulling me with him. "Let's get something to eat."

It wasn't a request as much as marching orders. He steered me to the buffet line, Carly right behind us.

"I'm so jealous of you and Bethany, getting to hang out up here. I miss my girlfriends from college."

"Where did you go to school?" I asked.

"I went to Penn State," she said with a toss of her blonde curls. "But first chance I got to escape the East Coast, I fled to California. I just love it here. Are you from around here?"

I nodded. "Sacramento. Just about two hours from here."

"Oh my God, I would love to live so close to Lake Tahoe," she said. Her voice sounded so sincere, I nearly believed her but then realized that she was totally lying.

"You'd hate it there," I said with a laugh. "It's a million miles from Hollywood. There are no movie premieres, no A-list actors, no glamour."

Carly picked some vegetables for her plate and eyed the bread basket with the type of lust-filled stare that was usually reserved for some of the actors she worked for. She sighed deeply. "Yeah, you're probably right. I do like my job. But I sure do miss carbs."

Quinn looked at Carly like she was out of her mind. "So eat the carbs."

She shook her head with a sad expression. "Are you kidding me? I'd never find a dress for awards season."

We sat down with our food, and I looked down with guilt at my own plate of a burger, pasta salad, and fresh fruit. "Isn't that months from now?"

Carly nodded. "Yes, but it's the hard truth of Hollywood. I tried to break into acting, but I'm too short and too fat. But I am truly the best personal assistant that anyone in Los Angeles could find. You can ask anyone. And one of the perks of this job is the designer clothes."

"First of all, you are tiny," I said. "And you get designer clothes?"

She speared a chunk of plain broccoli with her fork and grinned. "No, Lorelei is tiny. I'm average. And you should see the stuff that they throw at celebrities—clothes, shoes, makeup, phones, everything you can imagine. Lorelei doesn't even use half of it."

That sounded like a good perk. I mean, it explained Carly's expensive taste in lip gloss and electronics. But her job description made me sad. Who wants to live without carbs?

"So you work for the resort, right?" Carly asked. "What do you do?"

"I do some accounting," I said. "It's boring really."

She smiled widely. "But you're not an employee here, because I would have seen you before. Are you like, an auditor?"

I shrugged, not wanting to share too much and anxious to change the subject. "Sort of, yeah. How long have you been a personal assistant?"

Carly tossed her hair and her dangly earrings reflected the string of party lights with a sparkle. "About five years. I've learned so much about this business in the last few years."

"Have you thought about being an agent?" I asked.

She shook her head. "No, but I would like to produce movies eventually. I think I'd be really good at it. You have to be really organized and be able to juggle a lot of tasks. I am great at that."

I grinned at her confidence. "I can tell."

"But in the meantime, this job suits me well," she said. Her eyes flitted over the crowd, and she waved at someone with a smile.

It did seem to be a good fit, I thought, as I scooted my chair a little closer to her. And if there was anyone who would have heard about Max's competition for the Lucky Penny, it was Carly.

"So, have you heard anything about a group of celebrities who are interested in buying a casino here?"

Her eyes opened wide, and she nodded. "Oh my God, yes, I did hear about that."

"Who is involved? Do you know?"

She leaned forward as if we were conspiring together. "I've heard that it's some pretty big names. Like, uh, if you were to think of all the biggest actors who, say, were in a series of movies about casino heists, that would include a few of the investors."

Uh-oh. That was bad news for Max.

"And not only actors, but a lot of other heavy-hitters in the movie industry are involved, too."

My heart sank. Max really wanted that casino back, and not getting it would break his heart.

"Did you know that Jordan's family used to own it?"

I nodded. "I heard that."

"It's a pretty cool thing to have all these big time actors involved because they'll be up here all the time, and I'm sure tourists will go there just to see if they can spot any of the celebrity owners," she said with a grin. "I know I would."

I forced a casual laugh. "You probably already know them all."

She nodded and smiled widely. "I mean if I didn't already know them. It would be really good for the local economy, you know?"

"Yeah, sure," I said. "Is Denny Shawn Weber one of the investors?"

Carly glanced over at the director, still hanging out at the bar, the party lights reflecting off his thick, black-framed glasses.

"I think so," she said. "It's all very hush-hush, of course, until the deal's done. But I hear it's going to be quite the list of who's who."

"How about Reece?" I asked.

Carly shrugged. "Not that I've heard. Why are you so interested in this?"

It was my turn to shrug. "Just heard that the old casino on the shore might be getting new owners. It would be better than having an abandoned building at the lake."

Before she could reply, Lorelei appeared at her side like a ghostly apparition, and Carly popped up out of her chair. But Lorelei wasn't there for her assistant, or at least, that's not where her focus was.

Quinn must have felt the intense gaze of his former lover. He looked up from the discussion he and Mark were having, and his expression changed from casual amusement to concern. I could see why.

From a distance, Lorelei looked like a porcelain doll, but up close she just looked pale and wan. Her wide blue eyes were slightly glazed and sad, with dark circles underneath. She weaved a little as she gripped the back of the chair where Carly had been seated.

"Hi, Quinn," she said, her voice starting to choke up.

"Hey, sweetie," Carly said, taking Lorelei's elbow and pulling her away. "Let's get you home. You've got an early call."

Quinn started to rise, but Carly gave him a wave and shake of her head. She gently steered Lorelei back toward the garden gate, and then the two women disappeared beyond the lights of the pool and into the night.

The actress's dazed presence cast a pall over the table, and I couldn't help but feel a little sorry for her. I still hated her, but Quinn was right. There was something not right there.

"What's going on with her?" Jake asked, his eyes narrowed.

"Do you know her?" Bethany asked.

Quinn nodded.

"Yeah, I knew her a long time ago." He looked up at Bethany, ignoring Jake's question. "She and I used to be involved. Before I got arrested."

The look on Bethany's perfect face went from curious and slightly defensive to shock, but she quickly managed to cover it up with a neutral expression. She leaned back just a bit in her chair, a hint of distance from Quinn.

"Your arrest?" she asked.

Quinn nodded, not breaking eye contact with her. "I did two years in Lompoc on a drug charge."

Bethany swallowed and glanced at me, then back to Quinn.

I have never shown as much restraint in my life as I did at that moment because I did not jump up, throw myself across the round wooden table, and grab Bethany Boylan by her long pale throat and choke her until she passed out.

"Well, it's been a busy day," Jake said, standing up. "I think I'm going to go upstairs."

Quinn nodded, still watching Bethany, who was staring at him openly.

"Are you coming?" Jake asked, and she shook herself out of her stupor and stood up.

"Yes, of course."

They walked off, and Quinn and I sat in the dusk, alone and quiet. My stomach churned in anger, and my face flushed hot.

"I told you that you could do better," I whispered.

"Best to get these things out in the open right away," he said.

My hands had formed fists in my lap during the short exchange between Quinn and Bethany, and I slowly opened them, forcing my fingers to unfurl before I punched something.

"I really don't like her," I said, my voice still low.

He laughed, put his arm around my shoulder, pulled me close, and kissed the top of my head.

"I know you don't," he said.

But he does, I thought, and my hands balled up into fists again.

CHAPTER THIRTEEN

Dottie found me in the Pines Cafe, drowning my sorrows in a large carafe of coffee at a corner table. I'd barely slept the night before, tossing and turning and thinking up ways to torture Bethany Boylan for treating Quinn like he was some sort of criminal.

Okay, sure, technically, he had a criminal record. But even if he had done what he pleaded guilty to, it was a long time ago and he'd paid his debt to society. He was a nice man and deserved better than that snotty FBI agent.

I had just stuffed a large forkful of French toast into my mouth when Dottie sat down across from me and motioned to the waiter for a menu.

"Good morning," she said. "You look like you're dragging a bit this morning. Did you help close down that party last night?"

I shook my head and chased the syrup-soaked bread with orange juice. "No, I left pretty early actually. It was a nice party though."

Dottie placed her breakfast order with the waiter and then poured herself a cup of coffee, stirring in a large spoonful of sugar. "Nice party, but Max is already bitching about it, of course.

Turns out that Jordan comped the whole shebang, so Max is about at the end of his rope. Not only are they losing money on the film crew's lease, but now they're footing the bill for their parties too."

"Why did Jordan agree to pay for it?" I asked, topping off my own coffee.

Dottie shook her head. "Who knows with that boy? Now, what's on your schedule today?"

"I'm not sure yet. I wanted to finish compiling that end-of-quarter report, and I think I have everything I need for that. Everything else I wanted to do is on hold until I can see the complete version of the accountant's report," I said.

Dottie nodded and sipped at her coffee. "I got in touch with the accountant in Reno. I'm going to meet him this afternoon and pick up the report and talk to him about his findings."

"On a Sunday?"

She shrugged and grinned. "What can I say? I can be very persuasive."

The waiter appeared with Dottie's eggs Benedict and a fresh carafe of coffee.

"You know, you should take the day off and relax. There's not much left to do, and what's remaining can be finished tomorrow. We could be done by Tuesday."

That would be nice. Aunt Marie's wedding was Saturday at our favorite lakeside restaurant, about a half-hour drive from the resort. I had promised to go meet with the manager and make sure everything was ready for the big day. But if the film didn't wrap up by then, would I be stuck here pretending to audit the business while waiting for the wrap party?

"I did promise my aunt that I'd go check in at the wedding venue," I said. "But I don't have a car."

"Get that big strapping cowboy to give you a ride," she said with a wink that left no doubt as to her real meaning.

149

"We're just friends," I said quickly.

"Too bad. He's one good looking man," she said. "So how about one of the agents? Your neighbor, maybe?"

"Maybe." I wasn't opposed to being alone with Jake again.

"Which one of those fine specimens are you taking to your aunt's wedding?" Dottie asked.

"Oh, uh, neither. I don't have a date."

She looked at me over a fork full of eggs and frowned. "Pick one. You're too young to be a spinster."

"I'm not a spinster. Things are just a little complicated," I said.

Dottie pushed her plate away and reached for her purse. She left a generous tip and then stood up. "Whatever you decide to do today, have a good time. I'll be back this afternoon. Call me if you need anything."

I watched her walk out and thought about her advice. Quinn was already going to the wedding, but I couldn't count on him being my date because what if he already had invited someone. I mean, that was possible. Highly likely, even.

And I didn't want to be there with him. I mean, as friends, yes. But weddings are supposed to be romantic and having a platonic friend as a date is not romantic.

I pushed my now cold French toast around the pool of syrup while I considered my options. I was so lost in my thoughts that when Quinn sat down in Dottie's abandoned chair, it startled me.

"Good morning," he said with a warm smile. His blond hair was still damp from his shower, and unlike me, he looked bright-eyed and refreshed and ready to take on the world.

"Hello," I said. "How did you sleep?"

"I slept great. Haven't slept that well in years," he said. "And you?"

His playful grin said he knew that I was dragging.

"Pass the coffee," I said.

He poured more of the brew into my mug, then turned over another cup and poured some for himself.

"Are you going home today?" I asked. That had been the initial plan, well, after Carly found him in my room at least.

"Apparently, I'm going to stay a little longer," he said, looking away and taking a sip of the coffee.

I squinted at him. "Why? I got us all invited to the party, whenever it is."

Quinn turned his attention back to me. "Because in case you didn't notice, Lorelei is not likely to invite you along to any party that she's hosting or attending. But she very probably will invite me."

He had a good point there. Lorelei had so far acted as if I didn't exist, but that could change. She could freeze me out of her social circle, and that meant that Carly's invitation to play cards when the film wrapped could be rescinded. But from the way Lorelei was mooning over Quinn, he wasn't going to be frozen out.

"And, as your boyfriend pointed out, it would be best for you to have someone at your side if you do go to the party," he said.

"He's not exactly...wait. When did he say that?"

Quinn smiled. "This morning. Ran into him in the hall."

The waiter came back and dropped off another menu and yet another carafe of coffee. Quinn ordered eggs, bacon, and toast without looking at the menu. Once we were alone again, he leaned in.

"I told Barnes that I want to stay and help."

"But why? I know you're not exactly a fan of the federal government," I asked. I understood because, with one exception, I wasn't a fan either. Then I shook my head. "Not Lorelei. Please, tell me you're not staying because of her."

Quinn's blue eyes crinkled up at my plea. "No, that's not

entirely why I want to stay. Though I am concerned about Lorelei's mental state."

"So what are you going to do about it?"

He shrugged and spread his napkin across his lap and then helped himself to the basket of warm pastries.

"Well, since you're hanging out here, want to drive me down to Harmony Cove? I told Aunt Marie that I'd check in with the restaurant and make sure everything was in order for the wedding."

He shook his head. "Sorry, kiddo. I told my buddy I'd help him for a couple hours today."

"Okay, maybe the lodge has a car I can borrow," I said.

"Or you could ask Jake to take you," Quinn suggested.

I eyed him suspiciously. "You like him now?"

"I never hated him. I didn't know him. But he seems like an okay guy. You know, for a fed."

"As long as I don't have to take his wife with us, that would be fine," I said.

Quinn laughed and nodded toward the door. "Speaking of the happy couple."

I didn't even have to turn to know that he was speaking about Jake and Bethany. I pushed myself away from the table and stood. If I didn't escape, I'd be stuck making small talk with Bethany, and there was no way that didn't end without one of us wielding a butter knife.

"I think I'm going to scout out the spa for clues," I said, to Quinn's laughter.

"Good luck," he said, standing and taking my hand. He pulled me toward him, and I remembered that we were supposed to be a couple. As the only other people in the restaurant were from the film crew, it made sense to keep up appearances, so I didn't resist when he kissed me. Plus, he's really good at it.

"Did you do that for Jake's benefit?"

"I did that for my benefit," he said with a crooked grin. "Enjoy the spa."

I turned and found myself facing two glaring federal agents. Jake, I could understand, but what bee was in Bethany's bonnet? And was there any chance she'd have an allergic reaction to it?

"Good morning," I said as I walked past them at the hostess stand. "See you around—"

Jake grabbed my arm and steered me outside the cafe's entrance and around the corner. "Where are you going?"

"I don't know. Maybe the spa? You and Bethany should try the French toast. It's amazing," I said, glancing around the wide hall to make sure no one from the movie set was watching. We were alone but just a short distance and a wide open door from the half-filled cafe.

Jake seemed to realize that too and dropped his hand from my elbow. But he stayed closer than would be socially acceptable if he really were my best friend's husband. I took a step back and bumped into the wall.

"It's Sunday," he said. His eyes were lowered, and he slowly raised them to mine.

Oh, holy moly. His low voice vibrated through my entire body, and the resulting tremor practically shook my underwear off. I had expected a lecture about public displays of affection with someone other than him or being grilled about what I'd learned from Carly.

Instead, I was inches from him, staring into his deep brown eyes and wondering what would happen if I just leaned forward a little.

"How are we going to have a date when you're here on your honeymoon?" I whispered.

His lips turned down slightly. "Well, let's get out of here. Bethany can stay and keep an eye on things."

"I don't have a car."

"I do."

I swallowed hard and resisted asking if it had a backseat.

"I need to go to the restaurant where Aunt Marie is getting married Saturday."

"I need to stop at the local FBI office."

"Can we still call that a date?"

Jake's lips quirked up. "I guess that depends on how it goes."

The sound of footsteps in the restaurant interrupted us, and Jake took a couple steps back before several men walked out, turned down the hall, and left the lodge through a side door to the parking lot.

"I'll stop by your room and pick you up after breakfast," he said.

I remembered Carly wandering around the second floor and shook my head. I still didn't know why she was poking around our rooms, but I didn't want to run into her while Jake was knocking on my door.

"I'll meet you down here," I said. "I can get some work done in the business office."

He nodded and then turned back to the cafe. I watched him walk away, enjoying the view, then shook myself and went upstairs to get my purse and retrieve the binders that I never did get a chance to read.

Housekeeping had already cleaned up my room, and I relished the luxury of having a tidy room that I didn't have to clean myself. Humming an out-of-tune song, I grabbed my purse and added lipstick and sunscreen, then spritzed on a bit of perfume and ran a brush through my hair. Either the caffeine was kicking in or I was still high on the adrenaline rush of having been close to Jake, but I was feeling a thousand times better. We were finally going to have that date, and it had only taken a year or so. Or more, if you consider that I met him two-

and-a-half years ago when he arrested me. But that was in the past. We were finally moving forward.

I reached for the binders on the small round table and flipped open the first one, the profit-and-loss statements up through the last quarter. As soon as I turned the first page, something felt off. I stared at the chart, not seeing the numbers on the page, but looking at the rest of the binder.

My mind raced back to the day before when I had worked with the binders in the conference room. I had brought them up to my room to read but then never cracked them because I was at the party. I turned to the second page, and I realized what felt out of place. The first page was actually supposed to be the second page. The first page was missing.

I yanked my hand back as if the binder was on fire. The year-to-date income statement that had been at the front of the binder was gone.

Quickly, I flipped through more pages and confirmed that it wasn't in the binder. I moved it aside and opened the second one, which was the prior year's finances. The income statement was right in the front, where it was supposed to be.

I leaned back in the chair and felt my heartbeat in my throat. It was possible that I was mistaken about the pages I had read the day before.

Then I shook my head. No. It might be possible for other people to make that mistake, but I have a really good memory for these sorts of details. It was why I could memorize a long string of numbers, do complex math in my head, and count cards at the blackjack table. I closed my eyes and pictured the binder yesterday—and the statement was there. I could even recall the figures on the list.

I let out a long breath. The binder had been in my room all night and all morning. Where could it have gone?

I stacked the binders again, and a small piece of white paper floated to the ground. As soon as I picked it up, I knew what it was. The tiny slip of paper, ripped away from a page torn from the three-ring binder.

Fuck.

Who had access to my room?

The housekeeping staff, but the binders were in the same spot where I'd left them and were unmarked. I couldn't imagine that someone would have been curious enough to peek into them. And then why take only one page?

Quinn had a key to my room from yesterday. I had one for his room now. But he was with me at the party, and there was no reason he'd want information about Whispering Pines.

Jordan, of course. As a manager of the hotel, he had access to all of the rooms, if he wanted it. He had a stake in the audit's conclusions and had already tried to keep information from us by cutting out pages from the accountant's report. But this information was so easy to recreate, why would he take just this page? And Dottie was picking up a full version of the report today.

I looked around the room, and now the silence felt eerie. Instead of a tidy room, I saw a crime scene that had been wiped clean of evidence. Packing up my purse and the books, I left the room, making sure the door was locked behind me. Of course that was ridiculous, since it had been when I left for breakfast. And when I was at the party. Jordan—if it was Jordan who came in while I was gone—could have snuck away from the party to do a little breaking and entering. He had left pretty early in the evening.

I hurried down the stairs to the main floor, then into the business wing. The conference room was locked, but Dottie and I each had keys, and I let myself in. I unlocked the cabinet where Dottie had stored the rest of the financial information and looked at the stack of materials. It looked untouched from when we had finished work the day before. I added the binders to the stack, locked the cabinet, and then stepped out into the hall to lock the conference room door.

"Miranda!"

I jumped and whirled at the sound of my name and came face-to-face with Carly. I let out a long exhale and put a hand on my pounding chest.

"Hey, Carly. You startled me." I looked down the hall at the closed door to the lobby. "You're not supposed to be in this area."

She flashed me that dimpled smile. "I was trying to get your attention when you were walking across the lobby, but you didn't hear me," she said. "Are you busy? I'm going to go get a pedicure. You should come with me. Are you working? It's Sunday. You should take a day off and relax."

I guided her back to the lobby as she chattered away at me. "I think I'll pass on the pedicure. Isn't there filming going on today?"

She nodded. "We had an early shoot, but now we're waiting for the afternoon when the light's better for the remaining outdoor scenes."

I opened the door and ushered her through, then closed the door behind me. It wasn't locked, but it was marked with an "authorized personnel only" sign, which meant nothing to Carly, who had made herself at home in the resort.

"Well, have a good time at the spa," I said, hoping she would skip off down the stairs to get her pedicure.

Instead, she lingered with me. "What are you doing today?"

"Oh, I have some errands to run for my aunt. She's getting married up here next weekend."

I glanced around the lobby, hoping Jake didn't show up with Carly still hanging around. It would probably raise more questions if I were to take off for the day with the husband of my "best friend."

"What about Lorelei? She could go with you," I suggested.

Carly shook her head, and her sunny expression dimmed. "She's taking a nap."

More like a drug-induced stupor but whatever. I walked with Carly toward the staircase that would lead her down to the spa.

"Sorry you can't come with me," she said. "If you want to come hang out on set when you get back, just let me know. It should be a good one to watch because it's the scene where Frances finds out that Henry was killed in a battle on the Western Front."

This looked to be one dreary movie, but I smiled. "Sure, sounds like fun."

I practically pushed her down the stairs, but finally she went off to get her pedicure. A moment later, Jake stepped out from behind the huge stone fireplace that dominated the middle of the lodge. He nodded toward the front door, and I hurried to leave before anyone else saw us together.

Jake was driving a tan Honda that I'd never seen before. It was the beige-ist, most boring car I could imagine.

"Is this a stakeout car?" I asked, playing with the knobs on the stereo. No modern electronics here. The car came equipped with a cassette player. But it did have air conditioning, so I adjusted the temperature as Jake steered the car out of the resort and onto the winding mountain road that would lead us to the two-lane highway that circled the lake.

"Is it what?" he asked.

"This car. It's so boring, it's practically invisible."

"It's Bethany's car."

"Oh." Well, wasn't she a barrel of fun? "I bet it would be a good car to use on a stakeout."

Jake gave a small laugh and navigated a hairpin turn. "I'll tell her you said so."

"Ugh, please don't. She already hates me. Let's not give her more reasons."

He gave me a reproaching look. "She doesn't hate you."

"She doesn't like me."

"You don't like her either."

"We don't have much in common."

He gave me a funny grin. "You don't know that. Neither of you have given the other one a chance. You don't know anything about Bethany."

"I know I really don't want to spend the day talking about her," I said. "Where are we going first? The FBI office?"

"Yeah, I told Alex we'd meet him there at noon. It shouldn't take long."

The FBI office was in a nondescript building that sat back from a main road through South Lake Tahoe. There was nothing that indicated it was a federal office, probably by design, and it nearly faded from view thanks to the garish signs advertising the deli and bike shop that sat on either side. The door was unmarked and the windows tinted. Alex Marquez let us in and offered us seats in front of his wide empty desk. He shoved a stack of folders across the table to Jake.

"Here are the backgrounds on the movie set. Nothing too interesting, but a couple people have had some significant gambling debts."

Jake and I leaned forward, and Alex slapped a hand down on the stack.

"Uh, sorry, Ms. Vaughn," he said. "I don't think Agent Bonner would be happy if I shared this with you."

Well, that was no fun.

"Is it Denny Shawn Weber? I bet he has lost a lot of money on cards," I said.

Alex hesitated, then took his hand off the folders. "How did you know that?"

"Because I watched him play blackjack, and he didn't have any understanding of probability or strategy," I said. "But that didn't stop him from betting big and telling everyone that black-jack was 'his game.'"

Jake smiled at Alex. "Miranda may know more about your problem gamblers than you do. I don't see any harm in letting her stay while we discuss this."

After a moment, he shrugged. "Okay, just don't tell Gail. That woman scares me."

Jake flipped through the stack, noting things that might indicate someone was really into gambling or had a brush with the law in the past. A couple of misdemeanor assaults, both from bar brawls. A good handful of DUIs. Nothing on Reece Muir or Lorelei Arens. But, at least in her case, that only meant she'd never been caught for her crimes.

"And then there's Mark Tripp, who was sued by a casino for bad debt," Alex said, opening the last folder in the stack. "That caught my eye."

"How much did he lose?" Jake asked.

"More than forty thousand dollars," Alex said.

"He was playing poker the other night," I volunteered.

"He's been banned from several casinos in Las Vegas for nonpayment of his gaming debts," Alex said. "If anyone there would know how to find a poker game, it would be him. At least Denny Shawn Weber pays his debts."

"Mark was playing blackjack Thursday night at the Royal Palace, where Quinn and I ran into him," I said.

Alex made some notes. "I'll call over to the Royal Palace, see if they have any intel on him."

"You don't have any information on Carly Malone," I said, looking at the pile of folders but not touching, lest I get my hand slapped.

Alex frowned, and his brow furrowed. "No, I can't find anything on her. Do you know if she changed her name? Where she lived before?"

I bit my lip and tried to recall what she had shared with me. "She said she went to Penn State, moved to California as soon as she could escape the East Coast. She did some acting but couldn't find enough work to support herself, so she got a job as a personal assistant. Sounds like she's been really successful with that."

Alex wrote down the information and gave me a smile. "That's helpful, thanks."

He stood, and Jake and I followed.

"I'll let you guys get back to your weekend," Alex said, walking us to the door and unlocking it to let us out. "If you learn anything else, let me know."

I gave Jake directions to Harmony Cove, and we drove along the lake without talking for several minutes.

"Do you think it's weird that Carly wouldn't have any record?" I asked. The thought of her snooping outside our rooms made me uneasy. She was friendly and helpful, and I felt sorry for her a little, having to take care of her zonked-out boss. But she was a little too friendly, and a little too helpful. It could be off-putting.

Jake didn't answer right away. "It's not illegal to change your name."

"That doesn't answer my question."

He looked over at me and shrugged. "It's kind of weird."

"She was in the hall when I came out of the conference room this morning," I said. "She said she followed me trying to get my attention, but I don't know. I just didn't believe her."

"Why would she be there?"

I didn't have an answer for him. "I don't know. Maybe I was just on edge because—"

I looked away quickly without finishing my thought. I hadn't told Jake about the page ripped from my binder. It didn't make sense to me yet.

"Because of what?"

"Nothing." I shook my head. "It's nothing."

He gave me a long look, then pulled into the parking lot of the restaurant. He didn't believe me but didn't push me to answer.

"All right, then," he said, parking the car in a shady spot near a stand of evergreens. He turned off the ignition and gave me a wink. "Let's go see someone about a wedding."

CHAPTER FOURTEEN

Aunt Marie and Rob were in excellent hands for getting married. Harmony Cove was a favorite restaurant for locals on Lake Tahoe's North Shore, set among the tall pines and right on the water's edge. The family that had owned the property for two generations kept the menu up-to-date and it had a beautiful park-like garden with a gazebo for weddings.

The manager welcomed Jake and me with open arms and showed us around, even as the staff was setting up for a ceremony that evening. A long white carpet separated rows of white chairs set out on the lush green lawn and led to the white structure where the happy couple would exchange their vows. Bright flowers adorned the railings, and the bright blue water in the background completed the picture-perfect wedding venue.

After double-checking the menu and table seating arrangements, I made a command decision on the color of the napkins. Since Aunt Marie didn't want a shower or a bachelorette party, I had to do something to justify my role as maid of honor.

Jake wandered off to the bar to check out the selection of craft brews and the lunch menu, a reminder that my stomach didn't need, as it was already growling about not having eaten since breakfast. The manager handed me a reservation list that Marie had emailed the day before and showed me the seating arrangements for the wedding party.

"No date, sweetie?"

I scowled at her. "I haven't decided yet."

She smiled and glanced toward the bar. "How about that one?"

"It's complicated."

She raised an eyebrow. "That's a shame."

"Fine, put me down for a date."

She smiled and wrote in a plus one by my name on the chart. Jake returned with a menu and suggested we sit out on the patio.

"Do we have time? I mean, you've abandoned Bethany most of the day," I said.

He grinned. "They have fish tacos."

"Yeah, Bethany will be fine," I said, my mouth already watering at the thought of lunch.

"I thought you'd agree," Jake said, taking my hand and leading me out to the deck.

The fish tacos were as delicious as I'd imagined. The company was pretty perfect too. Jake and I managed to find plenty to talk about that didn't include his job, my trial, or our current investigations. By the time we paid the check, the late afternoon sun was casting long shadows on the patio. The shoreline and the long pier out into the crystal blue water were still bathed in bright sun.

"How often do you get up here, to your cabin?" Jake asked.

The Vaughn family cabin was technically at Lake Tahoe, but sat far up the side of the mountains that ring the western shore of the lake. If the weather cooperated, you could see a sliver of the water through the pine trees. And it was nothing like the luxury "cabins" at the Whispering Pines Resort. It was a rustic, one-bedroom A-frame cabin set in the trees. I had inherited it from my father, who had abandoned my teenage mother when I was born and whom I'd never met. Aunt Marie and I had spent many summer vacations hiking through the woods.

I had to sell it when I'd been arrested to pay for my legal defense, but I'd been able to buy it back after I'd been acquitted. It was my favorite place on earth.

"Not often enough. But Aunt Marie and Rob have been coming up one weekend a month," I said. "You grew up not far from here. Did you come up here with your family?"

He shook his head. "In the winter, we'd come up and go skiing, but in the summer, my dad liked to go camping at Yosemite. I haven't spent much time here."

Jake's cell phone vibrated, and he looked down and frowned.

"Let me guess, your wife is looking for you?"

He looked up, his expression almost pained. "I think I've had enough jokes about Bethany being my wife. But yes, that's who it is."

"Is everything okay?"

He smirked. "She ran into Carly, and they spent much of the day together at the spa."

The phone buzzed again.

"And apparently Carly never shuts up."

I smiled at the thought of Bethany stuck in a mud bath with a chattering Carly filling her in on the latest Hollywood gossip. "God knows what tales she's telling about our days in college."

He laughed and stood up, taking my hand. "Want to go for a walk?"

I followed him down the steps to the beach, a narrow sandy stretch that was dominated by a long pier that jutted into the water. A dozen sailboats bobbed offshore, tethered to buoys. The sun beat down on my shoulders, warming me after sitting in the shade of the trees. It wasn't hot enough that I wanted to stick my feet in the ice-cold water that I remembered from my childhood.

"That pier reminds me of camping at Sugar Pine Point. Aunt Marie used to haul me and a bunch of my friends up here to camp for the weekend. As soon as we arrived, my friends and I would dare each other to run to the end of the pier and jump in," I said, laughing at the memory. "Of course, the water is like ice here. So those of us who had been here before would stop short at the end of the pier and let the beginners learn that the hard way."

Jake laughed and shook his head. "That's terrible."

I nodded. "It was. We were rotten children."

Leaving the beach, we walked east along a footpath that rose above the shoreline and wove through the trees until we came to a clearing that had been carved out and ringed with a low rock wall. The quiet vista point overlooked a sandy beach below and had a view of the northeast corner of the shoreline. I pointed out the one blight on the otherwise scenic shore.

"And that is the reason why Max Emmerson is cooperating with you guys," I said, pointing at the spot where the Lucky Penny sat behind a chain-link fence. It was too far away to see how decrepit the abandoned casino was, especially compared to other properties, but even at this distance there was something tired about the old building.

"What is it?"

"The Lucky Penny Casino. Max wants to buy it. And to buy it, he needs a license from the Gaming Commission," I said.

Jake shook his head. "That's why you called us in?"

I shrugged. "Well, yes."

"What would he have done otherwise?"

"Probably just kicked everyone out of the resort," I said. "Which would have been in breach of his contract, would have resulted in a lawsuit, bad publicity, a lot of legal fees. Dottie convinced him that working with you guys was a better option."

Jake continued to squint across the stretch of water between us and the Lucky Penny. "This purchase of the property, is that why you're up here?"

It wasn't part of his investigation, so I didn't want to volunteer any information about Max and Whispering Pines that wasn't necessary. What if Jordan was embezzling from the resort? It wasn't my call whether to make a federal case out of that.

"It's just accounting stuff. Boring, really," I said.

But unlike Quinn, Jake wasn't going to be distracted by my glossing over the accounting issues. He sat on the wide wall, crossed his arms, and stared at me.

"You don't really think it's boring, do you?"

"Me? No, I don't. But most other people do." Most of the population found spreadsheets at best a necessary evil for tracking complex data and at worst, terrifying. I found them comforting, but I was in the minority there.

"What do you like about this profession?"

I shrugged. "Dottie says that forensic accounting is equal parts psychology and math. That's what makes what we're doing interesting. A budget or a bank statement tells a story about what someone values. What they are willing to spend money on. Where they are weak in management."

He nodded, a smile playing around his lips. "I never thought of accounting that way before."

The chirp of my cell phone interrupted us, and I saw Aunt Marie's number on the screen.

"The wedding is going to be perfect," I said, answering the phone.

"Thanks, sweetie," she said. "I heard you added a date too. Is it Jake?"

Well, that news traveled fast. "Yes, probably."

I glanced up at Jake and smiled. I guess I should ask him to go to the wedding with me.

Aunt Marie grilled me on the rest of the wedding details, and I confirmed that everything was taken care of, and the weather was perfect, and she could relax and enjoy her special day.

"And when are you coming home? Your dress is hanging in my closet," she said.

"Oh, yeah, there's been a small change in plans. I think by Tuesday. But I may have to stay a few more days. I'm sure I'll be home in plenty of time to gather up everything I need and get back up here on Friday."

My plan had been to stay at the cabin on Friday night with Sarah, so we wouldn't have to travel on the day of the wedding. But even if I had to drive home later in the week, it was less than two hours away, and I could easily make the trip home and then back to the lake in one day, if I had to. Well, not easily, but it wasn't impossible.

"Well, let me know if your plans are changing again," she said.

"I will, but everything is going to be perfect. Don't worry about anything," I said.

"I'm not worried. You have fun up there," she said.

I said good-bye and disconnected the call.

"Sorry about that. It was Aunt Marie," I said.

Jake's indulgent smile gave me flutters deep in my stomach.

"Let's drive over there," he said.

"What? Where?" I asked.

"The casino. I want to see it. Can we get close to it?"

"Sort of. There's a fence around the building and signs that say it's patrolled, but I didn't see anyone there when I went."

He nodded and took my hand in his. "We have to drive by there anyway to get back to the resort. Let's go take a look."

We walked back to the parking lot, hand-in-hand, and it would have been a really good time to ask Jake to come with to

Aunt Marie's wedding, but for some reason I couldn't gather my nerve to do it. What if he said no? Or, what if he said yes? Or what if I didn't ask him and just ate his filet mignon?

I still hadn't asked him when we pulled down the long tree-lined street that led to the Lucky Penny's parking lot. The chain-link fence surrounding the building looked almost as tired as the casino, with its faded siding and yellowing marquee.

"When did this shut down?" Jake asked as we walked along the fence toward the water's edge.

"In the mid 1990s," I said. "Max's family lost it in the 1980s, then it was bought by a couple different companies. The last people to buy it was the partnership that shut it down, but the partners have been in a legal battle over it ever since. Both partners died recently, so there's finally going to be some resolution to the fate of the Lucky Penny."

"And Max wants to reopen it?"

I nodded. "Yes, that's his plan. As long as his offer is accepted."

"And he gets his license approved." Jake glanced back over his shoulder at me. I nodded.

"And if he can raise enough money," I said. "Not only does he have to buy the property back, but it's in need of a lot of renovation."

Jake and I stopped at the corner where the fence turned ninety-degrees and cut across a rock retaining wall. Beyond the fence was a long-neglected water feature and what had probably been a picturesque landscaped garden. It would have been a lovely view from the tall, spired windows that faced the lake. The windows were dark and streaked with dirt. The casino was on the northern side of a small cove, so it was already in shadows, even though the sun wouldn't set for several more hours.

Jake jumped up onto the rock wall, where there was a foot of clearance on either side of the fence. He steadied himself then looked back to me with a smile.

"You coming?"

I glanced down at my leather slides with the slight wedge heel and then at the uneven rock surface.

"You'll be fine. You can hold on to the fence," Jake said. "Come on, haven't you ever wanted to explore an abandoned building?"

That did sound like fun, even if we were only going to walk around the outside. The Lucky Penny Casino was like a time capsule, untouched in twenty years. It wasn't a Roman ruin or an old church, but there was something evocative about the space.

I grabbed a handful of the fence and pulled myself up the short distance to the top of the retaining wall. I could feel the rocks beneath my feet wobble a little and gripped the metal links a little tighter. Jake was halfway across the forty-yard stretch of fencing, and I hurried to follow him. I glanced to my right and saw that the beach below was dropping away, and I was at least ten feet from the rocks on the shore. Keeping one hand on the fence, I moved forward as fast as I could while still making sure each rock I stepped on was secured to the wall.

When I reached the other side, Jake held out his hand and helped me off the wall and onto the ground that was thick with pine needles and years worth of fallen leaves. This side of the casino was harder to access, and there wasn't a path for us to follow as we walked toward the building. The trees were thick and with the breeze off the lake, it felt twenty degrees cooler than when we'd been sitting on the patio. With each step, I felt the snap of the dry twigs beneath my sandals and smelled the dusty scent of decaying green matter.

Unlike the other side of the building, on this side, the fence was not squared off but ran straight up from the water, then angled away as the building widened. The Lucky Penny's waterfront side was a striking angular wall of glass, but beyond that feature, it widened into a typical blocky hotel with a wall of square windows, some with balconies, rising about seven or eight stories high.

Where the two fences met, we stopped and looked at the empty building. It was the closest we could get to the Lucky Penny without climbing the fence. It was impossible to see what was beyond the tinted glass, but I could imagine it had been quite the sight when the Penny was in its prime.

A flicker of light bounced off the glass, and my eye was drawn to it, about halfway up the windows that faced the lake.

"Did you see that?" Jake asked, leaning toward the fence.

"Yes, but it could have been a reflection from the lake," I said.

Jake made a noncommittal sound and stayed still. I looked around the quiet patch of woods but saw and heard nothing. There didn't appear to be any buildings beyond the trees, at least not close enough to see through the thick branches and underbrush.

"There it is again."

I jumped at the sound of Jake's voice and looked back at the spot where I'd seen the flash of light. But this time, I saw a slow sweep of light from inside the building, casting shadows on the glass.

"Someone is in there," I whispered.

He nodded.

"It could be the security guard," I said.

"Maybe."

I stepped closer to the fence and gripped the metal links for support, but they wobbled, and I bumped into Jake.

"Are you all right?" he asked, putting an arm around me and steadying me.

"Yes, but look here," I said, pointing down at the corner of the fence.

Someone had cut the fence neatly with bolt cutters. The panel moved easily as Jake pushed it and left an opening that an adult could climb through.

Another flicker drew my eye up, but this time it was a flash of light, not the slow sweep of a flashlight. This was like a camera flash. Or a lighter. Moments later, a warm breeze caressed my face and carried with it an all-too familiar scent, wafting from the direction of the Lucky Penny. I turned to Jake to see if he noticed it too.

"Do you smell smoke?"

CHAPTER FIFTEEN

"Does your phone get a signal here?" Jake asked, frowning at his own cell phone and waving it to try to catch a connection to the nearest cellular tower.

I pulled my phone out of my pocket and saw that most ominous of modern warnings: no signal.

I shook my head and Jake's frown grew. He looked back at the massive building, then to me, and then around the empty forest behind us. The wheels were turning in his mind, and I imagined he was running through the possibilities—was it an arsonist in the building? Some stupid kids who were going to burn it down, or get themselves hurt?

He looked back to me, and I could tell he had no idea what to do with me. I shook my head. Whatever it was, I wasn't going to be told to stay here while he went into the abandoned building to investigate.

"Yeah," he said softly, more to himself than to me. "You go first and pull up the fence for me."

I dropped to the ground and scrambled through the dry pine needles and under the cut chain-link fence. I popped up on the other side, grabbed the metal links, and pulled up. Jake snagged his T-shirt as he squeezed through the opening, then dropped to his stomach and crawled through the triangle-shaped hole. He pushed the fence back down, but it was still curved up, and anyone who happened to walk by would see the hole cut in the fence.

It was unlikely that anyone would happen by this deserted side of an abandoned casino though.

Jake grabbed my hand and pulled me toward the building, across an empty walkway and toward a bank of doors. We were on a concrete pad that might have been a patio or another entrance to the casino but was now thickly covered with debris. The doors were locked, of course, but we kept trying them as we made our way to the corner of the building, where the glass doors ended, and we were facing a wall of concrete. Jake walked around the side, and I sniffed at the air. Definitely smoke, and it seemed closer now.

"Miranda, over here," he called, and I ran around the corner.

Jake held open a service door, and I stopped at the threshold and peered inside. I couldn't see anything, and more importantly, I couldn't smell smoke coming from inside.

"If it's the guard—"

"It's not," he said, showing me the door, which had been pried open by force, the edge of the frame ragged with fresh scrapes in the dull paint. "Just stay close to me."

I nodded and stepped in after him, the blackness enveloping us. Jake used his cell phone flashlight app to light a path for us down a bare hallway, our footsteps echoing off the walls and the linoleum. We reached the end of the corridor, and Jake pushed at the door, which swung open with ease. Jake studied the doorknob in the low light of the cell phone and pointed out the freshly damaged wood there too. Whoever was in the building had really wanted in.

We stepped out into a hallway, our footsteps muffled by the carpet. Jake closed the door behind us carefully, and I looked in both directions. Other than the weak beam from Jake's phone, the only light came from the windows facing the lake. The lower windows were boarded over with plywood, but the upper windows let in a beam of light that was filtered through two decades of dust and grime. The effect was a gloomy pall cast over the casino floor, where rows of tables covered by cloths lined up in the middle of the room. Raised platforms where the slot machines had once been now looked like empty planter boxes.

Cautiously, I sniffed the air for smoke. The interior was musty, as if there had been water intrusion at one point, and mildew thrived in its wake. But there was no smoke.

Silently, we made our way along the marble counter of the cashier's cage, past another cluster of covered tables and then toward a sweeping staircase that led to the second floor. A set of escalators sat to one side, but was stacked with chairs that were jammed in every which way, nearly halfway to the second floor. The only sound was the occasional scratch of the untrimmed pine tree boughs against the windows.

Near the base of the stairs, an overhead sign pointed the way to a ballroom and convention halls down a deep black hole of a hallway. I peered into the opening, but could see nothing. I pulled my own cell phone from my pocket, fumbled with it in the low light, then found the flashlight app and turned it on. While Jake studied the casino, listening carefully for any sound of the intruder, I scanned the dark corners of this part of the room.

I took a few steps into the darkened hall, and my light swept from left to right, illuminating forgotten musical acts, magicians, and upcoming car shows whose posters still lined the walls. With Jake nearby, my confidence grew, and I ventured farther into the tunnel. My flashlight beam bounced off a rack of tourism magazines from 1996.

I raised the phone's beam of light, and out of the darkness, a face emerged, pale and exaggerated—a wide mouth painted deep red, exaggerated black-rimmed eyes that bore into me.

I leapt backward, smack into something solid and warm.

"Eeek!" The cry escaped my lips involuntarily, and my phone dropped from my hand and bounced across the carpet.

Strong arms caught me as I scrambled to get away.

"It's okay, it's me," Jake said.

I tried to catch my breath as my heart raced. Jake raised his phone enough to light up the poster for a circus featuring the clown who scared the bejeezus out of me.

"I don't care what you say. That is scary," I said, pointing at the obscenely laughing painted face.

Jake hugged me tight, kissed my head, and then released me. I found my phone on the ground and followed him back toward the grand staircase, giving that clown poster a wide berth as I hurried past.

At the bottom of the stairs, I paused and looked up to the second floor balcony that overlooked the casino floor. My body was still trying to process all the adrenaline that clown had triggered, and my senses felt heightened—the sound of my heart thumping in my chest was clear and loud, and the dimly lit casino seemed brighter. I took a deep breath and exhaled slowly, trying to calm my nerves before we went upstairs.

Jake watched me carefully.

"Are you all right?" he asked, his voice barely a whisper.

I nodded but didn't say anything. He smiled and took my hand and started up the stairs. I followed but then pulled back, stopping him.

I pointed to the carpet three steps above the one I was standing on—and the footprint in the thick dust.

He nodded, put a finger to his lips and kept my hand in his grip. And then continued up the stairs.

Oh God, what are we doing here? My thoughts raced as we hit the second floor, a wide expanse of dusty carpet upon which a trail of footprints led to one side of the balcony and then back across to a hall. The sign over the entrance said that shops and restaurants could be found down the wide and darkened path.

And from the trail of footprints, so could our intruder.

Jake stopped and took out his phone again, this time snapping a few pictures of the footsteps. I held up a hand to stop him and looked around for something to use as a measuring stick. There was another full rack of tourism magazines near the top of the stairs, so I grabbed one and then went back to where Jake was kneeling by the trail.

The shoe print wasn't too distinct, but you could at least see that it was a running shoe of some sort. I set the magazine down next to the clearest impression, and Jake took a half dozen shots from different angles. Jake stood and dusted his hands on his pants.

"Smell anything?" he asked. Though his voice was low, it could have been a shout in the empty building.

I sniffed the air again, shook my head, then felt the tickle of dust and frantically rubbed at my nose trying to fend off the inevitable reaction to inhaling a nose full of 20-year-old dust. It was useless. My sneeze bounced off the windows and echoed down abandoned hallways and would have probably rattled the chandeliers, except it looked like the owners sold those off already.

"Sorry," I sniffed.

"Bless you," Jake said.

A second later, we heard a deep bang from the depths of the darkened hallway. Jake reached back to his waistband, under his shirt, and then pulled his hand back, empty.

"Damn."

"Where is your gun?"

Jake pressed his lips together. "In the trunk of the car."

"Why?"

He expelled a frustrated sigh. "Because we were having lunch. I didn't need to be armed."

Okay, so we were in a creepy abandoned building decorated with evil clowns, with an unknown person who might be up to no good, and Jake didn't bring his gun.

No problem.

Frozen in place, I listened for any sound that might indicate the other person in the casino was heading our way, but there was nothing. Jake took my hand and pulled me to the side, near the archway that led to the shopping center.

"Stay behind me. Stay close," he whispered and started down the hall, hugging the wall.

He didn't have to tell me twice. I practically stepped on his feet as we crept slowly along the gentle curving wall. The dark tunnel we were in opened to a shadowy atrium, with a round bench surrounding an empty podium that had probably held a statute or piece of sculpture. The seating arrangement looked out at the tall windows of empty shops. A gray light from glass panels overhead cast deep shadows that looked even creepier with the silhouettes of mannequins looking on from behind the dusty panes.

Passing what must have been a gift shop, now a locked room of empty shelves, we moved to the other side of the rotunda to a long stretch of shops. I'd seen some of the fabulous shopping malls in Las Vegas casinos, miles of elaborate and expensive boutiques that tried to recapture any winnings that casino patrons might be trying to leave with.

But the Lucky Penny's retail center was at best a miniature version of a suburban shopping mall. A small art gallery, its walls bare, sat next to a hair salon. Beyond that, a boutique with doors made of frosted glass and black lacquered wood that specialized in lingerie. Toward the end of the walkway was a gift store with the doors wide open and the merchandise cleaned out, except for a toppled rack of key chains near the entrance.

Had that been the sound we heard? Jake glanced around the empty room, then withdrew, and we continued to the food court where the short mall ended. The familiar logos were still mounted above the counters, but metal shutters closed off the kitchens. Dozens of tables still affixed to the floors dotted the tile floor, but the chairs were gone and there was simply no place to hide.

Jake moved quietly around the edge of the room to an emergency exit. The double doors were secured with a chain and padlock, which meant there was also no exit from this wing of the building.

The hair on the back of my neck stood up. As deadly quiet as the building was, we were not alone. I turned and looked back toward the rotunda that marked the entrance to the shopping center, but it was as still as it had been when we had walked through.

"Where could he have gone?" I whispered, staying as close to Jake as possible without him carrying me.

He shook his head. "Nothing seems to be on fire, at least."

"Is there another exit?"

He turned back to the emergency exit while I grabbed the handle of one of the metal shutters closing off a frozen yogurt counter. To my surprise, it rolled up several inches with a groan of creaky gears. Jake gripped the bottom of the shutter and forced it up a couple feet, the rumble echoing through the empty space.

A loud crash of metal to our left startled me, and I whirled around. Jake pulled me to the ground in a protective embrace, rolling us under one of the cafeteria-style tables as the sound reverberated off the metal and glass surrounding us.

"Are you hurt?" he asked, his voice low in my ear, barely audible over the pounding of my heart.

I shook my head and looked where the sound had come from but didn't see anything. Jake crawled a few feet away then jumped to his feet. He held an item the size of a softball in his hand and was staring back down the hall. At his wave, I climbed off the floor and looked around the room, and then back at the novelty snow globe that Jake held in his hand. It had bounced off one of the metal shutters, creating a lot of noise but no damage.

And that's when I heard the sound of footsteps, running fast and getting faint.

"Come on," he said, bolting forward.

I followed, racing after him, past the empty shops and the creepy mannequins waving good-bye from the shadows, into the dark tunnel that led to the casino. We burst out onto the wide balcony, but it was empty. Jake ran to the railing and looked over, and I saw the shadow of a figure darting into the hall, back to the door that would lead outside.

Jake took the stairs in double time, and I followed as fast as I could, but as I hit the second to the last step, my foot slipped off the wedge heel, and I tumbled onto the musty carpet. My head narrowly missed a collision with the base of a blackjack table, my arms coming up too late to protect me from hitting the carpet full on. I got a face full of carpet dust and had the breath knocked out of me, but I'd survive.

I rolled to a sitting position and felt my ankle—tender but not broken or probably even sprained. I flexed my foot and tried to stand.

A shock of pain shot through my ankle when I put weight on my foot.

"Ouch!" It was a little more injured than I had thought.

I hobbled closer to the table to get my phone, which had flown out of my hand when I stumbled and bent down. My hand closed around the phone, but something else caught my eye—a key chain.

A retro-style Lucky Penny Casino logo on a gold ring. Just like the ones we'd seen in the gift shop. I poked at it and noticed that it wasn't dusty like everything else in the building, and it must have come from the person Jake just chased outside.

"He got away," Jake said, not bothering to lower his voice as he stalked across the casino floor.

I leaned on the edge of the table to take some weight off my foot and felt the sticky grime from years of dust on the heavy fabric cloth covering the furniture.

Jake frowned. "Are you all right? Did you fall?"

I nodded, happy that he hadn't seen me do a face-plant onto the carpet. "It's not bad. Just a twisted ankle."

"Let's get out of here and get to where we can call someone."

"Who?" I asked

"The security company, to start. And Alex, who can decide whether the local police should be brought in," he said.

"Did you see who it was?"

He shook his head and put an arm around my waist to help me walk, but I stopped and pointed at the floor.

"Whoever it was, I think they dropped this. I didn't touch it, in case there were prints on it."

Jake carefully picked up the keychain by the metal ring and studied it. "Looks familiar."

He helped me across the room to the exit, then opened the door for me. I dropped my sandal on the floor and slipped it on my injured foot. It was already starting to ache less, and I was sure that a short visit with an ice pack would make quick work of it.

At the end of the dark hall, Jake pushed open the damaged door, letting in a bright beam of light. We stepped outside and were greeted with a haze that wasn't there when we had walked in a short time earlier.

And the unmistakable scent of smoke, heavy and close.

I looked around for a campfire, ready to go storm someone's picnic and educate them about the danger of wildfires in late summer in the Sierra Nevada, but there was no sign of smoke from the beach or the woods alongside the casino.

We moved as quickly as my bum ankle would allow, and my eyes were starting to burn as I crawled through the damaged fence. I looked back toward the casino before we started to walk away, and that's when I saw it.

A huge towering plume of white and grey smoke, reaching for the heavens. Not from the casino but from much higher up —from beyond the mountains that rimmed the lake. A steady breeze was pushing the smoke over the ridge and down the other side, right toward us.

And it was coming from just beyond the Whispering Pines Resort.

CHAPTER SIXTEEN

Jake drove Bethany's tan sedan like it was a Formula 1 racecar as I gripped the door handle and the center console and tried to put my foot through the floorboard.

"Call Alex, use my phone," he barked, hitting the apex of a curve on the mountain road.

"Where is it?" I asked.

"Oh, it's in my pocket," he said, moving so I could reach into his pants. It was far too intimate a move to be doing while in a car hurtling along a mountainside at high speed, but I ignored the heat on my face and managed to reach into his snug jeans and withdraw his phone without causing an accident.

When Alex answered, I put the call on speaker, and Jake filled him in on the casino. The connection faded and restarted several times as we wound our way higher up the road.

"I'll call the security company, but you guys aren't going to get to the resort. They just closed the road. They'll probably turn you around. They're not letting traffic through from Carson City on Highway 50 either," he said. "That fire on the east side of the mountains blew up fast and is heading right to the top of the ridge. You don't want to be anywhere near there."

Jake thanked him, said good bye, and I disconnected the call, leaving the phone in the center console instead of trying to insert it back into Jake's pants. We were only a couple miles from the resort, and we hadn't seen any signs of road closures yet. But it was hard to see anything with the smoke, which was growing thicker as we gained in elevation.

"Are you sure we should be going toward the fire?" I asked.

"They're going to need help getting everyone out of the resort if there's an evacuation order," he said. "And this is Bethany's car. I'm sure she'd rather not be left behind."

Out of the gloomy orange haze, the Whispering Pines gates emerged, and I realized we were closer than I had thought. The tops of the evergreens lining the long drive to the lodge were lost in the smoke. Instead of the view of the crystal clear lake below, our vista now ended in about seventy-five yards in a grey-brown smudge.

As the lodge materialized out of the haze, I saw a red fire engine parked by the front entrance, which made me breathe a little easier—or would have if the air wasn't thick with a choking smoke.

We parked Bethany's car and then walked to the wide porch as quickly as my wounded ankle would let me. I didn't want to stay out in the claustrophobic smoke any longer than necessary, but with each step, a stab of pain raced up my lower leg. Even the short walk left my eyes burning by the time we were inside the lodge.

Max and Jordan were at the front counter, talking with two firefighters who were bulked up by their fire gear. The four men pored over a large map spread over the marble counter.

"Whatever you need, you've got it," Max said, and I doubted that his generosity was about spa services this time. "A place to sleep, food, space to park your rigs. You just tell me or Jordan what you need."

Jordan nodded, his forehead furrowed. His dark hair had escaped its gelled confines. It softened his face, and there was no trace of the arrogant attitude he'd been carrying since I met him.

"Miranda," Max said, his face registering shock at seeing me and Jake for the first time. "How did you get up here? Isn't the road closed?"

"We must have just made it through," Jake said. "What's the status with the fire? Do we need to evacuate the resort?"

The taller of the two firefighters shook his head. "No, not at this time. In fact, we're asking everyone here not to leave, not to drive on the road. We're going to start bringing crews up to work on a fire line, and we don't want unnecessary traffic," he said.

The other man tapped the map. "The fire took out one cellular tower, could take out more, so you'll probably notice a drop in your service."

Max nodded. "The resort's phones are still working. For now."

His jaw tensed, and he looked around the cavernous lobby, and I followed his gaze. The heavy beams put in place by Max's grandfather, the stones in the fireplace set in mortar by his uncles and father. It wasn't just a business at risk; it was his family's history.

"Mr. Emmerson, I know it doesn't seem like it with all the smoke, but this is actually a pretty safe place to be. The fire's coming up the other side of the mountain because fires go up. Fires don't come down a slope unless it's grown to such a size that it creates its own weather system and wind pushes it downhill," the taller firefighter said.

"That's not going to happen here?" I asked, remembering the sight of the smoke billowing upward and spilling down over the top. We were under a heavy blanket of smoke that had been blown in our direction.

But the firefighter shook his head. "Let's hope not. There is a breeze that's funneling the smoke down into the lake basin, but at this point, it's just smoke. Keep everyone inside. Stay off the roads. But prepare to leave, if necessary."

The firefighters thanked Max for his cooperation and left, a rumble from the diesel engine announcing their exit.

"Someone is going to have to go talk to Mr. Weber about making sure his crew stays put," Max said, looking at Jordan as if it were a foregone conclusion who that would be.

Jordan nodded. "I'll go find Carly."

He grabbed a sheath of papers from the counter and flipped through them. "Do you think we should go door-to-door to make sure we get the word out?"

Max looked to Jake, who nodded. "I'm sure there are guests who are preparing to leave. You probably should stop them before they try to use the road."

Jordan looked down the list of names and room numbers. I glanced down and scanned the list quickly, noting that Cabin No. 7, where the party had been, did not have a name assigned to it, just said "crew." Jordan caught me reading the papers in his hands and yanked them away, clasping them against his chest. Shooting me a distrustful look, he backed up a few steps and then walked briskly away.

"Max, have you heard from Dottie? She was driving to Reno this morning," I asked.

"Yeah, she called a couple hours ago and said she was on the wrong side of the road closure on Highway 50. They were sending traffic back to Carson City, and I think she's going to have to spend the night there. She said she needed to talk to you though. You'll probably have to use the resort phones to get through," he said.

Jake put a hand on my shoulder. "I need to find Bethany and check in with her."

"And I need to find the rest of my staff and let them know what's going on," Max said, heading toward the Pines Cafe.

"Want me to help you get up the stairs?" Jake asked.

I shook my head. "I'll take the elevator. But maybe I'll get some ice before I go upstairs."

Jake frowned and steered me toward a padded bench near the elevator. "I'll take care of the ice. Stay here."

He followed Max into the café, and I leaned back against the wall, feeling the throbbing in my ankle grow.

A loud and colorful stream of cursing from the Grand Hall distracted me, and I twisted to see what was causing the commotion. Denny Shawn Weber stalked down the red-carpeted hallway toward the lobby. His thick curly hair, usually mussed from his habit of running a hand through it, was practically standing on end, and his eyes were red behind his black-rimmed glasses.

Two men trailed behind him—Mark Tripp and a man who had been operating the camera on the day I watched the scene in the library. Carly had told me that his name was Jean-Paul, but everyone called him JP, and he was the director of photography, responsible for ensuring the director's vision came to life on screen.

"It will look like fog. We keep shooting," Denny said.

Mark and JP exchanged worried glances.

"We can't do that. Everyone looks orange in this light. And if we go outside, their eyes will turn red from the smoke. Even if we move the shoot inside, the ambient light is orange. I can't work with that," JP said.

"It's just Reece coming out of the manor and walking away. Just filter it or something," Denny said.

JP threw his hands up. "I don't have a filter that will keep Reece Muir from looking like an Oompa Loompa in this light!"

Mark stepped forward between the two men and raised his hands.

"Denny, let's just wait a day. We're fine. We're not behind schedule," he said, his voice calm and reassuring. "It's just one day off. Everyone's been working hard. We all want this to be perfect."

Denny paced the hallway, just beyond the lobby and ran his hand through his thick tangle of curls again.

"Well, I guess we have no choice," he said. "Who wants to go tell the cast?"

Mark and JP each took a step backward, and Denny shook his head. "Fine. I'll do it."

He whirled around and stalked through the lobby, giving me a nod before exiting the building. I caught Mark's eye, and he grinned and shrugged.

"He's just upset because he can't direct the weather," he said, trailing slowly behind the director to the door.

I laughed. "Well, at least you get a day off."

"Yeah, is it any better down the hill? Maybe I'll go hit the tables at the Royal Palace again."

This wasn't a huge surprise, given what I'd learned about Mark's gambling problems only earlier that afternoon. "Only a little better. But the road's closed. We all have to stay here."

Mark's expression turned from amusement to concern. "We're stuck here? What about people trying to get here?"

"I don't know. They're bringing up a lot of heavy equipment and fire engines, so the roads are going to be closed to other traffic. Are you waiting on someone who's driving up there?"

Mark shook his head. "No one, just wondering," he muttered, hurrying now to the door.

As he left the lobby, Jake returned with a plastic bag of ice and helped me into the elevator, riding with me to the second floor.

"I thought you were looking for Bethany," I said, as he watched me unlock my room. "I'm fairly sure she won't be in here."

He smiled and helped me through the door. "Just wanted to make sure you're okay."

"I'm okay." I sat on the edge of the bed and put my foot up. Jake moved one of the chairs by the table to the edge of the bed, sat down and took my ankle, resting it on his knee. He removed my shoe, wrapped the ice bag in a towel and then placed it gently on my ankle.

"Feel better?" he asked, his eyes meeting mine.

Despite the ice, my body flushed hot at the way he was stroking my calf. I licked my lips and nodded.

"I don't know if we can call that a date, since you were injured," he said, a hint of a smile at the corner of his lips.

"You said it depended on how it ended," I reminded him.

His smile grew, and he moved so that he was next to me on the bed, my leg still outstretched with the ice pack on it but now resting on the bed. He leaned across me, resting his hand on the bed. With his other hand, he reached up and brushed my hair away from my face. My entire body was throbbing now, and I leaned in when he moved closer.

Our lips touched, gentle at first and then more insistent. *Yes, yes, yes.* This was what I wanted, what I needed. My pulse raced, and my skin tingled where he brushed his fingers down my neck, leaving shivers in his wake. Too soon, he moved away with a groan.

"I have to go," he whispered. "Stay right here."

His deep brown eyes met mine, and he kissed me again before I could respond, and my head spun. When he pulled away again, I was gripping his hard biceps with enough force that my fingerprints may have been preserved as bruises on his smooth tan skin.

"Right here," I agreed, once I found my voice.

He gave me a wink and then stood up. "I'll be back in a while," he said, adjusting the ice on my ankle. "Keep your foot elevated. It will help with swelling."

It was already feeling better, but I didn't mind him fussing over me, so I just nodded.

The door closed behind him, and I sank back into the pillows. As first dates went, it wasn't horrible. Even with the injury and the creepy clown poster and trespassing into the Lucky Penny, I could definitely say I'd had worse first dates.

A soft knock sounded at the door, and I sat up.

"Miranda," Jake said from the other side of the door.

I jumped up, careful of my now frozen ankle and hobbled to the door.

"Sorry," he said with a smile. "Bethany isn't in her room. I'm going to go look around for her."

"All right," I said, unsure why I needed the update. "What's the matter?"

He shrugged, but his casual gesture didn't match his expression. "I don't know. Her room is a little messed up, and she's, well, you know."

"Uptight. Anal-retentive. Fussy."

"Tidy."

"Whatever." I frowned at what he was implying. "Do you think she's in trouble?"

He frowned. "I don't know. She said she escaped the spa and was going back to her room. She wouldn't be outside with this smoke, so I'll walk around the lodge, see if I can find her."

"Okay. Good luck."

"So, when I get back, I don't want you to have to get up and answer the door," he said, and I saw a hint of a blush creep up his face.

I leaned back and studied his sheepish expression. "Jake Barnes, are you asking for my hotel room key?"

He grinned and gave me a shrug that made me laugh.

"Yeah, hold on. I have an extra key card here somewhere."

Jake was still in the doorway, leaning against the jamb, when I returned with the magnetic card. He reached for it with a smile, and I drew it back.

"Wait a minute, what do I get for this?" I asked.

He laughed and pulled me to him, kissing me deeply, causing my toes to curl into the plush carpet pile. Then his mouth slid down my neck, and I rolled my head and sighed. I was about to tuck the card into his pants pocket, when a movement in the hall distracted me.

I felt my eyes grow wide at the sight of Bethany Boylan stepping into the hall.

But not from her room. From Quinn's room, which faced Bethany's across the hall.

And she was wearing a plush, white Whispering Pines bathrobe.

At the moment that Quinn's door softly clicked shut behind her, our eyes met, and she froze. Bethany's long brown hair was tangled, her lips slightly swollen, and her entire look had a distinct air of "just rolled off a naked cowboy."

In that split second, a thousand thoughts raced through my mind. Every snub, every slight by Bethany queued up and flashed before my eyes. Every judgmental look she had cast my way. Each snide reminder that she wasn't entirely convinced that the jury had done the right thing in letting me walk free.

Jake was still nibbling on my ear and had no idea his partner was sneaking back from an afternoon spent in bed with a witness. I could easily say something and alert him, and puncture that image of the perfect federal agent who was so by-the-book that Jake didn't want to tell her about us.

Her eyes pleaded with me not to say anything, and in that moment, she no longer seemed like the uptight and prissy FBI agent but a woman who really didn't want to be caught in a comprising position by her coworker.

I grabbed Jake and pulled his face to mine, kissing him with a passion borne of, well, a lot of pent-up passion but also a bit of solidarity for Bethany. Jake didn't need to know what was going on with Bethany and Quinn. Frankly, I envied him that ignorance.

Jake reached around my waist and lifted me up, carrying me back into the room, shutting the door behind us. Pressing me against the wall, he kissed me until my breath was ragged and my body was on fire.

"Can I please have that key now?" he asked, his voice rough and low.

I slid the key into the front pocket of his jeans, and he groaned. "I'll be back later."

He slipped out of the room, and I leaned back against the door, my head spinning from the extended contact with him. But also my brain was trying to process the new information. I heard the shower turn on in the room next door and blew out a long exhale. If I couldn't find Dottie, at least I knew where Quinn was. And where he had been. I shook my head to empty my mind of that thought.

Remembering that Dottie had asked me to call, I limped back to the bed and used the hotel phone to dial her cell phone.

"Sweetie, I'm stuck here in Carson City," she said, her voice coming in clear despite the sound of clanging slot machines in the background.

"Are you at a casino?"

"Yeah, I got a room for the night, just in case the road doesn't get reopened right away."

I filled Dottie in on the fire situation at the resort but left out the adventure in The Lucky Penny.

"Listen, sweetie, I got that report from the accountants, and you're not going to believe this," she said.

"What is it?"

"That part that was cut out? It was a market study about whether using Whispering Pines as a film set would be profitable. It was done at Jordan's request."

"Why would he remove that? That was a really responsible thing to do."

"Well, it would have been responsible, but the accountants concluded that it wouldn't generate as much profit as renting the rooms out at the regular rate."

"And Jordan did it anyway? Why?"

Dottie gave a frustrated snort. "Who knows with that kid. The lease was signed after he asked for the accounting firm's opinion but before he got the report. Looks like he just made his mind up without any math to back him up."

That certainly explained why he would want to hide those pages from Max. It didn't show very good leadership. And Max had wanted to train Jordan to run the Lucky Penny Casino. This could make him change his mind.

But what Jordan had done wasn't illegal. It was simply a poor business decision. It might cause a bank some discomfort, but because Jordan was no longer in charge of the resort, it wasn't going to kill Max's financing plan.

"Hey, you stay safe up there, kiddo," Dottie said. "I'll see you in the morning when the smoke dies down. In the meantime, go enjoy Agent Dollface."

She disconnected the call before I could respond, and I leaned back on the bed. With the full report, we could wrap up the audit. That didn't mean I could leave, since I'd agreed to stay and make sure I was invited to the wrap party. And the wrap party was probably going to be delayed a day due to the smoke. Still, I should be able to get home for a couple nights before returning to Lake Tahoe for the wedding.

Ugh, the wedding. I had forgotten to invite Jake. In my defense, I was a little distracted at the time.

I promised myself that I would get to that as soon as I saw him next.

I heard a soft knock at the door and sat up again. Good thing my ankle wasn't as sore, because I was doing a terrible job of keeping it elevated, I thought as I opened the door.

Disappointingly, it wasn't Agent Dollface at the door. Instead, I found myself face-to-face with Jordan Swift. His face was red and covered with a thin sheen of sweet, and he was breathing heavily.

"I need to talk to you."

CHAPTER SEVENTEEN

"Yeah, well, I need to talk to you too," I said. "Dottie got the report from the accountants."

Jordan's face turned even more red, his cheeks practically purple. He looked down at the carpet, and his lips tightened.

"I meant to get that to you," he mumbled.

"I don't understand what hiding it will do. It's not like it's a secret that renting out the resort for the film was a bad decision," I said.

He jerked his head up. "It will pay off in the long run. Probably. Those accountants were only looking at the immediate payoff, but this film is going to win awards, be a modern classic. People around the world are going to see it and want to come here."

"So why not just explain that to your uncle and tell him the accountants are short-sighted?"

"Uncle Max has been doing the same thing for the resort for years. Do you know how long it took Angie to convince him to add a spa? More than ten years. And it was a huge success, but he didn't even want to hear about it for years."

"And what? You thought that since you had the reins for a

short time, you'd try out your ideas? Fine. But I don't see why you had to lie about it."

Jordan shook his head and straightened up. "I never lied about it. I just didn't tell Uncle Max about the report."

This was getting us nowhere, I thought with a frustrated sigh.

"I don't see why this is such an urgent matter," I said. "Dottie and I will get the audit completed in a day or so, and your disagreement on the direction of the business is irrelevant to our findings."

"Oh, okay. I thought you'd take Uncle Max's side on this," he said.

"That's not what we do. What you did was a business decision. A dumb one, maybe. But you didn't embezzle money or defraud anyone, so that's all we needed to know."

Jordan exhaled a long breath, and his face returned to a normal color. "That's a relief."

"Great," I said, starting to close the door.

"Oh, wait. No. That's not why I was here," he said, putting a hand on the door. "I can't find Carly anywhere. I went to do the door-to-door to notify everyone about the order to stay here, but I can't find Carly or Ms. Arens."

I frowned and pulled the door open again. "What do you mean you can't find them?"

"They're not anywhere. Not in their cabin and I can't reach Carly on her phone," he said. "I started to search the lodge, but I thought you and your friend had been hanging around with her, and I was hoping she'd be here with you, or you might know where to find her."

I walked across the hall to Bethany's room and pounded on the door. God help me if she was having round two with Quinn in there.

The Bethany who answered the door was the familiar one—polished, professional, and above all, fully dressed.

"Have you seen Carly? Jordan can't find her."

Bethany's FBI-mode kicked in, and she stepped out into the hall with us and faced Jordan.

"I was with her until early afternoon, around two or so, at the spa. Have you checked there?"

Jordan shook his head. "Not yet. But we sent the spa employees home hours ago."

Bethany glanced at me. "Where's Jake?"

"Looking for you."

"Oh."

"I couldn't very well call off his search without..."

I stopped talking as Jordan looked at me, then at Bethany, then back to me.

"Anyway, yes, you should call Jake, and tell him to keep an eye out for Carly and Lorelei," I said.

She nodded, reached into her pocket, and pulled out her phone. Then she frowned. "No service."

"The last cell tower on the ridge was in the path of the fire. We may have lost it," Jordan said.

"Jordan, you checked all the cabins?" Bethany asked.

He nodded. "I visited all the cabins to pass on the order not to use the roads. I didn't ask about Carly and Lorelei. And they weren't at their cabin."

"They may be in the lodge. Why don't we split up, go check the rest of the lodge for them?" Bethany suggested. "Jordan, you know the crew members who are staying in the lodge. Why don't you go talk to them, see who saw them last, where they were. Miranda and I will take the lower level and the first floor. Meet us in the lobby as soon as you're done."

He nodded. "Okay, thank you."

Jordan walked quickly down the hall toward the far end of the building where some of the crew was staying.

I stepped into the room and grabbed a pair of running shoes from the closet, then sat on the edge of the bed and laced them up, hoping to get better support for my ankle. I flexed my foot and didn't feel the dull ache any longer. Bethany lingered in the hall outside my room waiting for me.

"I'll take the main floor. I have a key to the business office, and Carly was there this morning," I said, striding toward the elevator.

"I'll take the lower level, the spa, gym, and restaurant."

We didn't speak in the elevator, and the uncomfortable silence was preferable to any discussion we'd have about her and Quinn. Or me and Jake. Thankfully, Bethany didn't seem to want to talk, either. The doors opened to the main floor, and I bolted toward the doors that led to the business office.

My sweep of the business office didn't take long—the offices were empty, and the conference room was securely locked, as it was when I left that morning. I checked it anyway, even looking in the locked cupboard to make sure the paperwork was still in order. It appeared to be untouched. I locked everything up on my way out and then walked past the reception area through the lobby and down the Grand Hall, peeking in all the alcoves for any sign of the missing actress and her assistant. But the ballroom, the small sitting rooms, and the Pines Cafe were all empty.

I hit the end of the hall and backtracked to the lobby. My ankle was feeling better, but I kept my pace slow so I didn't aggravate the slight ache. When I turned the corner to the lobby, I ran smack into Jake.

"*Oof.* Sorry. Oh, hi," I said, letting my hands linger on his chest for a moment.

"What are you doing down here?" Jake said. "You're supposed to keep that foot elevated."

"It's fine, really," I said. "I iced it. Lots better."

"You didn't find them?" Bethany asked, coming up from the stairs from the spa and restaurant level.

I shook my head, but before I could respond, I saw a pair of boots hit the top step on the landing, followed by the rest of Quinn, tall and lean and handsome. My eyes darted between him and Bethany and then to Jake, to see if he could see what was going on there.

"Where have you been?" Jake asked Bethany. "I just searched this building for you."

"Jordan can't find Lorelei and Carly," I said, trying to distract Jake from his partner's sudden reappearance. And hopefully from any chemistry between the FBI agent and the ex-con. "He went out to all the cabins, but they weren't at theirs, and we can't find them in the lodge. He's going to talk with the crew who are staying in the lodge."

Jake's puzzled and unhappy expression made me feel a little guilty about helping Bethany cover up her fling.

The elevator dinged, and Jordan stepped out, his face still anxious. "Did you find them?"

Bethany and I shook our heads as the front door opened, and Denny Shawn Weber walked in to the lobby, holding a handkerchief over his nose and mouth.

"You guys, this smoke is horrible," he announced, as if none of us might have otherwise noticed. "I'm really allergic to smoke, and this is killing me."

"Have you seen Carly or Lorelei?" I asked, ignoring the director's health updates. He wasn't the only one affected by the stifling pollution.

Quinn walked over and dropped an arm around my shoulders. I appreciated that he was trying to keep up our cover, but it was making my head hurt trying to keep up with all the lies. I knew about him and Bethany, but he didn't know that. Nor did Jake. And while Quinn and now Bethany knew about me and Jake, everyone else in the lodge thought Jake was the husband of my old college friend.

Ugh. My eye twitched.

"Carly had an appointment in town this afternoon," Denny said, his bloodshot eyes blinked behind his thick lenses. "Do you think she's stuck down there? What if she's trying to get back up here? Could she be in danger?"

Bethany zeroed in on the director. "When did you see Carly last? Where was this appointment? What time was it?"

Denny looked puzzled. "It was around four, I think. It was down near Stateline."

I exchanged a look with Bethany. What sort of meeting would a personal assistant to a movie star have in Stateline?

"Where was this meeting?" Jake asked. "Maybe we can call and find out if she's still there."

Denny shook his head. "Uh, yeah. I don't know about that. I'm just worried that she would try to drive back up here and get herself in trouble."

The elevator dinged again, this time disgorging Max and Reece Muir who were chatting excitedly as they stepped out into the lobby.

"Congratulations, Mr. Emmerson," Reece said, shaking Max's hand.

"Thank you, Mr. Muir," Max said. "I hope you'll be our first VIP guest."

"I'd be honored," Reece said with a wide smile that show-cased his famous dimples. He turned to the small crowd watching him and threw an arm around Max's shoulder. "Can I tell them?"

Max nodded and smiled.

"You're looking at the new owner of The Lucky Penny Casino!" Reece announced.

"They accepted our bid?" Jordan asked, the worry slipping away from his face.

"They did! I'm confident that we'll get the loan and be able to start construction within a few months," he said.

"What about the license?" Jordan asked.

Max stole a glance at Jake and Bethany, then smiled. "Let's just say, I'm fairly confident there too."

"Congratulations, Max. That's great news," I said. He reached out and pulled me to him, enveloping me in a bear hug.

"Thank you, Miranda. I just wish Dottie had made it back here in time to hear the news," he said.

"She'll be thrilled," I said.

Amid the congratulations being offered, I saw Denny Shawn Weber standing still, lost in his thoughts. His face was pale and his expression confused.

"Are you okay, Mr. Weber?" I asked.

He looked up from the floor and focused on my face. "I don't understand."

"What don't you understand?" I asked, alarmed at his reaction. His face had gone ghostly white at the first mention of the casino.

The front door slammed open, and three firefighters strode in—two tall and imposing and a third one leading them who was short and wearing fire gear that was far too big. The short firefighter took off her yellow helmet and tucked it under her arm.

"Gail," Jake said, stepping forward to greet her. "How did you get up here?"

"Hitched a ride with these boys," she said, jerking a thumb at the two men behind her. She shrugged out of the coat and pants with cuffs rolled up several inches and handed them to the firefighters. "Thanks, guys. I'll be staying here until the order is lifted. Appreciate the ride."

Gail strode forward and pulled a manila envelope from a messenger bag, slapping it against Jake's chest.

"Where is Miss Carly Malone? I need to have a little chat with her."

The rest of the crowd looked around and exchanged confused looks.

"That's the problem, Gail. She seems to be missing," Jake said. "We can't find her or her employer, Lorelei Arens."

That caught Reece's attention, and he stepped forward. "What? Lorelei is missing?"

Gail held up a hand and pointed at Reece. "You used to employ Ms. Malone?"

He nodded. "For about a year. She quit when Lorelei and I broke up, went to work for her. About six months ago."

Gail nodded. "Did you know her real name was Carlene Chubb?"

Reece shook his head.

"Nothing illegal about changing your name, especially considering—" My defense of Carly was cut off by Gail, who waved an angry hand in my direction.

"No. But what is illegal is luring your sorority sisters into a Ponzi scheme and then fleeing the jurisdiction prior to indictment."

A stunned silence descended on the lobby as everyone tried to reconcile that news with the image of a friendly, helpful cheerleader with blonde hair and deep dimples.

"Oh God," Denny moaned.

His breath was coming faster, and Jake moved closer, taking him by the arm and leading him to a bench.

"What's wrong? Is it the smoke?" Bethany asked, kneeling next to the bench.

"I just thought—I'm—there was a contract—and photos. She showed me photos," he stammered, reaching into his shirt pocket and pulling out his phone. "She sent me photos from her meeting with the casino people. It was a done deal."

"Photos of what?" Bethany glanced up at me and Jake, her forehead furrowed.

"The casino. The casino we're buying." Denny looked at her, imploring her to understand, but Bethany just shook her head.

Oh no. This was starting to make more sense. Was this why Carly was dogging me and asking about the resort's accounting? Maybe it explained why I found her in the business office this morning. If she knew Max was bidding, maybe she was trying to do reconnaissance on her competition.

"Who is buying what casino? *My* casino?" Max asked, but it was more of a shout.

"Carly. And a lot of other investors." The director leaned forward, rested his forehead on his knees, and tried to breathe normally.

"Oh, man, don't tell me you bought into that scheme," Reece said.

All heads in the room swiveled to the actor.

"What scheme?" Jake asked.

Reece shook his head. "Carly's investment opportunity. She wanted to buy a casino. Or rather, she wanted her rich friends to buy the casino. She'd just take a piece of the business as her fee for putting together the deal."

"Carly was trying to buy the Lucky Penny?" I asked.

He shrugged. "She tried last year to get something going in Las Vegas but got priced out. Too many competitors. So she focused on Tahoe."

"What made her think she could raise that much money?" Jordan asked.

Denny groaned, and Bethany patted his back awkwardly.

"Oh God. I gave her so much money. So much." Denny looked like he might be sick, and I took a step back to give him some space, bumping into Quinn.

"Who else gave money to Carly?" Quinn asked.

"I don't know. Lots of people," Denny said. "Important people. Actors. Producers. Crew members. If they had the money, she'd sell them a share."

Quinn squeezed my shoulder. "Did Lorelei Arens invest?"

My heart sank at his question, but I understood his concern. She did seem vulnerable, and her caretaker was possibly a con artist.

"I don't know," Denny mumbled into his lap.

Jake finished reading the papers that Gail had handed him and stepped forward.

"We need to find both Lorelei and Carly. Jordan, Bethany, and Miranda have checked the lodge. We need to search the cabins."

He quickly divided up the people present into pairs—but left me out.

"What about me?"

"There's just the upper cabins left, and you can't walk up," he said.

"I'm fine," I said.

"She can take the golf cart," Jordan volunteered.

Jake glowered, but I smiled. "Yes, I can."

"Not alone. Bethany, you go with her," he said.

My smile disappeared. "Why?"

"Because she's armed. And so am I. So Quinn and I will go hit up the lower cabins. You and Bethany take the upper cabins. Gail will escort Jordan and Reece and search outbuildings, the garden, and the footpaths," Jake said.

He glanced down at Denny, still rocking back and forth on the bench. "Max, you keep an eye on Denny."

Max nodded but frowned at the man-child in plaid, still moaning about his lost money. "Buck up, there, Weber. You have a contract, right?"

"A contract with a con artist!" he whined.

"Tough break," Max said, patting him on the back.

Quinn pulled me aside as Bethany and Jake ran upstairs to get their weapons.

"Are you all right? What did Jake mean about you not walking that far?" he asked, his blue eyes concerned.

"I just twisted my ankle. It's fine," I said.

He nodded, and I debated telling him that I knew about Bethany, but then his question about Lorelei made me pause. I really hoped he wasn't still in love with her. But he seemed so concerned about her. And right in front of Bethany. Who probably had no idea why because Quinn likely hadn't told her that whole sordid story.

So there was yet another secret I had to keep. *Christ.* I was just going to keep my mouth shut and not say anything until I could escape the resort and get back to my normal life.

CHAPTER EIGHTEEN

The golf cart was like driving a bumper car and would have been fun, if we weren't on a mission to find a con artist. And if we weren't navigating through thick brown smoke that had grown more dense and dark since I was outside last. The sun was setting, but we weren't getting a sunset tonight. I couldn't even see a horizon.

"Which one is Lorelei's cabin?" Bethany asked.

"It's toward the top of the loop," I said, urging the little car forward up a steep curve in the road.

There was no traffic on the narrow lanes through the resort, and all the guests were wisely inside, trying to escape the horrible air outside. This gave an eerie silence and sense of emptiness in the gloom. I brushed a light dusting of ash from my arm and realized that we weren't just getting smoke from the fire any longer. The road was also speckled with gray ash. I tried not to breathe too deeply.

"So, uh, listen. Thank you for not saying anything to Jake. You didn't have to do that. I appreciate it," Bethany said.

I kept my focus on the road ahead and gritted my teeth.

"Yeah, sure," I said. This just wasn't a topic I wanted to dive into, especially at that moment. But then my curiosity got the better of me. "What is going on with you two and why? I mean, you just met him. And he's a witness. And has a felony conviction. Doesn't this break all of the rules?"

I glanced in her direction, but it was hard to read her face in the dim light. If anything, she looked as puzzled as I felt.

"I don't know what happened. I just thought, for once in my life, I wasn't going to give up something I wanted, just because I was worried about what other people thought. I've never done anything this crazy, but it... I don't know. It felt right, even though I know it's not."

"You could have said no."

"Well, he wasn't exactly the one asking."

"What?" I turned toward her so suddenly, the cart swerved, and I had to straighten out before ramming a garbage can.

"I was trying to get away from Carly, and he helped me by manufacturing a phone call, said it was from you. I was able to get away from the spa and then ended up hiding in his room when she came looking for me. And one thing led to another, and I just went for it."

Huh. That wasn't what I expected to hear.

"All my life, I have done everything by the book. For once, I just wanted to have some fun."

Somehow, I didn't doubt that she'd always played by the rules. Mostly because she never looked like she was having fun.

"And now that you've had your fun, what are you going to do with Quinn? He's a great guy. He deserves to be more than your disposable sexy-times bad boy."

"I don't know. He's just incredible. I've never known anyone like him."

Her voice was softer and thoughtful. She ran a hand across her face, brushing off ash, but leaving a smudge under her nose that looked a little like a mustache. I started to tell her about it but decided against it. We might be talking, but it didn't mean we were friends.

"If you hurt him, if you are mean to him, if you treat him like he's a criminal and you're embarrassed to be seen with him—" I had no threat to follow up with, but Bethany nodded quickly.

"No, I would never do that."

"Yeah, right," I said, barely under my breath.

She shook her head. "I mean it, Miranda. Quinn is— He's not like other guys."

Her voice dropped, and she stared straight ahead, her serious expression only marred by her Hitler mustache.

"Anyway, I know you don't trust me, but that won't happen."

I shrugged. "Okay, we'll see."

She seemed sincere, but I'd seen her reaction when she learned about Quinn's conviction.

We rode in silence through the eerie, smoky, tree-lined street, past the cabins on the upper road. When the road stopped climbing, I pressed down on the accelerator, but the golf cart wasn't built for speed. Which was a shame because I really wanted to reach our destination as soon as I could before Bethany decided to resume our conversation.

"So, are you and Jake finally going to take the plunge and be open about your relationship?" Bethany asked, her voice hesitant.

There was no use denying it to her, since she'd just seen us in the mother of all lip-locks. But I wasn't sure exactly how to explain what was going on between us.

"We haven't had a relationship, until now."

"Really? He's crazy about you."

"Oh. Really?"

"Don't be an idiot. You know he is."

"Well, uh. Okay." I guess I knew that, but things were still unsettled and unsaid.

"Do you not feel the same way about him?"

"Of course I do," I said.

"Then why aren't you two together?"

"It's complicated."

"Because he's an agent?"

"Yeah."

"And you were once charged with fraud."

"Yeah. And because he was the one who arrested me, he works with the people who prosecuted me. He'll have to deal with the fallout of dating a former criminal defendant."

Bethany looked away, and her sharp features softened. "I didn't make that any easier for you two, did I?"

"No, you didn't. But it wasn't just you."

She sighed. "Well, the least I can do is draw fire away from you guys, I guess. I'll start dating an actual felon. That will give the gossips something to talk about."

She gave me a wry smile, and despite the tension and my long-held feelings for her, I laughed.

"That would probably help."

"Since we're talking and everything, I will admit that I had reservations about Jake and you, but it wasn't any of my business, and I tried to keep that to myself."

"But you were always giving me dirty looks."

"I wasn't giving you dirty looks."

I whipped my head around and stared at her—her direct eye contact, impassive, slightly judgmental.

"Yeah, you were. You're doing it right now."

She snorted. "I get that a lot. I've been told I have resting bitch face."

I bit my lip to prevent a laugh. "Oh. Well, that probably makes you good at your job."

Bethany laughed, but it sounded unpracticed and nervous. "I guess so. The bureau has made some progress in adding women to the ranks, but sometimes it feels like I have to prove that I'm tougher than any of my male coworkers. If I look like I'm slightly pissed off all the time, nobody messes with me. But it's hell on my social life."

I shook my head. I couldn't believe I was having an actual conversation with Bethany that didn't involve throwing jabs at each other. In fact, I even sort of felt sorry for her.

I parked the golf cart across the short driveway to Lorelei's cabin, and Bethany reverted to her usual all-business mode, bitch face and all. Stepping out of the cart, she pulled a gun from her holster and looked back at me.

"I don't suppose you'd stay here," she said.

I shook my head. "I'll stay behind you. I know the drill."

She nodded toward the house, and I followed her up the walk to the tall oak and glass front door. She knocked, waited, and then knocked again harder.

"Ms. Arens, open up. This is the FBI."

I jumped at Bethany's loud order and had a mini flashback to the FBI coming into my office more than two years earlier. Pulling myself together, I took a deep breath, immediately regretting that because of the smoke.

I turned away, rubbing my nose again from the irritants in the air and saw that our footprints left a trail in the ash on the walkway. And there was another trail leading away—a smaller and single set of prints. And they looked familiar, like running shoes.

Bethany tried the knob, and the door opened silently, a rush of cold air-conditioned air rushing out to greet us. Motioning for me to wait, she stepped into the foyer and then disappeared around a corner. I took out my phone to take a photo of the footprints but then realized that I needed something to indicate the size of the shoe-print. Glancing around, my gaze fell on a stack of magazines on a table in the entryway, so I stepped in and grabbed one. It was the same size as the tourism magazine that Jake had used, so I put it down next to the print and snapped a half-dozen photos.

"The downstairs is empty," Bethany said, appearing at the front door. "I'm going to check upstairs."

I nodded and stepped back into the foyer, feeling the chill of the air-conditioning on my arms. I shut the door behind me. The house was cold in contrast to the warm outdoor air, but it was also free of the heavy smoke.

Bethany didn't say anything, just started up the stairs, her gun in her hand. I followed several steps behind and listened for any noise, but other than the whirr of the air conditioner, the house was silent. At the top of the stairs, Bethany turned right and pushed open a door.

"Oh, crap."

She ran into the room, checked the closet and the bathroom, and then waved me in. Lorelei was lying on the tile floor in front of the fireplace, her long dark hair fanned out and tangled. Her face was even more pale, nearly blue-white, and when Bethany and I turned her over, her skin was cool to the touch.

I pressed two fingers to her neck and felt the faint pulse, while Bethany checked the bathroom and dressing room off the bedroom. "She's alive."

Bethany returned, gun in hand and constantly scanning the room. "They're clear. Stay here, and I'm going to check the other rooms up here. Call the main building, and get an ambulance."

I scrambled to the bedside table and dragged the phone with me to the floor, pulling a comforter off the king-sized bed too. I rolled Lorelei off the tile and onto the carpet and covered her body. The temperature in the house was in the low 60s—bearable if you were wearing clothes, but Lorelei was wearing only a thin cotton T-shirt that came to the middle of her thighs.

The lodge phone rang as I cradled the receiver between my

shoulder and ear, studying Lorelei while I waited for someone to answer. There was no blood on her head, no injury that I could see. Her lips were pale, nearly blue with cold. Her skin was clammy. Her pulse erratic. I glanced around the room, and my gaze fell on a plastic amber bottle under the bed. I picked it up and read the label. A strong prescription painkiller—a large bottle of it—completely empty.

Lorelei's behavior suddenly made much more sense. The blank expressions, the loopy and passive way she interacted with everyone. The way Carly made all her decisions, directed her off-screen, just as Denny had directed her on-screen.

Bethany returned, a handful of papers in her hand.

"These look familiar?"

She handed me the paperwork, and I handed her the empty bottle in trade.

"Damn it," I whispered, looking at the dozen pages of correspondence and other paperwork about the Lucky Penny Casino. Included in the paperwork was the page torn from my binder.

Carly had been the one in my room. The thought chilled me, as much as the cold air pumping into the room. Even more chilling was wondering where Carly was at that moment.

"Oh, shit," Bethany said, reading the label on the pill bottle. She pulled Lorelei up to a sitting position and shook her. "Lorelei! Wake up!"

"No one is answering at the lodge," I said, hanging up the phone.

"Let's get her downstairs and to the cart," she said.

"No-o-o-o," Lorelei moaned.

Her head lolled to one side, and her eyes fluttered open briefly.

"Come on, wake up," Bethany said, shaking her again. "Stay with me."

She pulled the limp actress up and dragged her to the bed, and then looked at me. "Can you help me get her out of here?"

I nodded, folded the papers and stuffed them in my pocket, and then between us we got Lorelei standing. I wasn't as helpful as Bethany needed, limping on a sore ankle, but we got the actress upright enough so Bethany could loop an arm around her waist.

"Sorry," Lorelei whispered.

"What?" I turned and saw her wide blue eyes were open. Glazed over and unfocused, but open.

"I never should have..." Her voice trailed off, and her eyes closed.

Bethany gave her a slight slap on the face and hefted Lorelei so we could drag her down the hall. She was so tiny, I'd be surprised if she was a hundred pounds. But it was a hundred pounds of dead weight, and it was taking both of us to navigate her down the stairs.

"Never should have what, Lorelei?" Bethany asked, trying to keep her awake.

Lorelei tilted her head back to stare at Bethany. "I'm a horrible person."

Her hoarse response was barely loud enough to hear. I would have nodded in agreement, but since the woman was on death's door, I kept my feelings to myself.

"I'm sure that's not true," Bethany said with a grunt, as she took the first step down the staircase, carrying most of Lorelei's weight. There wasn't room for both of us to go down the flight of stairs with her between us, so she turned backward and let Lorelei's feet bounce down the carpeted steps.

"It's true," Lorelei said, trying to look up at Bethany's face. "I ruined his life."

Yes, but this was not the time or place to talk about it.

"I'm sure you didn't," Bethany said, sounding like she wasn't paying attention as she maneuvered Lorelei around the corner and down the next short flight of steps.

"Quinn didn't deserve that. He was only trying to help me."

At the mention of Quinn's name, Bethany stopped and stared down at the actress in her arms and then up at me. I looked away. I couldn't confirm anything Lorelei said, as anything I knew about Quinn's conviction was covered by attorney-client confidentiality.

"What are you talking about?"

Lorelei's head drooped forward, her chin resting on her chest. I ran down the few steps to her and picked up her feet so Bethany and I could carry her that way out to the cart.

"What is she talking about?"

I shrugged.

"I didn't mean to...hurt him." Lorelei's voice was fading.

Bethany struggled not to drop her and get the front door open, and we managed to get outside and shuffle down the walkway in the now dark and gloomy night.

"I never meant for him to go to prison," Lorelei whispered, and the outdoor security light on the corner of the cabin caught the fat tear that rolled down her face.

"Oh my God," Bethany breathed, her eyes wide and staring at me.

"I should have done something. But I didn't. I can't do this any longer." She was crying now, openly, and with each ragged breath, her sobs grew. "I can't take it."

We wrestled Lorelei to the cart and leaned her against the hood, where she stood unsteadily and then pitched forward. We both reached out and caught her.

"What is she talking about, Miranda?" Bethany asked in a shaky voice.

I didn't answer right away as I considered what I could or should share with Bethany. As much as I'd love to shout to the world that Quinn had been set up, I couldn't. If Bethany wanted the truth, she needed to talk to Quinn. He could decide what to share.

"I can't say."

Bethany's lips pursed, and she blew out a frustrated breath. "Because you work for his lawyer?"

I nodded. "You should talk to Quinn about this."

She frowned and upped her bitch-face game. Then she turned back to Lorelei, put her hands on the actress's shoulders, and straightened her. Lorelei's head bobbled, her eyes blinked, but she looked at Bethany.

"Lorelei, what did you do to Quinn?"

"I don't think you should—" Lorelei was barely conscious. No matter how much I despised her, it didn't feel right to let a trained FBI agent interrogate the heavily inebriated woman.

"Lorelei, can you hear me? Tell me what happened."

Bethany ignored my protest, and Lorelei nodded slowly.

"It was my fault."

"What was your fault?"

"Those were my drugs."

I closed my eyes and felt a weight lifted from my shoulders, just having one other person know the truth about Quinn. When I opened my eyes, Bethany was standing still, holding on to Lorelei's shoulders. Her eyes were wide and her mouth slightly open.

"He went to prison for you?"

Lorelei's tears started again. "Yes."

For a moment, I thought she might drop Lorelei, but then she took a deep breath. "Oh God."

"Let's get back to the lodge," I said, taking one of Lorelei's arms and helping her to stand.

"I can't believe she— What a— Two years!"

Bethany's stunned reply was familiar. I'd had that same

thought when I'd snooped through Quinn's file and learned the truth of his conviction. It was an unfathomable act—to let someone take the blame for something you did and let them suffer the lifelong consequences of it.

"Why are we helping her again?" Bethany spat out.

"I'm sorry!" Lorelei's cry was loud and anguished and punctuated by sobs. "I can't stand myself. I hate that I did it."

Bethany and I froze, watching her pale face contort and turn splotchy in the orange glow of the security light.

"Why would you do that to him?" Bethany asked, her brow furrowed.

"Because I'm a horrible, horrible person," she gasped. "I have to see him. I have to tell him I'm sorry."

"Yeah, that will make it all better," Bethany muttered but then helped me get her closer to the back seat of the cart.

"That's why I took the pills. I can't stand it," she said, between hiccupping sobs.

I glanced between Bethany and Lorelei. "How many pills, Lorelei?"

Lorelei raised her face to mine, her expression defiant. "All of them."

"Oh, for fuck's sake," I said. "She needs to get her stomach pumped. We need to get her to the lodge now."

Bethany's emergency training kicked in, and she and I wrestled the petite and inconsolable woman toward the bench seat in the back.

"Just leave me alone," she cried suddenly, kicking me in the shin with her bare foot. It was barely a tap, she was so weak.

"No, damn it. You're not taking the easy way out," I said, trying to fit her between the seats and into the back of the cart.

She twisted as if to run away, but Bethany caught her.

"I don't want to—" Lorelei hiccupped again, sobbed. And then threw up.

"Oh, crap!" I jumped backward and was mostly able to avoid the torrent of what I assumed was a nearly toxic mix of mineral water and prescription meds. Bethany was not quite as lucky, and her bitch-face was cranked up to eleven as she stopped trying to be gentle and forced Lorelei into the back of the cart. Then she grabbed the keys from me and took the driver's seat. I jumped in the passenger side and turned to keep an eye on our patient, who was lying on her side on the bench seat, still crying loudly.

"Well, the good news is she doesn't have to have her stomach pumped now," I said.

Bethany scowled and started the golf cart, pulling back onto the road without saying anything.

CHAPTER NINETEEN

The little cart bounced down the road and around the hairpin turn and soon the lodge came into view. Bethany parked in the parking lot nearest to the front of the lodge. The ash swirled underfoot as we stepped out of the cart and wrestled the slightly less hysterical actress out of the backseat. She leaned heavily against Bethany as we started toward the front steps, and I peered into the darkness, looking for Jake or the rest of our search party. But all I saw were the yellow lights pouring out of the lodge's windows into the gloomy night and the orange glow that lit the sky to the east, where the fire burned steadily on the other side of the mountain ridge.

Inside, the lobby was empty.

"Hey!" Bethany yelled, dumping Lorelei on a sofa. "Anyone here?"

Footsteps in the hallway grew faster and louder, and Quinn and Jake rounded the corner. Relief flooded me at the sight of Jake. His dark hair was flecked with ash, and his black T-shirt now looked a mottled grey. He bent over Lorelei and tilted her head back. She opened her eyes briefly.

"What did she take?"

Bethany recited the prescription while Quinn and I stood back and watched them check her vitals.

"She needs a doctor," Jake said.

Quinn moved quickly to the reception counter, leaned over it to grab the phone, and dialed 9-1-1. After explaining where we were and what the problem was, he hung up and glanced around the empty lobby, looking as helpless as I felt.

"Where is everyone?" I asked.

"The director started having an asthma attack, so Max drove him out to the gate to meet up with a fire crew and get him some oxygen. They transported him down to the hospital," Quinn said, his eyes on Lorelei, who was lying limp on the plaid sofa.

"What about Gail?"

He turned and looked at me, his blue eyes serious. "She's still out with Jordan and Reece, checking the garden and pool areas."

Jake stood and left Lorelei in Bethany's care, walking over to the counter. "You got through to 9-1-1?"

Quinn nodded. "They're sending an ambulance, but they're not sure how long it will take to get up the roads because of the closures."

Lorelei moaned, and Quinn walked over to the couch, kneeling next to Bethany. Jake leaned back against the counter next to me, and we watched as Quinn reached up and wiped the ash mustache from Bethany's upper lip. Her hand flew to her mouth, and she blushed and gave him a small smile.

"I don't suppose there was any sign of Carly at the house?" Jake asked.

"There was this," I said, pulling my phone from my pocket, along with the paperwork from Carly's room. Leaving the papers aside, I found the photographs of footsteps in the ash. "Do those look familiar?"

Jake took out his phone and compared the two shots side-by-side. "You think it was Carly in the casino?"

"Denny said that she sent him photos. Maybe she was trying to convince her investors to send her more money to close the deal."

He nodded toward the documents on the counter. "What's this?"

"Bethany found it in Carly's room. It was taken from my room this morning. Or last night. I'm not sure when." I unfolded the pages and smoothed them out on the marble counter.

"Are you saying someone broke into your room?" Jake's jaw tensed, and his eyes darkened.

"Yes, I think so," I said. "But this doesn't make sense. Why would she just take this one page? It's just the front page of the latest financial report for Whispering Pines. I had the whole report there, which would have been more valuable if she were snooping for information."

Jake frowned. "Maybe she wanted more, but this was all she could get before she got interrupted."

"But why? I mean, this is important financial documentation for the resort, but it wouldn't be useful for her. Not unless she wanted to—" I stared at the page, my mind buzzing. "Wait, this isn't right."

I closed my eyes, pictured the page that I'd read previously. I could see the figures, the columns, the categories. I looked again at the page and noted the differences. The numbers were a little off, and this page didn't have the three holes punched in the side, but I could see the shadows of the rings. It was a copy of the original, and someone had altered the income levels to take off the first digits—dropping the income of Whispering Pines Resort by millions.

Thumbing through the pages, I found a fax cover sheet addressed to a company in Reno.

"Oh no."

Carly had faxed the financial statement to a company with a

note explaining that this was the correct version of the books, and any other reports were fraudulent. It wasn't signed but was on Whispering Pines Resort letterhead. Suddenly it made sense why Carly was kissing up to me.

"She's trying to sabotage Max's offer," I said.

"It didn't work," Jake said. "They accepted his bid."

I wished Dottie were here and not at a bank of nickel slots in Carson City. I could use her more experienced take on this. I took a deep breath and thought through the consequences of the fax. "We have the books, the bank statements, so we can show the true financial records."

"It's either a really stupid plan—" Jake said.

"Or she's desperate."

A desperate Carly could be resourceful. But could she also be dangerous? I spread the last of the documents across the marble top and glanced at them. One stood out, a fax cover sheet and a note written in loopy feminine handwriting.

"She faxed this to the Nevada Gaming Commission," Jake said, pulling the letter toward us.

To whom it may concern: I am an employee at Whispering Pines Resort at Lake Tahoe, and I have knowledge of an underground gambling operation on the premises. I can't tell you my name because I'll lose my job, but I wanted you to know that Mr. Emmerson and his managers are taking a cut of the profits. I have proof. Signed, A Concerned Citizen.

My eyes widened at the words. "My God. What is she up to?"

"Nothing good," Jake said. "Max is downstairs in the security office, looking through the surveillance video. I'm going to go down and see what he's found. When Gail gets back, can you tell her to come find me?"

I nodded, still staring at the papers and wondering how Max was going to take the news.

"Are you going to be okay here?" Jake said, putting a hand on my waist.

I looked up and met his eyes. "I'll be fine."

He glanced back at Quinn and Bethany, who were draping a throw over Lorelei, then gave me a quick kiss.

"Get your bags ready to go. I expect we're going to be evacuating the resort tonight."

I shivered at what that meant. The fire breaking through and burning over the ridge, racing down the mountain toward the historic lodge.

He checked in with Bethany, then took the stairs down to the lower level. I reached into my pocket to get my room key, but it wasn't there.

"Damn it," I muttered. It must have fallen out in the cart. I flexed my ankle, felt almost no pain, so I decided to risk the smoky air to find my room key.

I told Bethany and Quinn I'd be back in a few minutes, then left the lodge through the main entrance and stepped out into the thick haze. Immediately, my eyes itched, and after a few breaths, I could feel my lungs tighten. I kept my head down and pulled up the collar of my T-shirt, trying to use it as a mask.

I turned left at the parking lot and saw a figure dart between cars.

My heart rate soared as I recognized the small figure in trendy yoga pants and a black tank top. Her blonde hair was pulled back into a ponytail, and it was unmistakably Carly.

As I watched, she tried the handles of several cars, but they were locked. Facing away from me, she dropped an overstuffed gym bag on the curb and put her hands on her hips. She had no idea I was standing behind her, and I froze, wondering what to do. Go back into the lodge and get Bethany? By the time I got help, Carly would disappear again. And from the size of her luggage, that looked like her plan.

Before I could make a decision, she whirled around and saw me. Even in the dusky orange glow of the parking lot lights, I could see the emotions cross her face—shock, fear, anger. She quickly replaced that with a fake smile.

"Oh, hi, Miranda! What are you doing out here?"

Had I not known about her side business as a con artist, I'd never have guessed anything was wrong by the sunny tone in her voice.

"Hi, Carly, what are you doing?" I asked cautiously, unsure how much to tell her that I knew. If I could get closer, I could probably tackle her and pin her to the ground. She was small and carb-deprived. I could take her. But I'd feel better if I had Sarah's stun gun with me. I made a note to get one for myself.

Carly sighed dramatically. "Lorelei called. She needs her stuff brought to her, but I can't figure out in the dark which of these is our rental car."

"Lorelei called you? Where is she?"

"Oh, she headed out when the smoke started getting heavier. She's really sensitive to it. I'm going to meet her at the airport, and we'll be back as soon as Denny says shooting can resume."

I took a few steps closer and saw that she was wearing running shoes—brightly colored with pink laces and yellow accents. I would bet my last dollar that the tread would match the photos in the casino and leading away from Lorelei's cabin.

"The roads are closed," I said. "You can't leave until they give us the all-clear."

Carly swallowed and took a step backward. "Oh, I'm sure they won't mind if I leave. One less person to have to keep an eye on, right?"

Her giggle was so glaringly out of place in the smoky hell we were in, it sounded maniacal.

"Why don't you just come back into the lodge, and wait with us?"

223

She shook her head. "No, I really need to get to Lorelei. She's not doing so good with this smoke. We've got a plane on standby at the airport. As soon as I get there, we can take off."

I glanced at her bag on the curb. She was also wearing a smaller cross-body tote that rested at her hip. It, too, looked packed to the brim. Carly was trying to make a quick getaway.

Something on my face must have tipped her off, because the perky grin faded, and she squared her shoulders.

"I need to get out of here," she said, looking around. The valet station behind her was empty, but the door was cracked open, and she bolted for it, throwing the door open.

"Carly, no!" I shouted and ran after her.

She emerged from the station with a fist full of keys that she crammed into her small tote. Then she hefted her duffel bag and swung it at me, taking my legs out from under me. I landed in some soft mulch, narrowly missing an arrangement of three large rocks in the landscaped border between the curb and the manicured lawn.

"Son of a bitch!" I scrambled out of the dirt and tried to grab at Carly, but she darted behind a small hatchback. She fumbled with the keys in her bag but had so many that it was going to take her all night to match the right set with the right car.

"Carly, we found Lorelei. She was nearly dead," I said, testing my ankle as I stepped off the curb. It was still sore, but my fall hadn't injured it any further.

Carly snorted. "Nearly, huh. Not good enough."

That perky and caffeinated cheerleader persona was gone, replaced by someone bitter and resentful. Someone I suspected was Carly's true self.

"Max got the casino," I said.

She looked up and scowled, then moved to the next car. "Doesn't matter. I don't need to buy a casino now. Do you know how much money I have in the bank now?"

It was money she'd taken from Denny Shawn Weber and other people who trusted her.

"It's not your money. It's your investors' funds."

She shook her head and rolled her eyes as if she couldn't believe I was so naive.

"You need to come inside," I said, trying to channel Bethany's commanding tone. If it didn't work on Carly, maybe someone inside would hear me. Unfortunately, the effort to raise my voice only caused me to cough as the smoke irritated my throat.

"Come on, come on," Carly muttered, and I heard a click.

God damn it! How had she managed to get one of the cars open? I lunged for her but came up short when she whirled around, pulling her hand out of her tote.

In it she held a small silver handgun, which was pointed at me.

"Jesus, Carly," I said, my voice escaping on a shocked exhale.

"I'm leaving now. You're coming with me, so you don't go in there and raise all hell," she said, waving the gun at the car. "Passenger seat. Now."

CHAPTER TWENTY

I froze for a second, weighing my options. Run? Not a great plan, considering we were in a parking lot, and other than hiding behind a car, I didn't have many options for cover. Refuse to go? And then she'd probably shoot me. She was angry and apparently quite evil.

Carly fixed her gaze on me, a smirk on her face, and raised the gun. "Be a shame to shoot you, when you could just get out of the car at the bottom of the hill."

From behind Carly, I saw a figure move in the shadows and then heard a shout. A man emerged from the dark, his features obscured, but with his broad shoulders and crew-cut hair, I recognized him instantly as Mark Tripp.

"Mark! Go get Quinn," I yelled. "They're inside."

But instead of turning, Mark kept coming toward us, and I worried he hadn't seen the gun in Carly's hand.

"Get help!" I screamed, my throat nearly raw from the smoke.

Mark kept coming, and Carly smirked.

"Hey, cutie," he said, jogging up to the car. "You need some help?"

He leaned against the car and gave Carly a wink. I guessed that meant I wasn't "cutie."

"Put that in the trunk, okay?" Carly said, that buoyant tone back in her voice. "Miranda's going to come with us."

Mark glanced my way, raised an eyebrow, and then shrugged at Carly. "Whatever you want, babe."

These two were the worst couple ever.

"I'm not coming with you," I said.

"Yeah, you are," Carly said, tilting her head. "Because if I let you go here, you'll run in and tell your boyfriend. Or, maybe you'll tell your friend's husband. I know you've got a thing for him."

I didn't really want to explain all that, so I just shut up and stared at the gun. Mark slammed the trunk lid and opened the passenger side door for me. Carly climbed in the driver's seat and rolled down the window. Mark leaned in and kissed her.

"Aloha, babe," he said. "See you in a few days."

He jogged into the darkness. A few moments later, a motor cycle roared to life, and a lone taillight disappeared into the haze. Carly started the car and backed out of the parking lot, and my heart beat erratically in my throat. I'd taken a self-defense course and vividly recalled the advice: never get into a car willingly, never let your attacker take you to a different location.

My fingers found the window control on the armrest, and I pressed it. Carly hit the accelerator and poked the gun into my ribs.

"Don't even think about screaming for help," she said.

The road was passing by the front of the lodge, and I looked out helplessly at the large front veranda, knowing that two FBI agents with guns were just inside, and I couldn't do anything to get their attention.

The pressure in my ribs let up as Carly shifted gears, and

I said a prayer of thanks that she stole a car with a manual transmission. It gave me an opening. I reached across her and hit the steering wheel with all my force, sounding the horn.

"Stop it!" she screeched, throwing an elbow at my face. I ducked, but she caught me in the chin, and my head slammed back against the headrest.

As I sat there dazed, I saw the front door of the lodge fly open and a figure storm out.

"Jake!" I screamed.

Carly hit the gas, and the car lurched forward. I grabbed the wheel and yanked it to the right, trying to aim for the wide lawn that encircled the lodge.

I missed.

The little car hit the water feature with enough momentum that we were airborne for what felt like minutes, before plummeting back to earth with a bone-jarring thump. The car's airbags deployed, and I had the sensation that I was drowning—in the fabric bag, in the water, in the smoke that still lay like a blanket around us. I was tangled in the seatbelt and struggled to escape the car as water rushed in through the open window. Even though intellectually, I knew that the water wasn't deep enough to submerge the car, I fought frantically to extricate myself.

The door flew open, and Jake yanked me out of the car, into waist-deep water. Quinn raced to the other side of the car, pulling the driver's door open to rescue Carly, who was screaming and struggling against the seatbelt.

"Quinn, she has a gun!"

It was too late. An instant later, two loud pops sounded, and Quinn fell backward. He sat down hard on the rocks bordering the pond, his right hand clasping his left bicep, his legs still in the water.

Carly started wading to the edge of the pond, her gun held up and out of the water.

"Stay away from me," she screamed.

Jake pushed me behind him as Bethany raced past both of us. Sloshing through the water with impressive speed, she tackled Carly. They both went under with a splash, and the gun flew out of Carly's hand.

Bethany surfaced, her hair plastered to her face, and she pulled Carly out of the water and dragged her to the edge of the water feature.

"You bitch! You tried to drown me!" Carly's foot lashed out, catching Bethany in the side of the head.

I winced at the contact. Jake started toward the brawling duo, the smaller of which was starting to crawl away from the pond, still screaming.

But before he could get around the small car in the middle of the pond, Bethany rebounded and scrambled out of the pond, wrestling Carly to the ground. Carly swung a fist at Bethany, but Bethany blocked the shot, reared back and clocked the other woman in the chin. The blow knocked her silent, if not unconscious, and Carly's screeching was replaced by the metallic click of handcuffs being locked in place and the sound of water rushing over the fabricated falls and into the pond.

Once Carly was secured, Bethany ran to Quinn's side. Shouts from the lodge drew my attention, and I turned to see Gail and Jordan running toward us across the lawn.

Jake helped me out of the water, then read Carly her rights. She was stunned but not out for the count, so he helped her to her feet and handed her off to Gail.

Red lights lit up the trees as an ambulance rolled up the drive to the resort, adding to the surreal atmosphere. Jake flagged them down and pointed at Quinn when the driver rolled down the window.

"We've got a gunshot victim and, in the lodge, a possible overdose," he said.

The driver raised an eyebrow. "You've had a busy evening. But I don't know if we've got room for two."

"I'll drive Quinn to the hospital," Bethany said. "It's a flesh wound, not life-threatening, but he needs medical attention."

Jordan volunteered to get a car for her to take, then ran off. Jake turned to me.

"How are you? Are you hurt?"

I shook my head. I was sore from the impact when the car hit the water feature, but otherwise, I had no complaints. And in light of the other more serious injuries and medical issues going on, I wasn't about to mention my minor aches.

He grabbed me and hugged me tight with a sigh. I rested my head on his chest and listened to his heartbeat. My arms encircled his waist, and I never wanted to let go. Too soon, he pulled away.

"I need to help Gail with getting Carly booked. Can you help the EMTs with Lorelei?"

I nodded and reluctantly let go of him.

"Oh my God, Jake. Mark Tripp is still out there," I said, remembering the gaffer's good-bye to Carly. "I think he's working with Carly, and they're supposed to meet up in a couple days. I'd guess in Hawaii."

Jake grinned, then leaned down and kissed me quickly. "Thanks. I'll make sure and ask her about that."

The EMTs let me ride with them to the lodge, rather than make the squishy walk back to the lodge in water-soaked shoes.

I raced up the steps to the lodge and into the lobby. With all the excitement outside, I'd almost forgotten about Lorelei and hoped she hadn't choked on her own vomit or slipped into a coma or found more pills in the resort gift shop.

I didn't have to worry. Lorelei was sitting up on the plaid

sofa, resting against Reece Muir, who had his arms around her and was whispering in her ear. She still looked pale and wan, but there was a hint of a smile on her face. It wasn't much, but it was the happiest I'd seen her since I arrived at Whispering Pines.

Reece, too, looked happier as he looked up to see me and the paramedics run in. He held Lorelei's hand as they strapped her to the gurney.

"Can I ride with her?" he asked the young female EMT, who blushed and stammered an apology and something about regulations. I felt her pain. It was really hard to get to look at Reece and talk at the same time.

"Maybe you can ride with Bethany and Quinn," I suggested. "They're going to the hospital too."

He nodded, his eyes never leaving Lorelei's face. "I'll be right there. I won't leave you."

Her wide blue eyes filled with tears, and she nodded. "I love you," she said, her voice choking with emotion.

Reece bent down and rested his forehead against hers. "I love you," he whispered.

The EMT sighed, and her partner glared at her. I was on her side. That was romantic. Well, except that Lorelei had some vomit in her hair.

They wheeled the gurney out of the lodge, down the steps, and to the ambulance. I pointed out Jordan, who was at the valet station trying to find car keys that matched a car, thanks to Carly's grand theft auto.

"I can't thank you enough, Miranda," Reece said. "If you and Bethany hadn't gotten to the cabin, I don't know what might have happened to her."

I didn't want to think about that either. "Is she going to be all right? Do you know how many pills she took?"

He shook his head. "She's going to get help. And she's going to get away from people like Carly Malone. Or whatever her name is."

"Did you have any idea what she was doing?"

His jaw tensed, and his eyes narrowed. "Not a clue. When I look back, though, I think Carly was instrumental in causing Lorelei and me to break up. She's just always looking to move up to a larger target."

"What about Lorelei's drug problem?"

He looked down, and guilt crossed his handsome face. "I knew she took them for an old back injury. I had no idea she couldn't stop taking them. Or that Carly enabled her to take more and more of them."

We watched the ambulance pull out of the parking lot, the red lights flashing.

"That's going to be addressed too. And I won't let her go through that alone," he said.

"I wish you both all the best," I said, and to my surprise, I meant it.

Since I'd learned how Quinn had been duped into taking the fall for her on the drug charges, I'd held a deep grudge against the actress. But if Quinn could let that go, maybe I could too. As I watched Bethany walking with Quinn across the lawn, her arm around him and her head on his shoulder, I figured that if anyone wanted to carry that burden, she'd be just the one to do it.

Reece held out a hand, and I reached to shake it, but then he pulled me in for a hug. He smelled really good, but that might have been because I smelled like smoke and stagnant water. When he let me go, he gave me that patented smile, and it was like seeing an old crush.

"Hope to see you and Quinn again— Or is it Jake?" He glanced over at Bethany and Quinn and then back to me, then gave a shy smile and a shake of his head. "Sorry. It's not my place to judge."

"Oh, no, it's not like that—"

He held up a hand. "Hey, to each their own. I live in Holly-weird, so you can't shock me."

Oh God, my childhood crush thought I was a swinger. *Lovely*.

Before I could defend myself, Jordan managed to find keys to one of the cars in the lot, and Reece ran off to wave him down for a ride to the hospital. The car stopped, and Reece opened the back door for Bethany and Quinn, then climbed in the front with Jordan.

As the car drove down the lane toward South Lake Tahoe, another car drove in. Its headlights bounced off the trees and illuminated the drive. It wasn't another ambulance—it was a 1955 Chevy Bel Air. It was followed by a police car that stopped near the now-destroyed water feature where Gail and Jake stood with Carly.

Dottie parked in the road, threw open the door, and climbed out, surveying the scene.

"Well, looks like I missed all the excitement."

"Dottie! I thought the roads were closed. How did you get here?"

"Ha! I know a guy who works for the transportation department. Real mucky-muck. He got me an escort through the closed section," she said. Seeing my open mouth and shocked expression, she waved a hand. "Oh, they're going to reopen it shortly anyway. The fire's nearly contained. Just a lot of smoke now."

We walked back up to the lodge together.

"Well, we need to talk. First, you need to tell me what happened here."

"Carly Malone is a con artist who was trying to buy the Lucky Penny. Or maybe she was just trying to fleece her investors. Also, she may have tried to kill her boss with pills. Then she kidnapped me, and the car ended up in the water fountain," I said.

Dottie stopped at the top of the stairs and gave me a long look.

"How about that," she said slowly. "Okay, let's talk about your salary."

"My salary?"

"I'm not going to let someone who throws herself into her job so thoroughly get away," she said with a laugh and then patted my back, still wet from the pond. "Now, let's go get a couple of drinks, and you can tell me the long version of that story."

She held the door open for me.

"I think this is the beginning of a beautiful business association. If nothing else, I know you're going to keep me entertained."

CHAPTER TWENTY-ONE

A light breeze from the lake stirred the pine boughs, and the rustle mixed with the sounds of laughter and chatter from the crowd. All of the smoke from the fire last weekend had cleared out, and the skies were once again as clear as Lake Tahoe's famed water. The only clouds over Lake Tahoe this weekend were fluffy and white in the afternoon, turning a spectacular spectrum of pink and purple as Aunt Marie and Rob had exchanged their vows at sunset. Only a sliver of vibrant purple remained on the western horizon now, but the stars overhead in an indigo sky put on their own show.

"I have to say, I'm impressed at how well you held it together during the ceremony," Sarah said, appearing at my side with two tall flutes of champagne.

I was impressed with my resolve too, but only because I hadn't broken down in sobs while standing in front of eighty wedding guests. I tend to cry at weddings, but this one was extra special, so I had invested a good chunk of my income from Dottie in waterproof makeup. Then I really put it to the test, tearing up at the sweet and simple vows between two people I loved so much. Fortunately, most of the wedding guests were too busy dabbing at their own tears to notice how mine were flowing so freely.

"It was a beautiful wedding," I said, watching Aunt Marie and Rob pose for photos with friends from the bakery.

"It was," Sarah said, putting an arm around me. "Sorry Jake couldn't make it."

I was too. But, as usual, his job interrupted our plans. After Carly's arrest, Jake and Alex Marquez had tracked Mark Tripp to Hawaii. It had taken several days, but they had finally arrested him on Friday morning. It sounded like the FBI was building a strong case against him and Carly for taking millions from investors, though it was unclear when their plan changed from buying the casino to just running off with the investors' earnest money. But with all the extradition paperwork and procedures, Jake wasn't sure when he'd get back to California, so I was dateless at the wedding after all.

"So, that's an interesting development," Sarah said, nodding over the rim of her champagne flute toward Quinn and Bethany who were chatting with Rob's brother, a rancher from Tulsa, and Dottie Russell. Dottie wore another Chanel-inspired suit, this one an homage to Jackie Kennedy in pale pink with a stylish wide collar. At the end of a bedazzled leash, Duchess wore a matching pillbox hat, and Bub had gone with a white vest and mint-green bowtie.

I gave a noncommittal response, and Sarah looked at me. "I thought you and Bethany had raised the white flag, declared a truce in your ongoing feud."

"We don't have a feud. I just don't trust her. And she doesn't trust me."

Sarah shook her head. "Give her a chance. She's not that bad."

I whipped my head around and stared at my best friend. "You're taking her side?"

"If there's no feud, then there are no sides to take," she said. "I'm just saying that I sat next to her and Quinn during the wedding, and they seemed really happy."

I shrugged and downed the last of my champagne and studied the couple. Quinn had abandoned his suit jacket, and his left arm was in a sling. Bethany looked beautiful, of course, in a simple light green dress with matching strappy sandals. But instead of her usual confident posture, she hung back a little as Quinn introduced her to the other guests.

Was she embarrassed to be with him? I fumed at the thought.

"Didn't you read the Hollywood Tattler? You and Bethany are a crime-fighting duo responsible for saving America's sweetheart, Lorelei Arens. I read it online, so it must be true."

Sarah raised her glass in a mock toast. I groaned. The tabloids had been all over the story about Carly Malone, personal assistant to the stars, being arrested for fraud. The stories all quoted anonymous sources who sounded an awful lot like Reece Muir and Lorelei Arens. The scandal fueled Oscar-buzz around the two stars, even though the movie wouldn't be released for months.

"She's Canada's sweetheart," I corrected. "And she's in rehab for a pill addiction."

"I read that she's being treated for exhaustion. But, either way, it's all great publicity for *Purple Hearts*," Sarah said. "And you should make nice with Bethany. She's not going away."

I didn't respond, but I knew she was right. At least about Bethany not going away. She was Jake's partner, and now she was dating Quinn. Grabbing two glasses of champagne from a passing waiter, I made my way to the impossibly beautiful couple.

"Miranda, you look lovely," Quinn said, greeting me with a friendly kiss on the cheek. He looked happy and relaxed, and I tried to hide my inner anger at his date's reluctance to be seen with him.

"Thank you, and thank you both for coming. I know it means a lot to Rob and Marie," I said.

I held out one of the champagne flutes to Bethany who took it warily.

"Don't worry, I didn't roofie it," I said.

She smiled and laughed, then took a sip.

"I think Rob is breaking into a bottle of whiskey from one of his clients," I said, giving Quinn a nod toward the bridal table where several men were crowding around what must have been a very impressive bottle of booze.

Quinn grinned. "I can take a hint."

He turned to Bethany. "Do you mind if I leave you with Miranda for a moment?"

Bethany smiled, but her eyes betrayed her panic. She was clearly more skilled in reading body language than Quinn.

"Of course not," she said.

Quinn gave her a lingering kiss then made his way across the reception area. Bethany watched his retreating back with concern. Then she turned back to me.

"Did you want to talk to me?"

"Yeah. If you're so embarrassed to be seen with Quinn, why get involved with him?"

Her mouth opened at my blunt question, then slammed shut. She took a long drink of the champagne before answering me. "I don't know what you're talking about."

"Quinn Bishop is one of the finest people I've ever known. He's honest. He's a good man. You know he took the fall for someone else, someone who didn't deserve his sacrifice."

Her eyes widened at my anger. "I know that."

Her voice was low, nearly a hiss.

"You should be proud to be with him."

She took my elbow and steered me away from the crowd with the iron grip of someone who had been trained to do this.

"I am proud to be with Quinn. You don't know the pressure I'm under," she said.

"What, at work?" I asked. "If you can't be with him because you're a federal agent and he's a felon, then don't lead him on."

Bethany exhaled and gave me a steely glare. "You're a fine one to give advice about this. How long have you and Jake been sneaking around?"

It was my turn to be surprised.

"We're not sneaking around," I said, though that wasn't quite true. "And are you saying that Jake's coworkers wouldn't have a problem with him dating a former criminal defendant?"

She blinked and then looked down, but I saw a flash of something in her hazel eyes. Uncertainty? Guilt?

When she looked up, her expression had softened. "I've been thinking about what you said. I was wrong."

"What?" I wasn't sure I heard her right.

"I, uh, it's my fault. You and Jake not being together. It's my fault. And I'm very sorry. I treated you poorly. I believed rumors that I heard. I should have trusted his judgment. And I should never have judged you."

I sucked in a deep breath and then slowly exhaled, trying to absorb what Bethany was saying.

"I'm sorry." Her simple apology was sincere, and for the first time since I'd met Jake's partner, I didn't hate her.

"Oh." I had no idea what to do with an apology. "Thank you."

"And you're right about Quinn," she said, her face softening as she smiled. "He is great. I'm not embarrassed to be with him. Not at all."

I squinted at her. "You don't seem comfortable here."

She shrugged and sipped at the champagne. "Well, about a

third of the guests are defense attorneys who have cross-examined me. Including the groom."

Bethany gave a nervous laugh, causing my resolve to crack and a bit of sympathy to leak in.

"That's just their jobs. It's nothing personal."

She nodded. "I know."

"They're actually very nice people."

"I'm sure they are. I just wasn't sure how welcomed I'd be," she said.

I sighed. "Because of me."

She tilted her head and gave me a small smile. "A little."

Damn it. She was right. I was doing the same thing I accused her of doing.

"I am sorry about that. I wouldn't want you to feel uncomfortable here."

She gave me a curious glance. "Thank you."

Quinn cast a worried look in our direction, and we both smiled and waved. He looked relieved and returned to his conversation with Rob's former law partner.

"So, are we good?" Bethany asked.

"I guess so."

"I'm sure Jake will be happy to hear that. When is he going to be here anyway?"

"Last I heard, he was waiting for a flight back from Maui. He isn't going to make it to the wedding."

Bethany smiled and shook her head. "Didn't he call you? He and Alex were able to get a flight arranged to transport Mark Tripp back to Nevada. They flew into Reno this afternoon."

"No, he didn't mention that," I said, biting my lip. "I haven't heard from him since late yesterday."

Not that I was expecting Jake to check in regularly. I mean, technically, we hadn't even had a first date yet. Unless you count that whole breaking-and-entering episode as a date. Which I didn't. Still, knowing he had called Bethany and not me did sting a bit.

"Where's your phone?" Bethany asked.

"It's in my bag in the restaurant, where we got dressed for the wedding."

She laughed. "You're an idiot. Go check your phone."

Crap. She was right, again. I was an idiot. I headed toward the dressing room at the back of the restaurant, trying my best to dodge guests so I could confirm that Bethany was right. This was easier said than done. I was halfway across the patio when the cake was wheeled out, and I returned to watch Aunt Marie and Rob slice into a gorgeous creamy tower of buttercream-frosted wedding cake. Aunt Marie had made some beautiful wedding cakes in the thirty years that she'd owned the Sugar Plum Bakery, but this might be her best one yet.

Aunt Marie raised her glass of champagne and turned to me.

"I know it's customary for the maid of honor to make the toast, but I've never been one for tradition," she said. Her eyes started to tear up, and mine filled with tears in an immediate sympathetic response.

Clearing her throat, she continued, her free hand already wiping her eyes.

"I want to thank my beautiful and wonderful niece, Miranda, for being the best maid of honor," she said, her voice choking up. I blinked quickly in a vain attempt to keep my own tears at bay.

"Miranda, raising you has been the biggest honor of my life. I am so proud of you and love you so much."

I sniffed and swallowed the lump in my throat.

"And I know that a couple years ago, you were going through the lowest point of your life. But because of all the wonderful friends who are here today, who came together to support you and me, something incredible came out of that."

She turned to Rob with a shaky smile. "I found the love of my life."

The dam broke, and I sobbed into the paper I'd written my speech on. I wasn't going to be giving it now. I could barely see through the freely flowing tears. I managed to give the bride and groom a long hug, raised my glass with the rest of the guests and toasted their happy union. I caught a glimpse of Sarah dabbing at her eyes too, so I felt a little better about my public breakdown.

As soon as the restaurant staff began serving the cake, I grabbed my own slice and made a beeline for the dressing room in the restaurant. This time, I made it to the path at the edge of the patio before someone sought my attention.

"Miranda."

My first reaction was annoyance. But instantly that turned to recognition. I knew that voice.

I whirled around and found Jake standing just feet away. He wore his suit easily, somehow looking as comfortable in the formal attire as he did when hanging out in my backyard pool. The rest of the wedding guests faded away as I took all of him in.

"You look amazing," he said, stepping forward and running his fingers down my bare arm. The light touch left a trail of shivers.

"You're here," I said.

"I'm sorry I'm late," he said, his dark eyes sweeping over me from head to toe. I made a mental note to thank the small army of hair stylists, makeup manufacturers, and seamstresses who had conspired with me to create a look that inspired that hot, openly lustful gaze.

"I didn't think you'd make it," I said, wishing we weren't in a crowd.

"You can thank Max Emmerson. We flew back on his jet," he said. "I only wish I could have been here sooner."

"You're here now," I said with a smile. "Did you get your man?"

"Always."

"What happened?"

"He and Carly had planned to meet up in Maui then fly to Fiji, where they were going to pick up a boat and sail around the islands to avoid arrest," Jake said, a smile playing around his lips. "Well, that's the plan Mark thought they had. It's funny though. We can't seem to find any trace of an airline ticket for Carly, under any of her names. And the sailboat that she told him they'd bought doesn't seem to exist. And all the money they'd stashed ended up in an offshore account in her control."

I shook my head with a laugh. "She conned him too?"

"Before her lawyer stopped the interview, she tried to blame everything on Mark, but this scheme has her fingerprints all over it."

"Well, it sounds like you could use a drink after all that hard work," I said, taking his arm.

Our reunion was cut short by Rob, who slapped Jake on the back. "Jake! So glad to see you. Your partner was just telling me all about your adventures in Hawaii."

Jake raised an eyebrow. "Was she now?"

Rob put an arm around each of us and steered us toward the crowd, exactly the opposite of where I wanted to go. But we gave in to the groom as he introduced Jake and me to old friends, far-flung family members, and at least a dozen attorneys who Rob had known for years, including several prosecutors. It took about an hour and untold handshakes before Jake and I found ourselves on the edge of the party, blessedly alone.

Jake looked around with a mischievous grin and nodded toward the trail leading to the overlook where we'd been before.

"Want to go for a walk?"

I smiled and started down the path, but he didn't follow me.

"I'll meet you there," he said, disappearing back into the crowd near the bar. He hadn't said where, but I knew he meant the secluded spot on the trail where we had gone before.

It was a short walk to the overlook, and I sat on the wide rock wall, grateful for the chance to sit for a few minutes. My feet were sore from walking and dancing in heels all night. From my perch, I had a clear view of the Lucky Penny across the cove. It was still a black hole in the shoreline—no lights except for the security lights in the parking lot. But that was going to change shortly. Max had gotten his gaming license approved, and banks were lining up to lend him the money on the renovation. If everything went well, it could be open by next summer.

I heard his footsteps on the path, and when he rounded the corner, I laughed. He had two glasses in one hand and a bottle of champagne in the other. He handed me the glasses, then loosened the wire cage over the cork and, with a loud pop, opened the bottle.

He filled both the flutes and handed me one.

"What are we toasting to?" I asked.

"To our first date," he said, touching his glass to mine.

"Is that what this is?"

"I hope so." His eyes met mine, and my breath caught in my throat.

Before I could taste the bubbly, he took my glass and set it to one side, then slid one hand behind my neck. His lips touched mine, and the flutter in my chest grew to a tremor. I ran a hand up his chest, under his jacket, and then pulled him closer.

As Aunt Marie had said in her impromptu speech, something good had come out of that low point in my life. Two and a half years ago, Jake had cuffed my hands behind my back and marched me out of the investment bank where I thought I'd make my career. With our first meeting, he and his colleagues had sent my entire life crashing to its lowest ebb, irrevocably changing so many of my plans, changing me. Sending me into a deep despair, and deeper debt.

And as horrible as it was, I wouldn't go back and change a thing. The trauma of the arrest and subsequent trial had also shown me who my true friends were, and I made new ones, in Rob, Sarah and Burton, and later Quinn.

Now I couldn't imagine my life without any of them. Especially the man in front of me.

"I missed you," Jake said, leaning his forehead against mine.

"I missed you too. Even if it was only a week that you've been gone."

He smiled. "I meant this summer. I want this to work, Miranda. And for the record, I don't care what anyone thinks about it. I never have. Only you."

I blinked away the tears stinging my eyes. "Oh. Okay."

He smiled and kissed me again.

"Don't listen to Bethany—" he said, stroking my neck.

"No, she's okay."

He touched my face, possibly checking for a fever. "Bethany's okay?"

"Yeah, we talked."

He nodded and smiled. "Good. Glad to hear that."

"She says she's drawing fire from us by dating Quinn," I said with a smile.

He laughed and handed me my champagne, the relief evident on his face.

"Tell me about your new job," he said, running a hand down my arm again. I was pretty sure he didn't want to talk about accounting, but figured it was the equivalent of thinking about baseball. While we had found a quiet area, we were still in public.

"I'll start out part time, but there are some classes Dottie wants me to take, so I'll be studying..."

My thoughts trailed off as Jake's fingers ran up my neck. The only calculations I could make at that moment were how long a drive it would be to my hotel room and how quickly I could get Jake out of that suit.

"Studying to be a forensic accountant?"

"Hmm mmm," My thoughts were seriously scrambled, and I couldn't take my eyes off Jake's lips.

He raised his glass again. "To your nice, new *boring* job as a forensic accountant."

"It hasn't been boring so far."

He leaned in closer, and my pulse quickened.

"I'll make you a deal. You stay out of trouble at work, and I'll keep things exciting for you at home."

I closed the short distance between us. That was an offer I couldn't refuse.

ACKNOWLEDGMENTS

I'd like to thank my editor, Sandra Barkevich, who knows my characters as well as I do and always makes everything I write better.

Debra Sennefelder is the only person I trust to read my early drafts. Thank you for your wonderful feedback, advice, and support!

Thanks, too, to Gemma Halliday and T. Sue VerSteeg, for lending me your casino.

And finally, thank you to the readers. I appreciate that you choose to spend time in Miranda's world, where I let my imagination run wild.

ABOUT THE AUTHOR

Ellie Ashe has always been drawn to jobs where she can tell stories—journalist, lawyer, and now writer. Writing quirky romantic mysteries is how she gets the "happily ever after" that so often is lacking in her day job.

When not writing, you can find her with her nose in a good book, watching far too much TV, or trying out new recipes on unsuspecting friends and family. She lives in Northern California with her husband and two cats, all of whom worry when she starts browsing the puppy listings on petfinder.com.

To learn more about Ellie, visit her online at:
http://ellieashe.com